Her room had bee[n] had been emp[ty] documents she mi[ght have had were gone.]

But it would have been too much of a coincidence that the burglar was surprised by Marta coming back and killed her in panic. No. He had looted her room and then waited to do murder.

Why?

Because of something she knew.

And because Hooks had been with her, it would have been logical to assume that Hooks knew it too, whatever "it" was.

He closed his notebook in weariness. He understood two things.

One. That he was saved from being killed the night before by Marta's impulsive decision to send him to buy wine.

Two. Whoever the killer was would try again.

Hooks was now a target.

Another Fawcett Title by
Warren Murphy:

THE RED MOON

THE CEILING OF HELL

Warren Murphy

FAWCETT CREST • NEW YORK

A Fawcett Gold Medal Book
Published by Ballantine Books

Copyright © 1984 by Warren Murphy

Library of Congress Catalog Card Number: 84-90925

ISBN 0-449-12554-8

Printed in Canada

First Edition: December 1984

PROLOGUE

THE SMALL GROUP OF TOURISTS AND PASSERSBY STOOD impatiently outside the rear entrance to the large Washington hotel. Half a dozen bored District of Columbia policemen kept them behind rope barriers a dozen feet from the door.

"When's he coming out, Daddy?" a small boy whined.

"Just a few minutes, I guess."

"But I gotta go. Bad," the child said, and he began to squirm.

"Hold it," said the man. He checked the settings on his camera. "Not every day you get to see the President. Wait till you tell your friends."

"Well, he better hurry," the boy said, jamming his hands into his pockets.

A tall woman, dressed in a white frilly blouse and a blue skirt, glanced at her wristwatch, then leaned over to the small boy. She clutched a paperback book.

"He'll be out in less than a minute," she told him. She smiled at the boy and his father, and at that moment four men with cameras hurried through the doorway and took positions to photograph the President leaving the hotel.

"Here he comes now," the boy's father announced, aiming his camera. The spectators began shifting restlessly, pressing forward and straining for a look.

1

"Keep back," a policeman barked, spreading his arms wide and leaning against the group. "Stand back, please," another policeman echoed.

A burly man in a dark-blue suit came through the entrance first. He looked around, and was then followed by five other similarly dressed men, several of them carrying large attaché cases.

"Yeah, Big Steve," the woman in the white blouse called out, a happy lilt in her voice. She put her book in her purse, freeing her hands to clap.

A tall lean man in the group glanced over at her, smiled briefly and winked, then resumed a practiced, methodical scrutiny of the surroundings. His eyes were narrowed in concentration and his face was intense.

The woman leaned down to the small boy. "That's my husband," she said softly. "He's a Secret Service agent."

"No fooling?" the boy gasped, his eyes big. "Wow."

There was a ragged cheer and a smattering of applause as the President came through the doorway and paused briefly to smile and wave at the small audience while the news photographers dutifully recorded the event for posterity. The boy's father cursed softly to himself as he fumbled with the camera.

The burly man, who had been first through the door, opened the rear door of a long black limousine parked at the curb. The President began striding quickly toward the automobile, while still waving and smiling at the spectators.

Although they lied about it afterward, neither the boy nor his father heard the sound of the glass being smashed out of the fourth-floor window in the hotel, but the Secret Service men did. The tall lean man named Steve took one startled look upward, then spun toward the President, put both hands against his back and shoved him unceremoniously toward the waiting limousine.

There was a startled gasp from the spectators.

Then several women screamed in terror as the shooting began.

The burly man fielded the stumbling chief executive neatly, spun him around and lunged toward the safety of the bullet-proof limousine, protecting the president with his body.

He grunted as a bullet thudded into his neck; he then fell into the vehicle on top of the President. He groaned in agony. Blood spurted from his mouth onto the President's face, which was inches away. Then he collapsed, lifeless, his weight pinning the President helplessly to the backseat.

The confused yelling from the spectators almost drowned out the scream of pain from the tall, lean agent, who clutched his left leg and writhed on the pavement beside the limousine.

The press photographers, confused and afraid, automatically worked their cameras as fast as they could, aiming first at the limousine, then in every other direction at random.

"Get down, get down!" bellowed the policemen, clawing for their pistols and looking around wildly.

"Fourth floor," yelled a Secret Service agent, aiming his own revolver.

The attaché cases sprang open and small powerful automatic weapons appeared. Bursts of shots chipped brick and stone about the fourth-floor window and the young man with the shiny mail-order automatic pistol ducked back out of sight.

Then his hand appeared again, and he fired two more shots blindly toward the ground as the limousine sped away, with the door still open and two pairs of legs still visible from it.

The policemen joined the Secret Service agents in

shooting toward the empty window. Several men dashed back into the hotel.

There was a moment of shocked silence as the firing halted. Then a thin, quavering voice was heard. "Don't shoot. I surrender."

The afternoon sun glinted off the pistol that was thrown out of the fourth-floor window. It bounced on the sidewalk, then came to rest beside the body of the young woman in the frilly white blouse. She was sprawled limply on the ground atop the young boy.

"Daddy!" he screamed. "She's bleeding on me!"

CHAPTER ONE

THE LATE-AFTERNOON SUN TOSSED A SPEAR OF LIGHT INTO the hospital room. It fell in an irregular pattern across the face of the woman who lay in the bed, her eyes tightly closed, a faint frown on her face.

A short, chunky nurse was arranging the covers neatly over the woman when Steve Hooks pushed open the door, limped into the hospital room and stood quietly for a few seconds looking at his wife.

The nurse saw him and smiled tightly.

"Hello, Mr Hooks."

"Hello, Mrs. Bordino. How is she?"

"I was just getting ready to give her her massage. But I'll leave you alone for a few minutes."

"Thank you," Hooks said.

The nurse hustled toward the door of the room, but before she went out, she said, "I was sorry about today. I heard it on the radio."

Hooks shrugged.

"It's a damn shame," the nurse said. She shook her head. "I . . . well, I'm just sorry."

"I know," Hooks replied.

The nurse left. Hooks walked to the bed and folded his angular form into an armchair. He reached out and touched the limp hand of the woman in the bed.

"Hello, Joanna," he said. "It's Steve."

He squeezed her hand, but there was no response.

5

There had never been a response, not since that last wave she'd given him outside a Washington hotel ten months earlier.

He looked at the tubes that extended from her body into a small black machine on wheels on the far side of the bed.

"Well, they did it," he announced harshly. "I'm glad I didn't bet on it. I can't believe it." He spoke very slowly; there were long pauses between the sentences. Earlier in his wife's hospitalization, he had tried to speak in normal conversational tones, but he found that after only a few minutes he had nothing left to say, and he felt somehow guilty about sitting there in silence with the paralyzed, comatose woman. Now he tried to fill up the time by speaking slowly.

"It was unanimous," he said. "The whole jury. They all said that creepy little son of a bitch was insane when he shot you and me and killed poor Josh Quigley.

"I mean, anybody who buys a gun and flies two thousand miles so he can commit suicide on top of Jack Kennedy's grave, then changes his mind and tries to shoot the President, he's got to be crazy, right? So they're sending him to a funny farm.

"Too bad about poor Josh. But the twit didn't mean to kill Josh. He just wanted to kill the President. So Josh doesn't count. And too bad about you, too. Your tough luck for being around when a crazy decides to play bang-bang."

He placed his other hand over hers, massaging it restlessly between his palms.

"Right? An irresistible impulse, right? Shame on the government, expecting a paranoid schizophrenic to resist an irresistible impulse. And those twelve shits bought it. I hope that bastard gets out someday, and he goes and blows away every one of them. Maybe they can see how much compassion *he's* got."

His lips tightened in anger and he leaned forward urgently.

"I tell you, Jo, maybe if the President had been shot, maybe then the government would have been out for blood. Maybe the system would have nailed that guy. Maybe the law would have worked.

"But the President wasn't shot. Just you and me and poor Josh. And we don't count."

He sighed, released her hand and leaned back in the chair. Her hand lay lifelessly on the bedspread where he had placed it.

Hooks gave an exhausted sigh and tried to think of something else to say.

"I think I told you. My papers came through. Now I'm officially retired on a government disability pension. Good. I don't want to work for this government anymore. Now if I can only find some clients, maybe I can make a living. You know, all they were really worried about when I put in my papers was that I wouldn't embarrass the Secret Service? Ahh, I'm sorry, Joanna. I don't like to talk to you about this kind of stuff. I'd rather talk about nice things. What we're going to do when you finally get up and around and I can get you out of here. The places where we're going to go. We're going to learn to ski. Well, you, anyway. I don't think my knee's going to be much good for skiing."

He stood up and opened the drawer of the small cabinet next to the woman's bed. Inside was a paperback copy of *The Brothers Karamazov*.

"You know," Hooks said casually, picking up the novel that had been in his wife's handbag the day they were shot, "maybe I'll start to read you this book. Would you like that?"

He looked at the woman in the bed, but she was inert, motionless, her eyes still closed. He returned the

7

book to the drawer and stood alongside the bed and looked down at his wife.

"I thought about not telling you about the jury decision," he said. "I thought it might upset you. But I knew you'd wonder what happened, especially after hearing me all these months."

He stopped talking and just stood there, looking down. A tear glistened in the corner of one eye.

The nurse came back into the room, but stopped as she saw the tall man's broad shoulders heaving with sobs. She turned her back to him, cleared her throat and began fussing with one of the shelves in a large clothes closet near the door to the room.

"Time for her massage," the nurse said brightly. She waited a few more seconds before she turned around. Hooks had wiped his eyes of tears but moisture still glistened on the smooth tan skin of his cheeks. He ran his hands through his thatch of light-brown hair, in the unconscious gesture of frustration that the nurse had seen many times in the last few months. He was a handsome man with an intelligent face. There were little laugh lines in the corners of his dark eyes, and Mrs. Bordino thought, sadly, that there had been precious little laughter in the man's life for the past year.

"I've told her all the news," Hooks said as the nurse approached the bed. "I guess she needs her rest."

"Next week, maybe she'll be chattering away like a jaybird," the matronly nurse said.

"Let's hope so." He leaned over and kissed his wife gently on the forehead.

"See you next week, Jo," he said. "Maybe I can tell you about my first client. If I have one. I love you, hon."

He limped from the room. The smile faded from the nurse's face, and she shook her head sadly.

Then she bent to her task of massaging the limp body; she was careful not to dislodge any tubes or wires.

CHAPTER TWO

HOOKS WAS EARLY FOR HIS DINNER DATE WITH PATTI Maguire, but, as usual, she was late. He had almost finished his second bourbon and water when she rushed anxiously into the restaurant, looked around wildly and made a grimace of despair when she finally spotted him.

She hurried over to the table, and shed her light jacket en route. Tossing the jacket unceremoniously into the corner of the booth, she plopped down opposite him.

"Am I late?"

Hooks answered by cocking an eyebrow at her.

"I'm late," she admitted. "But not really really late. Anyway, it wasn't my fault. Traffic was a bitch. Somebody had a flat or something, and there was a traffic jam. Otherwise, I would have been here before you."

"That'll be the day," said Hooks. "You're worse than your sister."

"I know. It must be genetic or something, and I represent the high point of evolution. Joanna always used to say that when it came to being somewhere on time, she was bad, but I was the worst." She looked at him, and Hooks knew that she wanted to ask after her sister's condition but that she feared the answer would depress him. So he said simply, "No change. I was there today."

She nodded, and when a waiter approached Hooks drained the rest of his drink and ordered another. "And an old-fashioned for the lady."

9

Patti nodded even as she dove into her purse, pulled out a mirror, inspected herself and groaned in despair. She rummaged around for a moment, and, after finally producing a snaggle-toothed comb, she made emergency repairs on her tousled dark-brown hair.

"God," she said, "Jo always looked like she just came from the hairdresser. Even when she was a cheerleader, bouncing all over, her hair always fell right back. Me, I spend an hour brushing my hair, getting it just right, and as soon as I stand up, I look like the bride of Frankenstein."

"Let's face it," Hooks agreed amiably. "You're a slob."

"Too true, too true," she said.

When the waiter put their drinks in front of them, Patti frowned as Hooks scooped his up.

"That your second?" she asked.

He paused for a moment, then answered honestly. "Actually, my third. You were late, remember?"

"Oh, yeah." She plucked the cherry from her old-fashioned, ate it, then sipped at the drink.

"Does my drinking bother you?" Hooks asked.

"Only if you do too much of it," she replied. "And maybe you have since Joanna was . . ."

"Shot," he finished.

"Okay, right, shot. You've been drinking more and more since then. I can't help worrying about it."

"Try," he urged. "Try hard."

"Okay. None of my business. I know," she said, looking down at her glass, and he felt a pang of guilt for having been brusque with her. "Don't worry, Patti, it's not a problem. I'm not an alcoholic, and I won't be."

Mentally he crossed his fingers and wondered if he was telling the truth. Not that he really gave a damn anymore, except he didn't like upsetting his wife's younger sister. She had enough problems of her own.

"Joanna looked good today," he finally said.

10

"She always does since she stopped losing weight. She looks like she's asleep and going to wake up any minute."

"And she will," said Hooks, and Patti nodded silently. Suddenly her face, which had been studiously expressionless, clouded over with remorse.

"Oh, I'm sorry, Steve. You were in court today, weren't you?"

He nodded, and she said, "I'm sorry. I'm nattering away at you for drinking, and you've been in court watching them turn that bastard loose. Have another drink. Have ten. You deserve them."

"It's okay," Hooks said. "I'm over it now, but if I'd had a gun today I would have shot that swine where he stood. Aah, forget it."

They ate dinner in companionable silence until Hooks asked, "So how was your day?"

"Swell. Dear Lawrence called from Las Vegas. He says the divorce hearing is Tuesday, and then we'll both be free of each other. I could hear that chippie of his whistling in the background. She'll be whistling out of the other side of her mouth after a few months with that smooth-talking son of a bitch. *She'll* find out."

Hooks tried to picture a woman whistling first out of one side of her mouth and then out of the other. He gave up and concentrated on his chicken Parmesan.

Later he considered suggesting an after-dinner drink, but decided against it and settled instead for a cup of coffee.

"By the way, I may have my first client," he said.

"That's terrific. Who is it?"

"I don't know. Remember last week, I told you about Bob Pardin?"

"Oh, the genius who didn't want you to embarrass the Service when you resigned. He's a beaut."

"No, actually, Bob's all right; he was just doing his

job. I guess the Secret Service just wanted to be ready if I resigned and tossed a public relations hand grenade at them. Shut up, anyway. Whose story is this?"

"Sorry. Go ahead," Patti said.

"Anyway, Bob called and left a message on my answering machine that he might have a client. I tried to get back to him but there's no answer. I'll get him tomorrow."

Patti's eyes flashed. "Really, that's swell. You said it'd be months before you'd start making any money."

"It might still be. Don't get carried away. I don't know who the client is. I don't know whether they'll want me. Maybe I won't want them. I don't know."

"Trust me," Patti said with a smile. "It's General Motors, and they want you for a seven-year contract at a quarter mill a year and a brand new Cadillac every year."

"If it's General Motors, they'll probably offer me minimum wage, a watchman's job in Detroit and a bargain on a dented Chevette."

They both laughed, and Hooks looked at his sister-in-law affectionately. She was two years younger than his wife, but she seemed ten years younger. At thirty-four, she still had a fresh adolescent quality. She lacked Joanna's poise and her classic beauty, but in her own way she was still a head-turning knockout. Hooks had once thought that Joanna was opening night at the opera and Patti was the beach at Malibu. The two sisters shared a warm, open type of personality and a blind trust in the people they loved.

That had led to heartache for Patti, who had impulsively married a glib weakling with a fondness for hot dice and slow horses. But the misalliance had broken up more than a year before, and the senseless tragedy of her sister and her recently found job as an artist with a design studio had helped her put her husband, Lawrence, out of her mind and her heart, to Hooks's relief.

She had her own studio apartment now, and several months ago she had begun dating, in part at Hooks's insistence. He knew this was the right thing for her to do, but he was nevertheless dismayed to find himself sometimes wondering who she was out with and what they were doing.

He felt guilty and ashamed about those musings, especially when they took an erotic turn, but to his annoyance they had only grown stronger. He tried to lecture himself fiercely that he was Patti's older brother, but images of his sister-in-law making love to various men who were only casually mentioned names to him persisted in jumping into his head.

Hooks had never been unfaithful to Joanna, and he didn't want to start now, but he wondered how long he could withstand the steadily rising internal pressures of his body. And it wasn't as if the doctors held out any real hope for his wife's recovery. They were unanimous about that. She might stay alive. But that was all.

Still, if he ever did take another woman, it wouldn't be Joanna's trusting baby sister, he knew. That would be unforgivable.

Patti looked at her watch and emitted a squeak.

"I've got to run. I'm supposed to meet somebody at the National Gallery to look at some Calder sketches."

"So go," he urged. "See you next week."

"Before then, I hope," she said. "I want you to call me right away and tell me about this client."

"Good news or bad?" he asked.

"Good or bad. But it won't be bad. I've got a feeling."

She gave him a quick peck on the lips, then rushed away, tugging her coat on as she left. Hooks smiled after her. She was truly a sweet girl. More than just sweet, in fact . . . but that was dangerous territory.

He sat back down, beckoned to the waiter and ordered another bourbon and water.

CHAPTER THREE

ROBERT PARDIN HAD CHANGED LITTLE IN THE FIFTEEN years that Hooks had known him, Hooks thought. Perhaps he was a little more sleek, and he was certainly more well dressed, but he was still cold-eyed, poised, and alertly aware of his surroundings.

They had joined the Secret Service together after Vietnam, and while Hooks had drifted off into field assignments, eventually winding up assigned to presidential security, Pardin had immediately gone into administration and now was kind of a special assistant troubleshooter to the director.

Pardin sat across from Hooks at the luncheon table; he held a long thin cigar, and his eyes flicked from Hooks to the surrounding tables and back again. Hooks thought that with the right kind of mustache added, Pardin would be the reincarnation of a Mississippi riverboat gambler.

"What are you thinking about?" Pardin asked abruptly.

"That I wouldn't ever want to play poker with you. Your eyes are too shifty."

"Ahhh, but they're only a disguise for a warm and loving soul," said Pardin. His voice had the flat, almost accentless cadence of a native Californian. "Did you come here to eat lunch and abuse me or to eat lunch and find work?"

"Eat lunch and find work," Hooks replied. "I'm unemployed now. How's it going to look for the Service in two weeks when they see a headline that reads 'Hero Agent Goes on Welfare'?"

"Christ, I love it," Pardin said, as he lovingly knocked the ash of his cigar into an ashtray. "Off the job less than two weeks, and you've already joined the mercenary capitalist establishment. I didn't think you had it in you, Steve." The words were good-natured and buoyant, but Hooks saw there was no humor in Pardin's eyes, which were patrolling Hooks's face in an attempt to read it.

"Relax," he said. "I won't embarrass the Service. Now tell me what this job is about."

Pardin nodded and reached under the table to his attaché case, and then handed Hooks a thick hardcover book. Hooks glanced at the dust jacket. *The New Nazi Order* by Edward Kohl.

"Wordy and pompous," Hooks said. "But nevertheless an important warning for our time."

"You read it?"

"Naah, I'm practicing being a book reviewer. Is that the job you're offering me?"

Pardin screwed up his mouth in mock disgust reached across the table, and turned the book over. On the back of the dust jacket was a black-and-white photo of an elderly white-haired man with sunken cheeks; he was wearing dark-tinted glasses.

"That's your man," said Pardin.

Hooks read the legend under the name. "Professor Edward Kohl. All right, what's he all about?"

"Professor Kohl's coming to this country tomorrow," Pardin said. "He's doing some research for a book, and he thinks there are people who might like to see him put away for good."

15

"What makes him think so?" Hooks asked. "Threats? Any attempts on his life?"

Pardin shrugged. "I'm going to tell you what I know. Kohl made contact with the American Embassy. He told them he was coming here and asked for protection. He mentioned an assassination attempt. Our security people in Berlin asked the same questions you just did, but he was vague about it."

"Then he's a crank," Hooks said. "I don't do cranks."

"Maybe not," said Pardin. "Kohl is one of the leading experts on the new Nazi movement. A lot of people would like to have him put away or at least to have him not write any more books. That one right there stirred up a big fuss and almost overturned the German government."

"Come on," Hooks said. "Nazis. Christ, if there are any Nazis left, they're seventy and eighty years old."

"Their kids are younger, and there's a small, growing neo-Nazi movement in Germany, even though nobody wants to talk much about it. Give us the days of good old Hitler when Germany was respected in the world. That kind of thing."

Hooks sipped his drink. "All right," he said with a grin. "I'm convinced. I'll look under my bed before I go to sleep. Now what's this got to do with me?"

"So, like I said, this Professor Kohl asks for protection in America, and before you know it, the FBI's involved and the CIA, and they're both squawking that they can't do it, it's not their mission, so it gets dumped on us, and it's not our mission, either. But if we leave this Kohl naked and something *does* happen to him, it's egg on our face, and maybe worse. So it gets up to the director's office, and it's in my lap, and I thought of you. Kohl's willing to pay for a bodyguard. You've got the credentials, and you're in the business now."

"Not quite," Hooks objected. "If I ever get my

agency off the ground, it'll focus on security systems and electronic gadgets, not bodyguard work. Call the Pinkertons. They're good at it."

"And you need the work," Pardin pointed out.

"Not that bad," said Hooks.

"Okay. The Pinkertons aren't former Secret Service agents," Pardin said.

"Aha. The light comes on. With me, you can look like you're really giving the guy help, even when you aren't."

Pardin smiled slightly. "I wouldn't deny that that very thought crossed a few people's minds."

"Yours among them?"

Pardin's gaze drifted idly about the room for a moment before returning to Hooks. He leaned forward intently.

"Look, Steve. This is your pretty classical case of one hand washing the other and both hands getting clean. You get a good paycheck with no heavy lifting, and it's work you know something about. And we get . . . well, we get a 'well done' from some pretty influential people in Germany who like Kohl's work." He leaned back again and puffed mightily on the cigar. "And who knows? He may find out that the Supreme Court is riddled with Nazis and make us all look good. You'll be a star."

Hooks thought for just a moment and said, "Why not? I don't have anything better to do with my time right now. But I won't do it cheap. This Kohl's going to pay through the nose."

"That's up to you. Charge him what you want. We just don't want him going back to Germany with a chip on his shoulder. That comes under the heading of bad public relations, and we don't need any more of that."

"And if his research turns up anything interesting?" Hooks asked.

"I hope you'd let me know. Friend to friend."

"That's fair enough," Hooks replied. "So what do I need to know?"

Pardin produced a long envelope from his inside jacket pocket so smoothly that Hooks again had a fleeting image of the other man sitting at a card table, deftly sliding aces from his sleeve.

"Everything is in there," Pardin said. "Biography, background, the works. We'll have a man at Dulles Airport to meet him and introduce you two. You take him to his hotel—he's in the Mayflower—and make your own deal with him. If you can't come to an agreement, hand him the Yellow Pages, tell him to find his own and take a walk."

"Fair enough," said Hooks. He finished his drink, lit a cigarette, and pulled back from the table in an unconscious signal that the business portion of the lunch had been completed. Pardin motioned to the waiter for two more drinks.

"Why'd you think of me, anyway?" Hooks asked. "I thought the Service was just as happy being rid of me."

"Usual office politics, Steve. Sure, a couple of people held it against you that your wife was at the scene, that somehow it embarrassed the Service and gave the reporters something to yammer about."

"If it wasn't Joanna who was shot, it would have been somebody else standing there," Hooks said.

"I know that, and who cares what reporters think? They're airheads anyway. And your record was always outstanding. Truth is, I never really understood why you quit. Why didn't you just take a desk job? With the disability, it was yours for the asking."

"I don't know. I think it was when the President started gurgling about compassion for that freaked-out killer. I think that's when I didn't want to work for the government anymore, and I still feel the same way. Bob,

I'd like to have my hands around that creep's throat, just for a few minutes."

"You and me too," said Pardin. "And probably almost everybody else in law enforcement. The laws are ridiculous, the courts are a joke, the juries are jerks. We're drifting through life talking about detente and peace on earth, and there isn't even any peace at home.

"And you know, it's not going to get any better until we get somebody in the White House who's strong enough to sweep away all this mollycoddle of criminals and terrorists and Communists."

As Pardin puffed angrily on his cigar, Hooks eyed him with something close to surprise. He had never seen the other man exhibit such emotion. He certainly didn't seem like a professional gambler just now, but more like a shark that had just tasted blood.

"Anyway, there's always hope," Pardin said. "Enough of that. Call me at home after you talk to the professor. Let me know if you come to terms."

"And what the professor's plans are?" asked Hooks.

"That's more in the CIA or the FBI's field," said Pardin. "But we'll be happy to pass along anything interesting, of course."

"Of course," Hooks said.

CHAPTER FOUR

DRIVING TO DULLES AIRPORT THE NEXT AFTERNOON, Hooks realized he was looking forward to being a bodyguard for Professor Edward Kohl, and he also realized why. Anything would be better than sitting around in his small new office waiting for the phone to ring or for the postman to deliver the day's quota of junk mail.

The photograph on the back of the dust jacket of Kohl's book had given Hooks the impression that Kohl would be a short dumpy man, but instead he was almost five feet ten and gaunt to the point of emaciation. Pink blotches on his prominent cheekbones showed brightly against his sallow complexion. His eyes were barely visible through his dark-tinted glasses, but they looked rheumy and tired. The German's suit was baggy—its frayed cuffs brushed against the ground—and his gray hair straggled beneath an ancient stained felt hat. He carried a cane and walked with effort; it made Hooks aware again of his own limp.

They were introduced curtly by a young Secret Service agent Hooks had met briefly some months before. The agent left immediately, and Hooks retrieved the professor's two scuffed leather bags and led him to his car.

"Ach, a Porsche," Kohl grunted. "You must be wealthy."

"My one indulgence," Hooks said. "I have no children, and my tastes are inexpensive. Besides, I bought it secondhand."

"Secondhand?"

"Used. Not new. It had been owned by someone else before me."

"Ach."

As they drove the expressway back to Washington, Kohl looked about with obvious pleasure.

"You've been to America before, I understand."

"No . . . that is, yes, I have, to America, but this is for Washington my first visit," said the older man.

"You speak English well," Hooks said politely.

"I was taught as a child, and I make some mistakes and do not always say things right, but I can understand what is said to me. Except when I speak with young people. I do not understand clearly what your young people are saying."

"Neither do I," Hook said.

They traded polite talk until they reached the Potomac River, when Hooks began pointing out sights of interest to the visitor. At the professor's request, he drove past the Lincoln Memorial, the Tidal Basin with the Jefferson Memorial in the background, the Washington Monument, and the row of Smithsonian Institution museums as far as the Capitol, then back along the other side of the Mall and finally circled the White House before arriving at the professor's hotel.

He let the doorman take charge of his car and escorted Kohl through the registration process and to his small room, and he tipped the bellboy who brought the professor's bags. When Kohl admitted to a fondness for whiskey, Hooks ordered two double bourbons with water and ice from room service.

"You might as well try a native American drink while you're here," he said.

They quickly disposed of their business negotiations.

21

Kohl did not haggle at the three hundred dollars a day Hooks asked for his services, but he made it clear that he wanted more than just a bodyguard.

"Since you have been a part of the government of the United States, I am hoping that you will be able to give to me advice on how it is done to locate a person who came to this country many years ago," he said.

"Maybe. Who is it you're looking for?"

"A woman named Anna Mueller. She was born in Germany in 1920, and it is believed that she came to the United States immediately after the war."

Hooks whistled. "That's a pretty long time ago. Have you got any details? How did she come over? Do you know where she entered the United States? Do you have any dates? Any documents?"

The elderly German silently shook his head to each of the questions.

"Is she still alive?"

"I have no idea. It is possible," Kohl said.

"Is she a war criminal? Are there any grounds for asking the FBI to run a check on her? Is she wanted by the police anywhere?"

Kohl shook his head again. "She was not a Nazi, to the best of my knowledge, and she committed no crimes that I know of."

"Does her family know anything about her?"

"Her parents are both dead, but they did not know where she was. She disappeared during the last days of the war."

"Disappeared from where?"

"From Berlin."

Hooks threw his hands in the air in exasperation.

"For God's sake, Professor, she probably died during the bombings and was buried under a few tons of rubble. Or else the Russians grabbed her and took her back with them as a playmate. There are hundreds of things that could have happened to her. What makes you think she managed to get to the United States?"

Kohl shrugged his shoulders. "We have reason to believe that Anna Mueller came to the United States from Germany at the end of the war," he repeated stubbornly.

Room service delivered their drinks, and after commenting favorably on his first taste of bourbon, Kohl began to unpack while Hooks sprawled in an armchair and nursed his highball. He was amused to see that Kohl was traveling light. His one suitcase held only shirts, underwear and socks, while the other was filled with notebooks.

As the professor put his few garments into one of the dresser drawers, Hooks said, "Do you have a physical description of this Anna Mueller? A photograph, maybe?"

"I have a photograph of her in her confirmation dress and another when she was sixteen years old. She was about five feet and four inches tall and of a healthy physique. She had blond hair and blue eyes. She was athletic and had taken classes in gymnastics."

Hooks waited but the professor had nothing more to offer.

"No fingerprints?"

"No," Kohl said.

"Did she speak English?"

"I believe she spoke only German."

"Was she Jewish?" Hooks asked.

"No, purely German."

"She was Lutheran?"

"Any scars or birthmarks? Anything unusual about her appearance?"

"None that I know of."

"Any relatives here in the States?"

"None."

23

"Could she have married some American soldier and come back as his wife?"

"It is possible, but it is unlikely. It is believed she left Berlin before the American troops arrived there. She may have remained in Europe for some time, but I do not know."

"What's so special about this woman, anyway?" Hooks asked. "Why do you want to find her?"

Kohl had finished unpacking, and he picked up his bourbon and sat on the bed. "We want to talk with her. She may be able to give us some information about events during the final days in Berlin."

"You keep saying 'we' and 'us.' Who's we and us? Are you part of an organization?"

Kohl hesitated before answering.

"You are familiar with the books I write?" he asked.

Hooks thought of the book he had seen for the first time across a luncheon table the previous day. "In a general way," he lied.

"I have colleagues who help me to do my research. Not all of them wish for me to make public their assistance, because many in Germany do not appreciate the kind of history that I write."

"The neo-Nazis?" Hooks asked.

"And others," Kohl said with a nod. "Even those many who were not Nazis do not like to be reminded about Hitler and the war. They would be happy if I wrote no more."

He sipped at his bourbon and Hooks said, "Let's get back to Anna Mueller. *If* she's still alive. What does she have to do with the books you write?"

"There are some things that perhaps she could tell us about the last days of Germany under Hitler that we would find . . . I shall say interesting."

"Like what?"

"Let us find Frau Mueller first," he said.

"It might take months, if we can do it at all," Hooks told him.

"I plan to give the task ten days," said Kohl.

"Can't be done. You're wasting your time and your money."

"Perhaps, but we should try," Kohl said. He put his glass on an end table and fished into his inside jacket pocket. He handed Hooks a piece of paper which he unfolded and read:

ANNA MUELLER

Information is sought concerning Anna Mueller, who came to the United States from Berlin, Germany, in 1945 or 1946 at the age of 25. Anyone knowing the present whereabouts of Anna Mueller or having any information concerning her should contact Occupant, Room___, Mayflower Hotel, Washington, D.C.

Hooks read the paper and looked up.

"I would like for that to appear in your newspapers here tomorrow," Kohl explained. "As an advertisement."

"It's already too late for tomorrow's papers," said Hooks. "The next day."

"That will have to do, then," Kohl said. "It will be a start on our mission. And I'm sure you may think of other ways for us to carry on our search."

"Tough job," said Hooks.

"I know you will be of great help to me. And, of course, there is the other part of your work—protecting me against harm."

Hooks looked at him skeptically. "Do you really think that's going to be necessary, Professor? Have you received any threats?"

"There have been several warnings, you might say."

"Letters, phone calls? What?" Hooks asked.

"The most recent was a telephone message. It was . . . unpleasant. It frightened my wife and caused

25

me some concern. And sometime ago there was an accident involving my automobile."

"But that was back in Germany," Hooks reminded him.

"I am more vulnerable here than I would be in Germany. And planes fly from that country to this one every day."

"Perhaps the telephone caller was just a crank," Hooks said.

"Crank?"

"A neurotic person who wanted to upset you or frighten you. A crazy person."

"Oh?" Kohl smiled slightly. "And was it not decided that the young man who tried to shoot your President last year was merely a crazy person?"

Hooks's face hardened. "Yes, it was," he said bitterly.

"And yet some were killed by this merely crazy person?" Kohl said.

"With all due respect, Professor, you are not the President of the United States," said Hooks.

"For which you may be very grateful," Kohl replied and chuckled.

"Will you have dinner with me tonight?" Hooks asked.

"Yes. But first I must rest," Kohl said. "I always find travel exhausting."

Hooks and the professor agreed that the American would return for him at 8:30 that night and take him to dinner.

"I'll call you from the lobby phone before I come up," Hooks said.

"Fine," said Kohl.

"And put the chain on the door after I leave."

"I will," Kohl promised.

"I don't know, Bob. Maybe he's lost a few of his marbles, but he seems a decent-enough old coot."

Hooks was sprawled in an easy chair in Patti Maguire's efficiency apartment half a dozen blocks from the Mayflower. He nursed a bottle of beer and wondered why he had asked for it. He didn't even like beer, except on a hot day at the ballpark, but he realized it probably made Patti happier than if he'd poured himself a highball.

Bob Pardin's voice crackled back to him over the telephone. "Well, do what you've got to do, Steve. Go look for . . . what's her name, Anna Mueller. Take the money, send him home and just remember, I found you this cushy job."

"I'll say a prayer for you," Hooks said as he hung up the phone.

Hooks gazed at his sister in law pensively. She wore a faded flannel shirt with the sleeves rolled up to the elbow outside a pair of worn jeans with a rip in one knee. Her bare feet were tucked under her as she lounged on the couch in a position that only women seemed to find comfortable.

"Doesn't this professor realize that it's impossible, what he's trying to do?" she asked.

"I don't know. Maybe he's just stubborn or maybe he knows something he hasn't told me yet. Maybe he thinks he'll be lucky and just open a telephone book and there she'll be, waiting for him."

Patti looked startled at the thought, then reached for the District of Columbia telephone book on the table beside her.

"Don't bother," said Hooks. "I already looked. There are three dozen Muellers and no Anna. And if there were three dozen Anna Muellers listed, I'd bet a million dollars not one of them was the one he was looking for."

"I guess not," she said. "What about the death threat?" she asked anxiously. "And the car accident?"

"The car accident was an accident. He lent somebody his car, and it got broadsided in a hit-and-run. He wasn't

27

even in it. And the phone call, well, he didn't say it was a death threat. Just a threat. Whoever made it is probably still back in Berlin, calling other people at random and breathing heavily into the phone."

"Don't joke about that," Patti said. Hooks could see her shudder. "I got one of those calls once and it scared me silly."

"The professor didn't seem scared. He was kind of calm about the whole thing. I guess that's why I find it hard to take it seriously."

"Well, you just watch yourself anyway," she said.

He stood up from the couch, put the half-empty beer bottle on the table and turned toward the door.

"Steve Hooks, baby-sitter extraordinaire, must be off and about his duties," he said. "You finish the beer; it's too strong for me."

"Keep in touch, Steve. I want to know everything that happens."

"Highly unethical. Wild horses couldn't drag my client's secrets from me. My lips are sealed."

"I bet I could unseal them," said Patti.

"I'll bet you could," Hooks agreed.

As he waited for the elevator down the hall, Hooks wondered if Patti had meant anything special by her threat to unseal his lips, and he thought how easy it would be later to come back to her apartment, then plead tiredness and ask if he could sleep on her couch, or simply drink enough to worry her. She had been in a car crash with a drunken driver as a teenager and still hated the thought of anyone driving after they had been drinking.

No, Patti would never refuse to let him sleep over, not her big, kindly brother-in-law. It would be an easy first step.

The elevator door opened. He stepped inside quickly and jabbed the button for the lobby.

CHAPTER FIVE

FOR DINNER, HOOKS TOOK PROFESSOR KOHL TO A Japanese restaurant on Connecticut Avenue. It was the German's first encounter with Japanese cooking, and he found the experience delightful.

After several cups of warm sake, he said. "What I have been missing all my life. We must come here every night. Are there places like this in New York and other cities?"

"Sure. Lots of them," Hooks told him.

"I will visit them all. Maybe I will marry a Japanese woman, and she can cook like this for me back in Berlin."

"Breakfast, lunch and dinner?" Hooks said. "You might get tired of it after a while."

"I will tell her to make schnitzel for variety."

"And what will be your wife's position on all this?" Hooks asked.

The professor chuckled. "Aahh, well," he said. "Another beautiful plan ruined by the brutal facts."

They were still laughing when Kohl unlocked the door to his hotel room, turned on the light and walked inside, closely followed by Hooks. As the American began to close the door, he saw with a shock that a man was standing behind it.

The next moment, the side of his head seemed to explode.

I'm dead, Hooks thought as he slumped forward, falling against the door.

He heard a muffled shout from Kohl and the slam of the door closing as he hit the floor. He heard a groan from the professor and looked up in time to see a black leather shoe swinging toward his own face. It connected with the side of Hooks's jaw, and he groaned and rolled over on his back; he was stunned but still fighting to stay conscious.

". . . hard head," he heard a voice say.

Then the top of his skull burst open, and he fell into blackness.

He was hurting, and he didn't know why.

He didn't even know where he was, but it was dark, and he was lying on his face on a scratchy surface.

It came to him slowly. He was lying with the side of his face pressing against a rug. It was silent, except for the faint sound of automobile traffic. He must be indoors because the traffic sounded far away.

Was he in his own apartment? he wondered. Had he tripped and fallen, hurting himself?

But why were the lights out?

Belatedly, he remembered Professor Kohl and choked back a curse. He listened intently for a moment but heard nothing to indicate that anyone else was near.

Cautiously, he pushed himself up so that he was on his hands and knees. His head spun for a moment, then the vertigo passed. The room was not completely dark after all, he realized. There was a faint rectangular patch of light not too far away. He stared at it intently, finally recognizing it as a window with drawn drapes.

He put out his hand cautiously. The dark bulk directly ahead of him was a bed. He had been lying with his head almost under it.

He turned his head slowly and saw a thin line of light

at floor level. It puzzled him for a moment until he realized that it came from under the door to the room.

The outside of his head was throbbing, and the inside seemed to be stuffed with soggy popcorn. Every thought had to be slowly, laboriously pursued to reach a logical conclusion.

Stand up, he ordered himself. Go to the door. There's always a light switch beside a door. Find the light switch and turn it on.

He examined that sequence of action, decided it made sense and began to put the sequence into effect.

Except that when he staggered erect, the room promptly turned upside down, depositing him onto the bed. He rolled off helplessly and fell with a skull-thunking thud back onto the floor.

Good going, Hooks, you're right back where you started, he snarled to himself.

The second time, he modified the sequence by crawling on his hands and knees to the door; he then stood up carefully and braced himself against the wall.

He groped fruitlessly for the light switch before it occurred to him that it must be on the other side of the door.

It was. He flipped the switch and gave a yelp of pain as light blazed into his eyes from several fixtures. He put one hand over his eyes and slowly moved the hand away as his eyes became accustomed to the brilliance.

He leaned against the door and slowly turned around to look back into the room. Professor Kohl's body was sprawled limply on the floor at the foot of the bed, the feet toward him, the face staring blankly toward the ceiling.

He saw a telephone on the nightstand next to the bed and tried to walk to it.

He fell again and crawled toward the telephone. His hand brushed something smooth and his fingers closed around the object, as he used his other hand to pull himself up onto the bed. He shoved the object into his pocket as he forced himself into a sitting position, then reached out, picked up the phone and stabbed the button at the bottom marked O.

"Operator," a woman's bored voice informed him.

He thought with horror for a moment that he could not speak. Then he heard his voice croaking: "Police. And a doctor. Quick."

Then his thoughts seemed to drift away. He heard urgent sounds coming from the telephone's earpiece, but he lowered it from his throbbing head and let it swing idly at his side.

He heard an authoritative rapping on the door and considered what that meant and how he was supposed to react, but before he came to any firm and final conclusions, the door opened and people began coming in. There were loud, excited noises. When he focused on them for a moment, he realized that someone was asking him questions, but he couldn't seem to understand what was being asked of him.

He felt the telephone being taken from his hand, and he wondered why anybody would do something like that to him. It seemed cruel and inhuman. After all, he was going to call somebody, wasn't he?

If he could only remember who.

He decided to reach for the telephone again, but he couldn't. Something was preventing him from bringing his arms from behind his back.

And the telephone was being used. A big man in a blue suit had it in his hand and was talking to someone. Straining, he made out a few senseless words whose meanings should be clear to him, he knew somehow, but that might as well have been in a foreign language, one he once knew but had long ago forgotten.

"Sergeant . . . dead . . . spaced-out . . . bloody . . ."

You know those words, Hooks, he told himself fiercely. Think. Remember what they mean.

But he lost interest in this as the pain in his wrists became more acute and began traveling up his arms and into his shoulders; it almost rivaled the pain in his head. Another word began taking shape somewhere in his mind. He focused on it intently until it finally came into clear view. He examined it with surprise and a dull growing anger. Finally, involuntarily, he heard himself say the word aloud.

"Handcuffs," he croaked.

Then the word disappeared into darkness and he followed it gratefully.

CHAPTER SIX

"ALL RIGHT, HOOKS, LET'S GO OVER IT AGAIN," SUGGESTED the short detective in the rumpled brown suit. "You say you think this guy behind the door was white, right?"

"Let's go fuck yourself," Hooks snapped. "I've been through it three times with you, and enough's enough. I've told you every damn thing I know about what happened. I wish it was more, but the doctors say I'm lucky I can remember that much, with the beating I got. Go away and leave me alone. I've got a hell of a headache."

"And we've got a dead body on our hands," the detective snapped back. "Even if you were still with the feds you'd have to answer our questions, and you're not a fed anymore, just another high-class private eye, so get off your snot. This is a murder investigation."

"Take it easy, Jerry," the bigger detective chided. "Can't you see he's hurting? Maybe he needs a shot of something. You on any medicine or anything, Hooks?"

Hooks sighed. "All I want is aspirin. I've got a headache, not withdrawal pains."

"Okay, we'll get you some aspirin, then. I know what it's like to get hit in the head. I've had a couple of concussions like yours, and they hurt like hell."

The smaller detective jumped to his feet. "You've been hit in the head too often, Conroy. I don't give a damn about his headache. I just want to know who was behind that door."

"Hey, Jerry, how about you go tell the nurse that Mr. Hooks wants some aspirin?"

"Maybe a pacifier too? Maybe a teddy bear?" the short detective named Jerry snapped.

"Go get him some aspirin," said the other detective, and when Jerry stomped from the room he eased himself onto the vacated chair with a wheeze.

"You got to understand; Jerry's tour was supposed to end at midnight and he's still going. He's really a good guy, but he gets grouchy."

Hooks closed his eyes in pain. This was about as clumsy a "rough and smooth" routine as he had ever seen. The two cops must have learned it from a training film starring the Three Stooges.

"Why don't you think back, Mr. Hooks? Maybe you can come up with something to make Jerry happy," Conroy urged hopefully.

"You've got it all," Hooks answered and his eyes shut. "There ain't no more."

He heard the door to the room open and looked up hopefully, praying for someone in a white uniform. Two men in conservative suits and wearing hats were entering the room. One flashed a document billfold briefly in Hooks's direction. "We're from the FBI," he announced sternly.

Hooks closed his eyes again with a groan.

Two hours later, Hooks sat beside the hospital bed wearing a robe that Patti had brought him from his apartment. He toyed listlessly with the orange Jell-O she had bought in the hospital's all-night cafeteria.

Patti sat huddled in the armchair across the small room and stared at him wide-eyed. "Eat it," she urged. "You need your strength."

"This gives strength?" he said, but he took a small spoonful.

"You look awful. The side of your face is all swollen.'

"So's the top of my head," said Hooks.

"But you're going to be all right?" she asked anxiously.

"Just your normal run-of-the-mill concussion," he assured her. "Nothing to worry about. I'll be out of here in a couple of hours."

"I'll take you to my place. You can stay with me until you're better," she said.

"Don't be silly, Patti. I just got a knock on the head. Several knocks, actually, but there's nothing wrong outside of a headache."

"Sure. That's why you staggered when you got out of bed."

"I was just woozy for a moment. Thanks anyway, but I'm going to my place, not yours."

"All right. I won't argue," she said. "If it makes you happy, we'll stay at your place. That's probably better, anyway. You'll be more comfortable in your own bed."

"Patti, little sister-in-law, I love you dearly, but I don't need anybody to look after me. I'll just go to bed and sleep for a day or so."

"Right. And not even think about feeding yourself. You've always looked after me when I had my troubles, Steve. How could I face Joanna if I didn't look after you now?"

And how could I face Joanna with the thoughts I'd be having with you in the same apartment with me? Hooks wondered, looking at the bright-faced young woman across the room. Something of his concern must have flickered across his face because Patti looked puzzled and a little hurt. She shifted her position uncomfortably and asked, hesitantly. "I wouldn't be interfering with anything if I stayed over, would I, Steve?"

He found the question confusing for a moment, then gave a startled laugh as he realized what she was wondering.

"Good God, no, Patti. You think I'm playing around with someone? Forget it."

She blushed and looked at the floor.

"Well, it crossed my mind. I mean, it's been a year and . . . Well, I know how tough it must be for you."

Oh, no, you don't—and you won't, Hooks thought, distractedly attacking the Jell-O again.

"Then it's settled?" she said.

"If it makes you happy, stay as long as you like."

Jo, I need you, Hooks thought. He said, "I still don't like Jell-O."

"It's good for you," she said.

"New rule. No food that bounces is good for you. Keep it in mind for when you move in with me."

They were interrupted by a sharp rap on the door. It swung open immediately, and Robert Pardin peeked in. When he saw Hooks sitting behind the small table, he walked in; he was followed by a portly man with snow-white wavy hair.

"Hello, Steve. Glad you're up. This is a colleague of ours from another department. Can we bother you for a few?"

"Sure," Hooks said, with a cheerfulness he didn't feel. "This is my sister-in-law, Mrs. Maguire. Patti, this is Bob Pardin. He's with the Service."

Patti greeted the man with wary politeness, then stood and said, "I've stayed long enough, Steve. Call me at the house and let me know when to pick you up."

He nodded, and she pecked him on the check and left the room with a cheerful wave at the two visitors.

"We didn't mean to interrupt you, Steve," said Pardin.

"It's all right. She was going anyway. What's up?"

"This is Frank Casey. He's with the CIA."

Hooks raised both eyebrows in surprise. "Aren't I the popular one? First Curly and Moe from the local homicide squad, then Tweedledum and Tweedledee from the FBI. And now the Secret Service and the CIA. When's the Border Patrol due?"

"The FBI? What did they want?" Casey barked belligerently.

"They wanted to know who killed Professor Kohl. I think they were hoping I'd tell them that whoever did it had a red star tattooed on his forehead and was carrying a hammer and sickle."

"Did you get their names?" Casey grunted.

Hooks handed him a pair of business cards from the end table. "Keep them. I don't expect to be calling them," he said.

Casey glanced at the cards and stuck them in his jacket pocket.

"I gather that nobody thinks this was just a hotel sneak thief who got caught in the act and panicked," Hooks said.

"Not likely," said Pardin. "German author says he's been threatened. Author requests protection. Private protection. Author is killed accidentally by sneak thief. It wouldn't seem to scan."

"Then who did it? And why wasn't I killed too?"

"'Cause you didn't see anything," Pardin speculated. "You couldn't recognize him. Or 'them,' if there was more than one. No reason for a massacre."

"And if they knew who you were," Casey added, "they might think twice about killing someone with ties to the federal government. The same as killing a cop. It just makes for a lot more heat."

Hooks nodded. It seemed to make sense.

Pardin said, "If you don't mind, Casey would like to ask a few questions that aren't covered in the reports."

"Why? How does the CIA figure into this?" Hooks asked.

"We're not sure that we do. That's what we want to find out," said Casey. "Tell me. Did Professor Kohl say anything to indicate who it was that threatened him back in Germany? Did he mention any individuals or groups that might be gunning for him?"

"No. I mentioned neo-Nazis to him, and he said maybe, and also maybe some people who'd just like to forget about Hitler and World War Two. But nobody by name."

"All his notebooks were stolen. You know what was in them?" Casey asked.

"No," Hooks said.

"Do you think he expected to be killed here in the United States?" Casey asked.

"I don't think so. He thought someone might have tried to kill him in Germany, but he didn't seem worried or anything. But he did hire me, so he had something on his mind."

Casey pulled a pipe from his jacket pocket, hesitated, then replaced it.

"Go ahead, I don't mind," Hooks told him.

Relieved, the CIA man quickly filled and lit the pipe and began puffing away. Then he jabbed the stem at Hooks.

"Who is Anna Mueller?" he asked.

"Beats the hell out of me," replied Hooks. "That's the question that's been bugging me all along."

"Tell me what you can about her," Casey requested.

Hooks patiently relayed all that Kohl had said about the mysterious woman, while Casey puffed meditatively on the pipe, his eyes fixed on Hooks.

"I was going to go to the newspapers today and put the ads in for tomorrow." Hooks shrugged. "Too late now," he said.

"Too late for a lot of things," said Casey. "None of that helps much. I still don't know who the hell Anna Mueller is."

"No," Hooks agreed. "But with you guys and the FBI interested, you might just be able to find her. Immigration. A Social Security card. Maybe there's a wedding license. An arrest record. Something."

Casey had surrounded himself with a cloud of smoke from his pipe, and he got up and went to the window and opened it.

"How do you feel about all this, Steve?" asked Pardin.

"How do you think I feel? I'm fed up and I'm not taking it anymore. My first client hires me to protect him, and he's dead eight hours later and with me right there. I get hit on the head and kicked in the face. If I ever get a chance, if I ever run into that guy, I'll blow the bastard away and dance at his funeral."

"Can't say I blame you," Pardin said. "But until that happy day, what are your plans?"

"I don't know. I think I'll get out of here in the morning unless I start leaking blood out of my ears. I'm going to spend a day in bed. Then, when I get up the nerve, I guess I should write a letter to the professor's wife saying some nice things about him. You know, I didn't even get paid. Not a cent."

"You earned every cent of it too," Casey groused from near the window.

"Hey," protested Hooks. "I don't need your sarcasm, pal."

"Calm down," Pardin said. "About the professor's wife, you may be able to tell her in person about her husband."

"She coming here? I don't want to see her."

"No, she isn't," said Pardin. "But you could do us a favor by going over there."

"What are you talking about?"

"Kohl's body will go back to Germany in a day or two," Pardin explained. "It occurred to us that you might go back with it. You could tell the German authorities what happened, and you could talk with Mrs. Kohl too. She might appreciate that."

"And then again, she might not," Hooks said. "She might just hit me over the head with a hasenpfeffer and start kicking the other side of my face. No thanks. I don't want to talk to any bereaved widows, especially when I let her husband get killed. You go."

"Not really feasible," Pardin responded calmly. "After all, Kohl wasn't under our protection when he was killed."

"And the Service has no desire to see its name mentioned in connection with his death," said Hooks.

"That goes without saying," Pardin said.

"You surprise me, Hooks," Casey said from the window. "You just going to walk away from this whole thing?"

"What else?" asked Hooks, surprised. "I'm not with the feds anymore. And even if I were, I wouldn't be involved in this. It's a matter for the local cops, that Mutt and Jeff act that were in here before. If you want to do something, you and the FBI can track down this Anna Mueller. I couldn't do that if I spent years at it."

"But you could stay involved," Casey said quietly. "Go back to Germany. Find out what Kohl's family knows about this whole affair. See if you can make some sense out of it. We can't. Our people over there are scratching their heads, and so are the German authorities. They don't know what's going to happen next."

"Who says anything's going to happen next?" Hooks snapped. "And what are the German authorities involved for? It happened over here, not Germany."

"If the professor was killed by some Nazi-connected

group, it might happen over there next time. Take my word for it, they've got a problem."

"I'd be a fish out of water over there," Hooks protested. "I'm not an investigator. I was a bodyguard with the Service. I know a little electronics. A detective? Never. I couldn't find my change in my pocket."

"You're selling yourself short," Casey said. "You're well trained and you're competent, and because you were with Kohl, you can talk to his family the way none of our other people could do. Also, your background is open. No one's going to suspect you of being a CIA man snooping around. And another thing. Just maybe you'll find out who kicked your face around. Unless you're afraid of going another round."

Hooks glowered at the CIA man. "Why do I get the impression that you've never taken a course in how to win friends?"

"Because I am obviously a cold, cynical, mean-tempered son of a bitch," Casey answered. "I am also being completely straightforward with you. This thing has a potential for trouble, but it's no big deal. Not yet, anyway. But you could help us out by doing some digging for us."

He tromped solidly over to Hooks's chair, pulled an airline ticket envelope from his jacket and dropped it on the table.

"My card is in there. If you decide to go, let me know, and we'll make all the arrangements. Expenses on us. If you decide against it, no hard feelings. In either case, take care of yourself. And stay out of dark alleys."

He nodded curtly and walked toward the door. Pardin followed him. "Keep in touch, Steve. I'm sorry the way things turned out."

But the Secret Service man waited until the door had swung shut behind Casey, then added hurriedly, "Listen, Steve, if you don't want to go, tell the CIA to go take a hike. You don't owe them anything."

"Okay," Hooks said. "Take care."

He puzzled briefly over Pardin's last remark. If there was some kind of internal dispute between the Service and the CIA, he knew where his sympathies were. But he found a growing appeal in the thought that maybe, just maybe, he might help uncover what lay behind Professor Kohl's cold-blooded murder.

He might even get an opportunity to kick a certain goon in the head, not just once, but several satisfying times.

He took that cheerful thought to bed, but his dreams that night were about an elusive, shadowy woman.

CHAPTER SEVEN

PATTI'S EYES WERE WIDE WHEN HOOKS FINISHED DESCRIBING the conversation in the hospital room during the early hours of the morning.

"I'm glad I wasn't there," she said. "I hate the smell of pipes. They're almost as bad as cigars."

He blinked in surprise, then laughed. After all the years he had known her, it still took him by surprise when Patti made remarks that went off in a wildly illogical direction from the subject under discussion.

"Don't laugh," she ordered. "I'm getting scared."

"About pipe smoke?"

"No, you goof. About the CIA and Nazis and people trying to kill you."

"I'm still alive. If somebody had wanted to kill me, I'd be dead."

"Any law against their coming back for seconds?" she asked; she then began scrambling in her purse for a cigarette.

She was sprawled comfortably on his couch, completely at home in the one-bedroom apartment overlooking Rock Creek Park. She had shared the apartment with Hooks and his wife for several months after the breakup of her marriage.

Hooks wished she were wearing her familiar faded jeans. He was uncomfortably aware of the slim shapely legs carelessly displayed by her hiked-up full skirt. It

44

was touching evidence of her casual, trusting sisterly relationship with him, but it was also putting an increasing strain on his self-control.

She found the battered pack of cigarettes, lit one and eyed him seriously.

"So what are you going to do?"

"I don't know."

"But you're thinking about going, aren't you?"

"Yes, I am. It's sort of flattering in a way that they'd ask me. And I can use a little flattery right now. Yesterday wasn't exactly a rousing start for my new career."

"It wasn't your fault," she said. "You almost got killed."

"And my client *did* get killed," he said.

She took refuge in her cigarette and he said, "You don't want me to go."

"I didn't say that. But I'm afraid. When I went to that hospital and saw you lying there with bandages around your head . . . You're all I've got left in the world, Steve. I don't want to lose you too."

"You've still got Joanna," he pointed out quietly.

"Do I? Do you really think she's going to recover?"

"I hope so. I keep telling myself that she will."

"And I love you for that, Steve. But if it weren't for the thought of you, going up there every couple of days, sitting there, holding her hand, talking to her . . . if it weren't for that, I don't know if I could force myself to visit her at all. Because it just tears me up, that's all. Every time I see her, I go home and cry for hours. All I can think of is our mother lying there in bed, drugged to the eyeballs with morphine or whatever they used, wasting away with cancer. At the end, I'd sit with her and hold her and talk to her, and she didn't hear a thing I said. And I'd think to myself, This isn't really my mother. This is some other woman who just looks like my mother.

And I'd feel so awfully guilty for those thoughts, and I'd force myself to keep visiting her anyway, but it was awful, Steve, just awful."

She stabbed out her cigarette furiously in the ashtray and sent sparks flying.

"I hate to say it, but I feel that way now about Jo. I look at that poor woman lying there with all those horrible tubes and wires, and I think, What am I doing here? Why am I in this room? That isn't my sister, not anymore. That isn't Joanna Ridley, my beautiful older sister who married Steve Hooks. That's someone else. I can't help wondering if that someone else just wouldn't be better off dead, instead of being kept alive the way she is now."

Patti fumbled in her purse for a handkerchief; she wiped away the tears streaming down her face and blew her nose loudly but thoroughly.

Hooks used the heel of his hand to brush away tears that had formed in his own eyes.

"Patti, what else can I do? I don't have any more family than you do. Joanna and the Service were my whole life. Then I started getting less and less pleasure out of my work, and after that crazy bastard put a bullet into her head and crippled me, I had to drop the Service. So what can I do except keep telling myself that Jo is going to be one of those rare cases that finally do wake up and start living again? I have to keep hoping, Patti, or I have nothing to hope for."

"I know. But how long can you take it?"

"I don't know," he answered somberly. "I guess I'll just have to find that out the hard way."

Patti wiped her eyes again and flopped back on the couch; she sighed and placed her arm over her face. Both Hooks and Patti were lost in their thoughts, picturing Joanna, the helpless beauty who had once been so alive and loving.

"You're going to hate meeting Kohl's family," she said from under her arm.

"I didn't say I was going yet," said Hooks.

"Oh, you're going," she said. "You're going."

"All right," he snapped. "Then I'm going. A free trip and it might be a change. I was in Germany before I went to Nam. It'd be interesting to see how it's changed." Suddenly, he heard himself say, "You want to go with me?"

She turned her head slowly, gazed at him intently for a moment, then smiled widely. "Oh, that's really nice of you to say, Steve. But I couldn't take the time off from my job. Not now."

"Well," he said lamely. "It was just a thought."

She nodded. "A nice thought," she said, then her gaze sharpened. "Haven't those pills taken effect yet?"

"Now that you mention it, I am starting to fog out a little."

Patti catapulted off the couch; her long legs flashed. "On your feet," she ordered. "Beddy-bye time for you."

She took his hands and helped him to his feet. He stood unsteadily for a moment, but when he took a step his left knee gave way under him, and he fell back to the sofa and pulled Patti down on top of him.

"I'm sorry," he said, releasing her hands as if they gave off electric shocks. "I don't get around so well without that knee brace. Where'd you put it, anyway?"

"It's hanging in there on the bedpost. Come on, you slug. On your feet. I'll help you inside."

He got up again, put his arm around her shoulder and let her lead him into the small bright bedroom. He sat on the end of the bed while she turned down the covers and fluffed the pillows.

"Hop in," she said and held out her hand for his robe.

"I'll undress when you leave, if you don't mind. I've still got my dignity," he said.

"All right. You're a big boy now. I'll be at work, but I'll be back to fix supper. Call me at the studio if you need anything."

"I'll be fine. Git."

She bounced out, started to close the door behind her, then stuck her head back in just as he was starting to untie the sash of his bathrobe. As he looked up, startled, she grinned, gave a quick wolf whistle then closed the door.

He shook his head groggily and climbed wearily into the lonely double bed, so empty now for so long. Was Patti just teasing him? Or? . . .

He dismissed the thought and was asleep within minutes.

He awoke slowly, and it took him a moment to realize that he was feeling the pressure of a cool hand on his forehead.

"Open your mouth," Patti's voice said. "I want to take your temperature. Your forehead's kind of hot."

He started to protest but stopped as she deftly slid the thermometer into his mouth. "Keep it under your tongue," she ordered.

"Mmmmmm."

She opened the venetian blinds, and he saw it was late afternoon. She came back and sat on the edge of the bed and waited. Finally she plucked the thermometer from his mouth and took it to the window to examine it.

"Not bad," she announced. "If you were a stock market, it'd be a modest rally. Up a point." As she bustled from the bedroom, she said, "Go brush your teeth. Dinner will be ready in fifteen minutes."

Hooks considered drifting back into sleep, but the smell of steak and a pang from his suddenly alert stomach changed his mind, and he got up and limped heavily toward the bathroom.

He concentrated on eating while Patti chattered about an argument she had had with a client concerning the layout for an advertisement. "He won, of course, because he's paying the bill, but he's wrong, dammit. Now it's all cluttered and fussy and looks like crap, and nobody's going to read it, and it serves him right."

Later, while Hooks drank a second cup of coffee, she did the dishes and virtuously scorned his offer of help.

"When are you going to Germany?"

"Who said I'm going?"

"You're going. The question is when," she said.

"You may be right," he said.

"I'm always right," she replied.

"I thought you said the client was always right."

"No, I said the client always wins. But generally the client is wrong. Except when he agrees with me. Then he's right. When are you going?"

"Day after tomorrow, I guess. Offer to go still stands," he told her.

"I'll pass this time. Try me on your next trip," she said.

CHAPTER EIGHT

"I'm glad you can't see what I look like right now, Joanna, 'cause you'd have a fit. Remember the time that nut in Seattle swung the 'Peace at Any Price' sign at me and broke my nose, and I was walking around for a week with two black eyes? I thought you'd have a heart attack when I walked into the apartment.

"You never could stand the sight of blood or even the idea of people hurting each other. You couldn't even watch the prizefights on television with me.

"So you wouldn't be happy looking at me right now. I'm all banged up and it looks pretty awful. But I hardly feel it, honey, and it'll be gone in a day or so, so don't get excited."

Hooks squeezed Joanna's hand reassuringly. From force of habit, he looked for a response. There was only the faint rise and fall of her chest under the thin covers.

"I guess we'll have to wait a little bit before I start reading you *The Brothers Karamazov*. Maybe I'll take it with me so I can underline the good parts. Oh, I didn't tell you. I'm going to Germany for a little while. Patti thinks I'm jumping to attention because the government whistled, but it isn't that. It's really just kind of an obligation I have to Professor Kohl. I was supposed to keep him alive, and I didn't. If there's even a faint chance that I can help find out who killed him, I've got to go for it.

50

"There's another reason too." He paused for dramatic effect. "You've got a rival, Joanna." He smiled sadly at her stone face, unmoved by his revelation.

"I'm haunted by this woman, Anna Mueller. I hate the thought that I might go through the rest of my life not knowing who she is or at least who she was. What happened to her? I'm sure she existed. The professor wouldn't have just made her up. But I'm pretty sure he wasn't telling me everything he knew about her. And I think she's important. Maybe she even had something to do with getting him killed. I don't know. Maybe she knew something about the neo-Nazis who hated him.

"I just don't know. I don't know who she is, and I'll probably never find out. Even if the FBI or the CIA did get into it and managed to identify her, they wouldn't be likely to let me know. So this is my chance to find out on my own. And it won't cost me anything but a few days out of my life."

He sat silent for a while, studying his wife's face. Was she looking a little thinner, a trifle more shrunken? They said they had controlled the weight loss, but maybe it had started again.

He tried to picture the glowing smile on the beautiful young woman who had walked trustingly down the aisle to join him at the altar . . . the apprehensive look when she awaited him in their inexpensive hotel room bed that night . . . the cheerful, confident grin she gave him while waving to him that fatal day in front of the hotel.

"Yeah, Big Steve," she had called. They were the last words he had ever heard from her.

But the pictures of her life were growing dim and indistinct in his mind, and when he tried to superimpose them on the woman who lay limply on the hospital bed, they didn't seem to fit.

This was still his Joanna, he told himself fiercely, the

girl he had loved and married and laughed and fought with. But she was also another Joanna that he didn't know, an older woman, frail and withdrawn, slowly slipping further and further out of his life.

She was gone from him, he admitted bitterly to himself, sent alone into the darkness by the whimsy of a madman's bullet. Her body was still here, her hand cool and pulsing faintly in his, but her mind was shut away, her soul already voyaging far into the uncharted realm that lay beyond reality.

What would it be like to join her? he wondered. That had almost happened two nights before. Someday, it surely would. Would he find her then again? He would pray for that.

But how could he live his life until that moment with this growing sense of guilt and shame? What kind of man could walk away from his helpless, paralyzed wife to blithely seek joy and happiness? How could he do that and still face himself?

What was he going to do about Patti? What was he going to do about himself?

Hooks bowed his head and kissed Joanna's lifeless hand, then held it against his cheek for a while, lost in his tragic musings. Finally, he replaced her hand on the bed and kissed her forehead.

"I have to go, Joanna. I have a lot of things to do before I leave. I won't bother to send you a card, but I'll pick up some little souvenir for you and bring it back.

"And I'll be back, Jo. I'll always come back to you, as long as we both shall live."

52

CHAPTER NINE

THE MOST EVENTFUL PART OF THE EIGHT-HOUR PAN AM night flight to West Berlin was trying to get on the plane.

Hooks set off the metal detector while passing through the airport security check, so he dutifully emptied his pockets of keys and coins and walked through again, and set the detector off again. For a moment, he was puzzled, and then he understood that his metal and canvas knee brace was triggering the machine.

He felt like an idiot, standing in the long walkway with his left trouser leg rolled up above the knee while an airport security guard swept his body with another hand-held metal detector, before allowing him to pass through.

On the plane he skimmed through some promotional material on Berlin and West Germany; he then leaned back in his seat and tried to call back the few days of leave he had spent in Berlin during his brief two months in Germany before his army unit had been shipped to Vietnam.

But all he could remember was drinking oceans of beer with his buddies, Joe and Frank, and looking for women. They weren't hard to find, he remembered. In fact, he had almost been the object of a fistfight between two eager ladies of the night—although the one he eventually found himself in bed with certainly had not turned out to be a lady.

He smiled pityingly across the years at the memory of how shocked he had been at her casually matter-of-fact suggestions concerning the range of activities she would perform for him if he increased the agreed-upon price, and, thinking back, he regretted that he had been so timid and stuffily conventional at the time. Most of her suggestions had been outside of his experience, although he would soon lose all his inhibitions in Vietnam.

They were not the kind of sexual variations he would have felt comfortable suggesting to Joanna, or would ever have expected her to suggest to him.

He wondered if Joanna had ever wished for a greater variety in their sex life than they had enjoyed over the years but had just been too shy to let him know. He doubted it, but he couldn't be sure.

Too late now, he thought, and then winced at the realization that increasingly he was thinking of his wife in the past tense, as if she no longer existed.

He lost himself in staring out the window for a while, then smiled again at that young man he once had been; but he wished he had been more interested in the German people and their largest city than he had been in satisfying his sexual urges. He could remember nothing now of Berlin that promised to be of any use to him.

He wondered if he would see that same woman again. Surely she could not still be plying her ancient trade. Then he wondered if Anna Mueller had been a prostitute.

The thought excited him for a moment. Could that be a way of picking up her trail? Then he dismissed the idea with a snort of disdain.

He dozed off, his head on a small pillow supplied by a smiling stewardess. In his dream, he was walking through the vaguely familiar streets of a dimly remembered Berlin and was peering intently into the faces of middle-aged women, but all the faces seemed blank and featureless like mannequins in a store window. They looked back at him without curiosity, then walked on, ignoring his constant question:

"Are you Anna Mueller?"

Then he saw a woman walking quickly away from him, and he knew it was Anna Mueller. He tried to run after her but his feet were leaden. It was like running through molasses. She turned into a doorway, her face averted so that he could not get even a glimpse of her features. He struggled on and eventually reached the huge, thick oaken door, so massive and strong it seemed like the entrance to a castle. He tried the handle—but it was locked.

He pounded on the door and sobbed with frustration and fear. If he didn't reach Anna Mueller quickly, something dreadful was going to happen to him, he knew. But the door was as immovable as a wall of stone.

Above and behind him, he heard the sound of a window breaking. Oh, God, the shooting was going to start again. He spun around, reaching for his gun—but his wounded knee betrayed him, and he stumbled and fell, the gun falling from his hand.

He stretched out his arm but couldn't reach the gun, and in the window above a shadowy figure was raising its arm, a shiny glint of metal in its hand. And something had hold of his shoulder and was keeping him from escaping. . . .

He awoke with a start, his forehead covered with sweat. The blond stewardess was leaning over him and gently shaking him; a concerned look was on her face.

"Are you all right? You seemed to be having a bad dream." Her English was spoken with a soft Germanic accent.

He gasped for a moment, unable to speak, almost unable to breathe. Then he shook his head.

"I'm all right, thank you."

She looked at him dubiously, then gave him a bright, professional smile. "Another two hours to landing. Can I get you anything?"

"No, thank you. It was just a bad dream. I'll be all right," he assured her.

She smiled again and left him. He shifted his position and willed himself to get a little more sleep. And no dreams.

To hell with Anna Mueller.

At Tegel Airport, Hooks soon found himself standing with hundreds of other passengers, in long lines, passports in hand. He was rescued from the normal bureaucracy by a page over the loudspeaker. Hooks reported to a security officer, who led him to an office. There he was greeted by a tired young man who introduced himself as Burton Sellers of the Foreign Service office. His light-blond hair was clipped anonymously short and his eyes were a strikingly pale water-blue. Sellers spoke briefly with an airport official, and after answering a few perfunctory questions from a bored immigration officer, Hooks was reunited with his luggage and in a taxi with the younger man.

"They've got you booked at the Excelsior Hotel," Sellers informed him.

"So they told me. I had nothing to do with it."

"It's a good hotel," Sellers said.

"I'll be satisfied with hot water and a good bed," Hooks replied.

"It's got that," said Sellers. He was silent for a few minutes, then asked, "How come you're limping?"

"Bad knee. I've got to wear a brace."

"That's not from when you were with Professor Kohl, is it?"

"No, I got it before that," Hooks said.

"Kohl's death made a little bit of a stir here. Hit the front page of a couple of papers."

"I'm not going to have to talk to any reporters, am I?" Hooks asked.

"I shouldn't think so. No reason for them to come after you. I don't even remember that your name was used. One paper said something about a bodyguard being beaten, but no name." He looked at Hooks's face. "You're all right now?"

"A couple of headaches, but I'm all right," Hooks said.

"You look like hell," Sellers said matter-of-factly.

"I'll improve after my beauty rest."

They had missed the morning traffic rush, and the five-mile ride from the airport passed quickly. As they drew up to the hotel, Sellers handed Hooks a thick manila envelope.

"There's some walking-around money in there. Dollars work all over Berlin. Do you have any credit cards?"

"American Express."

"Good. Use it, and we'll reimburse you. You speak German?"

"I can be very polite if somebody sneezes, but that's it."

"Every little bit helps, but most of the people here can speak some English. Anyway, there's a tourist phrase book in the envelope and a map of Berlin and directions for getting in touch with Frau Kohl. If you need any help, call me at the number that's in there. If I'm not there, somebody will take the message or give you any help you need."

"Suppose I call at three in the morning?" Hooks asked.

"Someone'll be there."

"I thought that might be the case," Hooks commented quietly.

Sellers flashed him a look, then shrugged and smiled slightly. "Give us a call if you need any help, but try to stay out of trouble. I want to retire with the reputation of having kept the lowest profile in history."

A doorman in splendid livery opened the door to the cab while the driver jumped out to remove Hooks's luggage from the trunk.

"What about Kohl's body?" Hooks asked.

"It came in on an earlier plane. The funeral's tomorrow morning. You going to go?"

"Not a chance," Hooks said. "Besides, if there's any newspaper interest, that'd be asking for trouble."

"You're probably right. Give the widow and the daughter a little time to get over it before you see them."

Hooks nodded. "Can I buy you a drink?"

Sellers looked at his watch. "Sorry, got to run. Listen, I'll take care of the cab. You get some rest, you look beat."

"*Jawohl,*" Hooks said with a smile.

"Not bad," said Sellers. "Give me a call if you find out anything interesting."

"Sure. And remember, the telephone works both ways." Hooks shook Sellers's hand and climbed wearily out of the cab. His head was hurting again, and he was beginning to regret having agreed to make this trip.

Not only a widow but a daughter, too, to be faced.

Hooks checked into his room, surprised and pleased at how easily the entire hotel staff seemed to deal with English. After hanging up his clothes, he unstrapped his metal and canvas knee brace and lay down on the bed for a few minutes' rest.

He woke up two hours later, feeling stiff and grimy. His head hurt, his knee hurt, and he was hungry.

He undressed and, even though he knew it was foolhardy, hobbled without his brace to the bathroom, where he took a shower, brushed his teeth and swallowed four aspirins. He dressed in clean, casual clothes, restrapped his knee and went down to eat a simple meal in the hotel restaurant. After dinner, he stopped in the bar and noted with amusement that it served a wide variety of tropical drinks. He downed two Drunken Bastards, a vile rum concoction that he remembered having once in a California cocktail lounge, then he went back upstairs to sleep.

He took Joanna's paperback copy of *Karamazov* from his end table and started to read in bed, but he had gotten only a few pages into the history of the family when he became tired; he turned off the light and closed his eyes.

His sleep was fitful. He awoke several times but managed to drop off to sleep again each time.

It was still dark when he awoke for good. For a heart-stopping moment, he thought he was back in his Washington apartment and that somebody was in the room with him. The realization that he was half hoping it might be Patti jolted him fully awake, and he cursed his insubordinate body for responding so eagerly to the thought.

He took the manila envelope Sellers had given him and hobbled over to the small table near the window, where he sprawled into an armchair.

There was five hundred dollars in American money in the envelope, enough, he decided, to do a fair amount of "walking around."

On the map of Berlin, he saw that his hotel, located on the Hardenberg Strasse, was near several museums and the zoo, which he remembered was one of the largest in the world.

One quick glance at the phrase book was enough. Languages had never been his strong suit, and maybe he would just carry it with him and point out the words for things he wanted.

There was a thick packet of material on Professor Kohl. A native of Berlin, the professor had been a high school-level history teacher when World War II started. Then, in his twenties, he had eventually been drafted into an infantry division and was a junior officer when he was captured during the Battle of the Bulge.

He had married after the war and had one daughter, Marta, now almost thirty. She had been married and divorced and was working as a stewardess for Pan Am. Hooks wondered for a moment if she had been on his flight. Could she have been the pretty blonde who'd awakened him from his nightmare? Of course not. Marta Kohl would be home preparing for her father's funeral.

After the war, Kohl had finished work on his doctorate in history. His dissertation had been on the economic causes and consequences of the Franco-Prussian War of 1870. He had accepted a position with the University of Heidelberg and seemed destined for a quiet academic life.

Then he had written his first book, *The Wolves of War*.

A blistering attack on Germany's long militaristic history and the men and events that brought about World War II, the book was a runaway commercial success throughout Europe and the focus of a firestorm of personal criticism in Germany itself. Whether by choice or of necessity, Kohl soon left his tenured college post and began a new career as an author and lecturer. He established the Institute for Contemporary Historical Studies, which functioned out of a small office in

Berlin, supporting it from his own earnings and from grants by sympathetic individuals and organizations.

The Institute's handful of employees helped Kohl with his research, which increasingly focused on the activities of the Nazi party and the industrialists who had profited from Hitler's mad dreams of glory.

His second book, *The New Nazi Order,* warned that the same forces that had spawned Hitler and his madness were again abroad in the land. It named names and places and dates, and it seemed to split Germany's cultural community in half.

Some were friendly toward Kohl, but many others looked upon him as a crackpot and a nuisance. They were annoyed, embarrassed and uneasy about his revelations concerning people and events they thought were better left forgotten.

And a small but determined minority of Germans obviously hated Kohl. His lectures were often disrupted by hecklers, he was assaulted several times, the Institute's office was firebombed twice, and at least one serious attempt was made to murder him.

Each attack only strengthened his position as a martyr of Nazism and his own determination to continue his work.

Hooks wondered what had inspired Kohl to make opposition to Hitler and his regime his life's work. Was it some experience from the army? Was it the sight of Berlin after the war, with entire blocks reduced to monstrous piles of rubble? Had he lost just too many relatives and friends to the war?

He dismissed the speculation and glanced through several magazine articles either by Kohl or about him. Only one was in English, from an American literary magazine, and it helped fill in the personal picture of the man who had put himself in Hooks's hands for safety and who had been killed.

The article told how Kohl's eyesight had been failing for years and how he was now racing against inevitable blindness to finish his third book. Kohl's description of the book, to the article's author, was a sequence of tantalizing shadowy hints.

The book would be entitled *The New Messiah*. Kohl said he had uncovered startling new evidence that showed that Hitlerism, far from being dead, was a threat not only to Germany, but to the entire Free World. His research was not yet completed, and he hoped that God would give him the strength to finish his work before his end came.

Hooks wondered if Anna Mueller were part of that research; and all those notebooks that were missing from Kohl's room after his murder, did they contain the only record of what he had been working on? A life's work, lost to a thieving murderer?

The article dribbled off into a series of personal anecdotes about Kohl's likes and dislikes, and Hooks found himself studying the photographs of Kohl and his family that illustrated the magazine articles.

The latest one, apparently taken only a year or so earlier, showed a somber, slightly pompous man standing stiffly beside a middle-aged woman, slightly plump and wearing a self-conscious smile. Next to them was a taller young woman, dark-haired and pretty, poised and unsmiling, with a slightly sulking look on her face. There was a touch of arrogance in the younger woman's stance and more than a hint of sexuality. She was lovely, Hooks thought, and she seemed to know that fact quite well. Probably a spoiled bitch, he decided.

He looked more closely at the professor's picture. Much of his face was hidden by his dark glasses, but he appeared to have weighed more when the photo was taken. He seemed sturdier, and his face was fuller. It reinforced Hooks's initial impression at Dulles Airport that Kohl was either seriously ill or just recovering from an illness.

When he replaced the clippings in the envelope, he noticed that it had grown light outside. Frau Kohl and her daughter probably were already out of bed; they were probably dressing for the funeral, which would take place in several hours.

He shuddered at the thought, but a nagging voice in the back of his mind told him that he should be there for the service. Under the circumstances, it was almost an obligation of sorts . . . and it might relieve some of the guilt he felt about Kohl's death.

Reluctantly, he considered the idea. It might not be too bad if he sat in the rear of the church and made no attempt to speak to the family. He would feel better if he went. But no way would he go to the cemetery for the burial. That was out.

He sighed heavily, went to the closet and took out his dark-blue suit.

After a quick breakfast, Hooks took a taxi to the small Lutheran church several blocks from the Kohl residence in Zehlendorf, in the American sector, some ten kilometers from the heart of the city and near the southwest border with East Germany that surrounded the free city.

He waited down the block until a large number of people had entered the church, including two women in black who he decided were Frau Kohl and her daughter. Then he entered the church and slipped quietly onto a rear bench.

Professor Kohl's casket stood in front of the altar, but it was closed and Hooks gritted his teeth as he realized it was probably because of the savagery of the beating the professor had undergone before being strangled to death.

The service seemed to drag on forever. The elderly

minister mumbled and several men delivered long eulogies, one of them in an impassioned voice that stirred the congregation visibly; he concluded by shaking his fists defiantly at the sky, and his words drew a shocked sip of air from a dowdy woman seated in the front of Hooks.

Only the choir provided any relief from the tedium. Hooks remembered the melody of one of their offerings from his boyhood churchgoing with his parents. When the service was finally over, he watched Kohl's widow and daughter come up the aisle. Both wore heavy veils, however, and he could only dimly make out their features.

He was among the last to leave the church; he used a side door just in case the family or any reporters were still out front. He walked for fifteen minutes until reaching Grunewald Strasse, where he flagged down a taxi and returned to his hotel. As he got into the cab, he saw a man in a white raincoat looking toward him from a block away. Had he been followed? He rejected the idea and spent the rest of the day wandering through the Berlin Zoo. He found the aviary especially interesting, as did several thousand youngsters. Their cheerful laughter echoed oddly against his memory of the grim funeral service, and he found himself wishing for the thousandth time that he and Joanna had been able to have children of their own.

CHAPTER TEN

THE TAXICAB DREW UP IN FRONT OF THE KOHLS' SMALL home. Hooks was almost a quarter of an hour late for his two o'clock appointment, but he didn't mind because he hated the thought of meeting the professor's family. He hoped that Mrs. Kohl was bearing up under her loss, and he vowed that if she began crying, he was taking the next plane back to the United States.

Marta Kohl had answered his call that morning asking for the appointment. She had not seemed surprised to hear from him but had consulted briefly with her mother before telling him that they would be happy to see him. Her voice had been cool and composed, he noted with relief.

Mrs. Kohl answered the door. She was a small woman, and she peered up at him intently as he identified himself, speaking very slowly so she might understand his English. She smiled at him, took his arm and led him into a front parlor.

Marta Kohl was in the parlor and Hooks realized that the grainy reproduction of the magazine photograph had not done her justice. She was not just pretty, but breathtakingly beautiful. Her black hair had almost a blue animal sheen to it, and her eyes were jade-green, set wide apart in a face whose skin was so flawless it seemed to shine with an inner glow. Her mouth was wide, and her lips were full and turned out slightly as if ready to be pursed for a kiss.

Mrs. Kohl, speaking slow but very adequate English, introduced them, then seated him and insisted upon serving him coffee and cakes. Hooks accepted out of politeness. Coffee had never been one of Joanna's strong suits, he remembered, and it disturbed him that the memory seemed from long ago in a former life.

Marta Kohl was looking at him intently. "You were in the church yesterday," she announced suddenly. "You were sitting in the back."

"Yes . . . I was there," he said, and he felt relieved when Mrs. Kohl came back in from the kitchen with a large tray holding a coffeepot, cups and sweet rolls.

"Why did you not come to greet us?" Marta asked.

"I . . . well, it didn't seem like the right thing to do. I didn't know if you would want to see me at all and certainly not at that time."

Marta looked at her mother, who poured the coffee and said, "I think perhaps you were right, Mr. Hooks. But that was yesterday, and this is today. We are very glad that you have been so kind to visit us. It is thoughtful of you."

"Are you here in Berlin on business or did you come just to meet us?" asked Marta, frowning slightly.

"My government paid for the trip. We thought you might want to know firsthand what happened back in the United States."

"That is kind of your government," Marta said coolly, then leaned back in her chair. "We have read the report sent us by your State Department, and we have read the newspaper stories, of course, but we would like you to tell us what happened."

"Ach, yes," agreed Mrs. Kohl, sitting next to her daughter on the sofa. "Tell us."

Hooks thought for a moment, took a sip of the strong and flavorful coffee, and began by briefly outlining his own background. As he started to recount his time with

Professor Kohl, he realized that it was ridiculously brief. He had ridden with the man in an automobile, sat with him for a few minutes in a hotel room, eaten one meal with him and then allowed him to be murdered. But he tried. He talked of the sights they had seen driving into Washington. He told how the professor had seemed to like bourbon, and the women smiled when he told them how the professor seemed to fall in love with Japanese cooking. Their faces grew stern when Hooks described what he could of the assault in the hotel room. Marta's lips tightened, and she muttered something savagely in German. Her mother sighed and dabbed briefly at her eyes. Hooks tensed and felt he would bolt from the room if she lost control.

"So that's how it happened," he finished lamely. He reached for the coffee cup to cover his confusion, but it was empty.

"Ach, let me pour you more," Mrs. Kohl said. She sprang to her feet and offered him the plate of cakes again.

"Delicious coffee," Hooks mumbled.

"It is from Jamaica," the elderly woman said. "My husband insists upon it. I must make it extra strong for him and add just a touch of chocolate."

She was talking about her husband as if he were still alive, Hooks realized, and he glanced sympathetically at Marta. The woman had a right to, he thought. Was it any different from what he was doing? His wife was alive, and he was speaking of her as if she were dead. Marta's return gaze was stiff and impassive.

"Do you think your police will find the killer?" she asked. "Or killers?"

"I don't know," Hooks said. "I doubt it. If they had been sneak thieves, maybe yes, but I think we were dealing with a professional assassin."

"No fingerprints?" she asked and Hooks shook his head.

"Do you think it was an American or a German?"

"I don't know. I didn't hear anybody speak."

"They were probably Germans," Marta said.

Hooks shrugged and sipped his coffee.

"And all my father's notebooks were gone?" Marta asked.

"That's what the police told me," Hooks said, and in that moment, he realized that the missing notebooks were proof that the killing had been an intentional assassination. He had never felt that it had just been sneak thieves; neither had Pardin and the CIA man, Casey. But if it had been, the thieves would have taken the two men's wallets and jewelry and cash. They certainly would not have bothered with notebooks, especially notebooks that were probably written in German. Had the reasons behind the search for Anna Mueller been in those notebooks?

"Did your father have duplicates of those notebooks?" he asked Marta.

She shook her head. "I do not think so. There are none here."

"And how of yourself?" asked Mrs. Kohl. "The newspaper stories said you were seriously hurt. Are you now recovered?"

"I'm all right," he said. "I guess I have a hard head. I still get some headaches, though, and I have a lump."

Marta rose with practiced gracefulness from her chair, strolled over to him and put a slim, cool hand gently on his head. She fingered the swollen area delicately, made a hissing noise and said something in German to her mother.

Mrs. Kohl clucked anxiously and hurried to Hooks to inspect the injury herself.

"Ach," she said. "They were cruel, those men. You are lucky still to be alive. You must be very strong."

"And very dumb," he said. "I feel great guilt, Frau

Kohl. It was my duty to see that nothing bad happened to the professor, and I failed."

"And this is why you are here?" the older woman asked, and Hooks nodded mutely.

She patted his cheek gently. "You are a good man," she said. "You mean well, and you tried. But who can defend against assassins? If not there, someplace else they would have killed him. He knew this but went on with his work."

"It was that important?" he asked.

"It was," she said.

"But what was it?" Hooks asked.

The woman smiled. "He did not discuss his work with Marta and me. I'm sorry."

Hooks stretched his legs out beneath the heavy wood coffee table. They used space-age plastic for auto bodies and aspirin bottles and television sets. Why did they still have to use metal and canvas for knee braces? He thought idly that if he ever became rich, he would instantly become eccentric. Conduct all his business from a swimming pool where his leg would never have to bear the weight of his body.

He noticed that Frau Kohl was looking at him, almost expectantly.

"I know the professor offended a lot of people with his work," he said. "A lot of bad people."

"Yes, he did," agreed Marta.

"But I can't help but wonder if this Anna Mueller had something to do with his . . . his . . ."

"Murder," Marta said.

Hooks nodded. "All these years after the war, it just seems strange for the professor to start looking for her. Unless she really meant something to his work. He told me he hadn't any idea of her friends or relatives. No records. It almost made me wonder if she ever really existed."

Frau Kohl's eyes widened in surprise.

"Oh, but she did," she said. "I knew her well. We were in school together, and she was one of my best friends."

Hooks felt as if he had just been hit on the head again.

" . . . and so I saw little of her during the last year of the war," Frau Kohl concluded. "She was very afraid from the bombing. We all were, of course, but she was very brave and kept working at the hospital. And then she did not come home one night. Ach, her poor mother. She came to our house the next day to see if we could give her any information, but my mother had to tell her that she had not been there."

She shuddered at the memory, more upset than Hooks had yet seen her, and he frowned.

"Perhaps she was killed in a bombing attack and buried under rubble," he suggested.

She shook her head firmly. "No bombs fell that night."

"Perhaps someone kidnapped her and took her away?"

Marta coughed and her mother nodded hesitantly. "It could have been that," she said.

"The Russians?" Hooks asked.

"No, not then. They were later."

"Then who?" he asked.

Mrs. Kohl shrugged her shoulders and sighed. "Poor girl. So pretty. So young."

Hooks tried to picture Berlin in the closing days of the war—the constant wail of air raid alarms, the Russian juggernaut remorselessly advancing, the stunned realization that the war was irretrievably lost. He snapped his fingers. "The hospital. Somebody there must have known what happened. A doctor, a nurse, somebody."

Mrs. Kohl shook her head again. "That was the first place Frau Mueller went the next day. They said she had left early in the evening to go home. She was alone when she left."

"I wonder if anything unusual happened at the hospital that day, concerning Anna Mueller," Hooks said. "Did a patient make any trouble for her? Or did she have a boyfriend at the hospital?"

"You are asking very good questions, Mr. Hooks," Marta commented. "Unfortunately, Frau Mueller died many years ago so she cannot tell us now what she found out then. In any case, now you know that there really was a woman named Anna Mueller. What happened to her is a mystery, but—"

The doorbell rang and Mrs. Kohl jumped to her feet. "That must be the minister," she said, glancing at an elaborately scrolled clock on the wall. "He said he would drop by. And Frau Kallman said she would be here, probably with her sister."

Marta stood up and spoke briefly in German to her mother, who nodded and answered her. Hooks rose uncertainly to his feet as the older woman hurried to the door. He winced from the brief flash of pain as the blood, cut off by the knee brace, again began to surge through his leg.

"You may stay if you wish, Mr. Hooks," Marta said, "but I suggest you will not enjoy it. Friends and neighbors will be in, and since you speak no German you may find it awkward and uncomfortable. Can I drive you to your hotel?"

"That would be very kind of you. But I hope you are not leaving on my account," he said.

Her green eyes sparked. "Oh, no, I would be leaving now anyway. I have a flight tomorrow, and it gives me a good excuse not to sit here for hours making polite conversation with people I barely know. Come. They will think you are a gentleman friend paying me escort."

She linked her arm snugly in his and led him from the room, pausing briefly to say a few words to the elderly minister Hooks had seen in the church the previous day and to several ample women who were fussing around Mrs. Kohl. Hooks nodded dumbly to the group.

Mrs. Kohl joined them for a moment at the doorway and said something rapidly to Marta, who put on a look of surprised innocence, one hand on her heart. Her mother frowned and Marta laughed indulgently, then leaned down to kiss her on the cheek and whisper briefly in her ear. Mrs. Kohl shook her head disapprovingly at her daughter, then extended her hand to Hooks and pumped his firmly. "I am glad you came to see us. I hope you will come again."

Hooks bowed slightly. "I am only sorry the occasion was not a happy one," he said. *"Auf wiedersehen."*

"Auf wiedersehen," she replied and smiled at his hesitant pronunciation. "And remember, Anna Mueller was a good girl, not like some girls today."

Marta Kohl gave a snort of laughter, took Hooks's arm firmly in hers and led him from the house. He tried very hard not to limp.

Marta Kohl's Opel sports car was tiny, but like most European cars it allowed Hooks to spread his legs out in front of him and ease the pain from the knee brace. He thought of the afternoon's conversation, from time to time flinching as Marta deftly zipped through the heavy traffic. He had a strong feeling that things had been said, or left unsaid, that he did not understand.

He glanced over at Marta Kohl. She was one of the few women he had noticed who was as beautiful in profile as she was in full face, but in profile her features were stronger. She seemed less a shy, sleepy kitten and more a lioness from the side.

"Fraulein Kohl, I—"

"Call me Marta," she ordered brusquely, her eyes on

the road as she swerved expertly around a bus, nipping in front of a large truck.

He closed his eyes for a moment, then relaxed. She seemed to know what she was doing.

"Okay, Marta. What I wanted to say was, I think maybe I was followed yesterday when I left the church."

She glanced momentarily at him, then turned her eyes back to the road.

"By who?" she asked.

"I don't know. I thought I caught a glimpse of a man in a white raincoat. He seemed to be following me when I walked for a taxicab."

"You did not see his face?" she asked.

"No. He was too far away for that."

"Forget it," she said. "It was probably your imagination."

He thought about that for a moment, then nodded. "Probably," he agreed. "By the way, I don't want to get personal but could you tell me what was going on there when we left your house? I had a feeling I was missing something."

"You don't speak German, but you speak people very well," Marta said. A smile brushed across her mouth.

"Meaning?"

"My mother is a very old-fashioned woman, Mr. Hooks."

"Your turn. Call me Steve."

"All right. My mother does not approve of the way I live my life. I don't like Steve. Steven," she said.

"What way is that?" he asked.

"As I please."

"She doesn't like the fact that you're a stewardess?"

"Please. Flight attendant. Where have you been for the last ten years? No, actually, she worries about that, but that is not what bothers her."

"What does?"

"She was brought up to believe that I should be

73

tamely at home having babies and cooking meals and keeping my house clean. She wants grandchildren to fuss over."

"You have been married?" he asked, already knowing the answer.

"For a brief while. A nice boy, but a boy. And he was soon jealous that I was away so much and enjoyed my work so much. He began making scenes and then tried to force me to become pregnant."

Her lips drew down sullenly, and she swerved the car violently around a long black sedan.

"He lost the argument, I gather."

"Yes, and he lost me too."

"Do you ever regret it? Is flying that important to you?"

"Being free is important to me. I enjoy my work, but it was more than that. Karl was fun when we were dating and when we were first married, but too soon he became a . . . how do you say it, a wet towel. He bored me, so I left, and I have enjoyed myself very much since then."

"Wet blanket," Hooks said.

Marta turned and gave him a sudden, dazzling smile. "I am happy, Steven. Be happy for me."

"I am," he said, confused but touched by her candor. She nodded, reached over without looking and patted his knee gently.

They both pursued their own thoughts for a while. Hooks couldn't help thinking resentfully of how he and Joanna had wanted a child with increasing urgency and concern but couldn't seem to produce one. I would love to have a child, he thought, and I don't blame Frau Kohl for wanting grandchildren.

They were stopped for a traffic light several blocks from his hotel, when Marta said abruptly, "If you were any kind of gentleman, you would offer politely to take me to dinner. Or at least buy me a drink."

"But I thought that you—"

"You have other plans for the evening, of course. That's all right," she said in martyred tones.

"No, I don't. I have no plans at all. I just assumed that you—"

"I accept your apology and your kind offer. Where are you going to take me?"

Hooks held up his hands helplessly.

"Very well," she said. "I know a few nice places."

"I believe you," he said.

The Opel leaped across the intersection the instant the light changed, barely missing a fat woman walking a poodle. Hooks closed his eyes again.

"I know a few not-so-nice places too," she said. "Which would you prefer?"

"I am completely in your hands. Just don't take me to East Berlin."

"I won't," she said, patting his knee again. "Do you wish to go to your room first?"

"No need," he said cheerfully, remembering that he had meant to telphone Patti. Well, too late now. And there was nothing really to tell her. Just about his visit with the Kohls.

"This is very kind of you," he said. "It won't interfere with your flight tomorrow, will it?"

"It is a late-afternoon flight. I can stay up all night and still get plenty of sleep."

"That's good," Hooks said, wondering what he would tell Patti when he called her. He wondered if she would get the wrong impression of Marta.

And he wondered if her wrong impression would be the right impression.

CHAPTER ELEVEN

THE RESTAURANT WAS SMALL, DIMLY LIT AND INTIMATE, and its menu carried more French items than German. It was almost empty when Marta and Hooks arrived—the hour was too early for chic dinners—but by the time they had finished their leisurely meal, every table was full.

The food had been excellent, but Hooks was almost glad that the dry martini he had ordered had been made backward, mostly vermouth with a splash of gin. He had almost gagged on the first swallow and afterward had taken only token sips, leaving his glass almost full.

He had also drunk sparingly from the bottle of white Moselle that Marta had selected. Meanwhile, Marta had happily consumed two frothy pink concoctions before the meal and put away several large glasses of wine while eating. Now she toyed with an after-dinner liqueur and eyed him quizzically.

"You don't drink very much," she said, nodding at the barely touched martini.

"Well, it's a lousy martini to start with. And I'm on my good behavior tonight."

"Whatever for?" she asked.

"I don't need to drink to enjoy your company, Marta."

She smiled broadly. Her teeth were long, perfectly straight and shone like pearls. She patted his hand across the table and said, "I like you, Steve. I am glad you are no longer in the Secret Service with people shooting at you. And I am very sorry about your wife. That was terrible."

There was nothing for him to do but nod.

She had begun the evening by prattling merrily about her work, describing unusual things that had happened on various flights and the antics and foibles of pilots, flight attendants and passengers. She had seemed disappointed when he had failed to be shocked as she told him about an unofficial "30,000 feet" club of airlines personnel whose sole requirement for membership was having made love six miles above the ground.

Then she had insisted that he tell her about his own work and experiences, and he had let her deftly lead him through his past, curious if a pattern would emerge from her questions.

She had seemed genuinely stirred by the traumatic attempt on the President's life and the havoc it had brought to his life. He had described the events in a flat monotone, but she had reached out and squeezed his hand hard when he'd reached the climax, and she had asked several questions about Joanna and her condition.

The pattern of her questioning had been slow to emerge but Hooks now felt it coming, and he felt uncomfortably like a mouse passing too close to a cat's paw.

Finally, between the dinner and the dessert, he said, "Marta, let's level with each other."

"I thought we were," she said.

"No. We're playing around. For the next five minutes, you ask me anything you want to know. Then I'll ask you anything I want to know. And then we'll have all our business out of the way and we can enjoy the rest of the evening."

He smiled at her and she studied his face for a few seconds before she smiled back.

"All right," she said. "Who goes first?"

"You go first."

"Are you working for the CIA?" she asked.

"No. I no longer work for the government."

"How did you get the job to guard my father?"

Without even hesitating, he decided not to tell the whole truth. "I was a bodyguard for the President," he said, "before I opened my own company. What I imagine happened is that your father asked at the American Embassy about getting protection in the United States. The State Department probably routed it through a few agencies in Washington, probably the FBI, the CIA and the Secret Service. The FBI and the CIA probably ignored it; they don't handle protection. The Secret Service does and probably the geniuses there figured it would be a public relations black eye for the U.S. if anything happened to your father and word got out that he had asked for and been denied protection. I probably seemed to be a good alternative. An ex–Secret Service bodyguard who runs his own firm. So I got a call about the job."

"From whom?" she asked quickly.

And again he lied. "A secretary in the director's office. I don't know who else."

"You said your government sent you here. Who in your government? Why?"

"Secret Service again. Sorry, the same secretary, Miss Blodgett, I think her name was. She said they wanted to express regrets about your father's death, but I think part of it was to make sure that you weren't angry with us and going to take a rap at the American failure to provide the professor with security. Maybe they thought I could find out something about who killed your father, or maybe the killers are somehow a threat to the President. The Secret Service would be interested in that."

"And have you found out anything about who killed my father?" she asked.

"I know no more now than when I was left unconscious on that hotel room floor," Hooks said, very honestly.

She pursed her lips, nodded and said with a small smile, "Now it's your turn."

"Why was your father looking for Anna Mueller?"

"I don't know."

"Does your mother know?"

"No. One day, out of the blue, he asked her about Anna Mueller. She told him what she knew, and he never mentioned the woman again," Marta said.

"What was he working on? His new book, *The New Messiah*, what would it have been about?"

"All I know is that it was about Nazism outside of Germany, in the other countries of the world."

"Including America?" Hooks asked.

"Yes, I believe so."

"Do you think American Nazi sympathizers killed him?"

"I think it is possible," she said.

"All right. The professor's notebooks. What was in them?"

"Notes for his book, I imagine."

"I find it hard to believe," Hooks said, "that your father, a scholar, an intelligent man, would travel halfway around the world with his life's work stuffed into a suitcase, trusting it to the lunacy of airline baggage handlers."

"Easy on the airlines industry," she said with a smile.

Hooks didn't smile. "Where are the copies of his notebooks?"

"I don't know. After the assassination attempt on him two years ago, my father stopped working at home. That was an effort to protect my mother and me. I know that

79

he often worked at his institute. I suspect he had another place, a secret hideaway, where he worked also. If he kept copies of his notes, they would be there. They are not at the Institute because that was the first thing I checked when I heard of his death."

"You know, those notebooks might tell us who had him killed," Hooks suggested.

"I know. That's why I have tried to find them," she said.

"All right," he said. "I'm done. You done?"

"I'm done," she said.

"Let's enjoy the rest of our dinner," he said, and they made bright small talk through dessert and her after-dinner drink; now she patted his hand again. "I think it is time for us to leave here. The waiters would like to clear this table. Would you like me to take you to a wicked nightclub where people do shocking things?"

He considered the suggestion, then shook his head. "Not really. This evening has been much too nice. I don't think it needs that kind of memory added to it."

"Good. I have long ago stopped finding any interest in watching other people do such things for money, but I know many men find this very exciting so I thought I would offer the opportunity to you. Do you have anything else in mind to do?"

"Nothing that I care to confess," he said politely and truthfully.

"The night is yet young. Is it that you are tired and wish to retire?"

"No. I slept late today. I just don't know what to suggest that might interest you. A walk, perhaps?"

"You are very kind to offer that, even with your bad knee," said Marta. "But if you do not object, I think what I would like to do is have you go with me to my apartment. I will mix you a dry martini as it should be made, or a cup of coffee as my mother makes it, and we will talk some more and perhaps listen to music on my phonograph."

"That sounds very pleasant," he said quietly, wondering if she could hear his heart beating. She could probably feel it from the pulse in his fingers where her hand touched his, and he removed his hand to light a cigarette.

"Good," she said. "Settled. Do you have money for the bill or would you like me to take care of it?"

"Don't be silly." He reached for his wallet, pulled out a sheaf of bills then looked helplessly at the bill which was in deutsche marks.

She smiled, plucked the money from his hand, selected several bills and gave him back the rest.

"Are you leaving a decent tip?" he asked suspiciously. "Women often don't."

"I am not women," she replied. "And the tip is part of the bill. Have you been leaving tips for waiters here in Berlin?"

"Yes."

"You have been taken," she said. "Ah well, better that you spend your money on a hardworking waiter or waitress than on some woman of the streets."

"Not my style," he assured her, remembering with embarrassment his musings during his flight.

"Very good. We will go," she said.

They went.

Marta Kohl's large efficiency apartment was in the center of Berlin, not far from his hotel, high in a building overlooking a small park with a pond. She had furnished the apartment sparsely but elegantly with teak Scandinavian furniture, a large Rya rug, an angular wooden sofa with overstuffed cushions and a bewildering array of stereo equipment. The walls were bare except for two large modernistic paintings, bright blobs of color with no meaning at all to Hooks.

A small dining table with four chairs was in an el beside the tiny kitchenette, and an unmade double bed and red lacquered triple dresser almost filled an alcove.

She waved her hand negligently at the bed. "I can't be bothered making it every day," she said. "Besides, it lets the sheets air out."

"The old air-out-the-sheets trick," Hooks murmured.

"Excuse me?"

"Nothing. A stupid remark," he said.

"Sit," she ordered, pointing at the sofa. She went to the stereo, flipped several levers and put a cassette into the tape deck. Moments later, the uninvolved sounds of the Dave Brubeck Quartet came from the huge speakers. By then Marta was already in the kitchen, and in a surprisingly short time she emerged with two large martini glasses and a half-filled martini pitcher.

As she poured the drinks, Hooks said, "You'd better watch out or you're going to have a nasty hangover."

"Not so. I have a very hard head for liquor."

"Okay. If you get blotto, don't blame me."

"It will not happen. I have never met a man I could not drink under the chair," she said.

"Table. You won't get any competition from me. Lately, liquor puts me away quicker and quicker."

"Perhaps that is because you want the liquor to put you away," she suggested shrewdly.

"You may be right," he said. He sipped the martini and pronounced it perfect.

"Good." She picked up her own glass and sat on the couch next to him, then laughed softly. "My mother would be shocked to see us sitting here together, alone."

"Right," he said. "But what do mothers know?"

"Generally everything their daughters know. It's just that they forget it."

"I guess so, but I wouldn't know. I'm not a mother. I'm not even a father."

"For want of trying?" she asked.

"No," he said.

"Good." She put her glass down, removed her feet from the table and swung around to face him. She gently removed the glass from his hand and placed it beside hers, then she framed his face with her hands, stared into his eyes for a long breath, leaned forward and placed her lips gently against his.

The kiss continued on and on, growing steadily in intensity. Feeling foolish with his hands hanging empty in the air, Hooks placed one on her waist and the other behind her shoulder. He squeezed her, and she abruptly broke the kiss, leaned back and stared again into his eyes.

"Do you want to make love to me, Steven?"

He opened his mouth to tell her gently that he was a married man, faithful to his wife, no offense intended to her, but found to his astonishment that he had forgotten how to make sounds with his mouth.

She dropped one hand from his face to his leg and quickly moved it up the inside of his thigh. She paused there with a satisfied smile.

"You want me," she purred and leaned forward to mash her lips against his again. Her tongue darted eagerly into his mouth, and her hand tightened on his body. Without willing it, Hooks found his own hand sliding up from Marta's waist to explore her full, firm bosom. He cupped the other hand behind her neck and he pressed her mouth even closer against his.

Finally, she freed him from her grip, placed her hand on his chest and pushed herself gently away from him. He released her head reluctantly, and she stood up. Then she began removing her clothes slowly, smiling down at him.

Hooks thought of Patti. Then he thought of Joanna.

Then he thought that he would think of them tomorrow. He stood up and began to take off his jacket.

Marta was quick to help him.

Hours later, lying in the rumpled bed with his arm under her neck, he felt Marta toy with the hair on his chest.

"It was good for you," she observed clinically.

"Mind-blowing," he said. She giggled and because he knew the joke going through her mind, he added quickly, "Not just mind."

"It was very good for me also, Steven," she said. "It has been a long, long time since anyone has treated me with such passion. You were very masterful."

"I was very rusty," he said honestly.

"Rusty? How long has it been since you have been with a woman?"

"A year or so," he said.

"Oh, you poor man," she breathed, kissing his cheek. "You make me feel proud of myself. Or should I feel ashamed?"

"No, you shouldn't," he said. "You didn't put a gun to my head, and even with my bad knee, I could have escaped you, if I'd wanted to. I'm glad I'm here, and I'm grateful to you."

He rolled toward her and kissed her closed eyes and the tip of her nose, then buried his face in the softness of her neck. His free hand caressed her hip, then slid softly, delicately across her stomach.

She gave an involuntary shiver at the touch. "You can't be serious," she said. "Not again." Her hand fumbled toward him and stroked him and she said, "You *are* serious."

"Let me show you how serious," he said, and then rolled over into her eagerly awaiting arms and legs.

CHAPTER TWELVE

HOOKS WOKE UP, ALONE IN THE BED, FEELING VERY
pleased with himself. Bright sunlight streamed through
the windows of the apartment, and as if from far away he
could hear the sounds of West Berlin's raucous traffic.

"Marta," he called out, but there was no answer. He
sat up on the edge of the bed and saw his knee brace
hanging on the bedpost where Marta had put it after
unstrapping it from him. He thought to himself that it
looked, with all its metal bars and canvas straps, like
some kind of insidious rat trap.

He called Marta's name again, louder this time, and
decided she might be in the bathroom showering. He
did not want to put on the brace because he thought he
would look ridiculous, walking around her apartment
naked except for the support device.

Carefully, favoring his weak left leg, he hobbled
toward the bathroom. The door was closed but there was
no sound inside, and after his knocks on the door
produced no response, he found the bathroom was
empty.

Then he saw the note on the coffee table.

Dear Steven,
  I have had to run some errands and don't know
exactly when I will be back. Stay if you wish. If you
are here when I return, I will be very nice to you.

Very nice. If you must leave, I will call you when I return from my flight tomorrow.

Marta

Very nice, he thought. She had already been "very nice" to him. He went back to the bed, lay down and smoked, and tried to relive the memories of the night's strenuous love bout.

But something kept digging into his mind, something that had happened earlier, and with an effort he wrenched his mind away from Marta and sex and tried to focus. What was bothering him?

The most obvious thing, he realized, was the lack of emotion over Kohl's death shown by both his wife and his daughter. Was it natural? Italians were supposed to scream and carry on at wakes and throw their bodies over the coffin. The Irish were supposed to drink and sing and wind up fighting in the kitchen while the body was lying in state in the living room. Were the Germans just matter-of-fact about death? Were Mrs. Kohl and Marta just ethnic stereotypes of the dour, stolid unexcitable German? He didn't know, but he did know that Mrs. Kohl had seemed more concerned about the quality of her coffee and cakes than about the memory of her slain husband. And Marta . . .

Again he put Marta out of his mind.

The beautiful brunette faded from his thoughts, and her place was taken by a shadowy woman. He saw her walking down a dark street; she wore a long coat, but her face was hidden from him.

Anna Mueller.

Who was she?

Why was the professor seeking her out?

The answers lay somewhere.

Not for a moment did he believe that Mrs. Kohl and Marta knew nothing about Anna Mueller, but they had chosen not to tell him, and that was that. He had no official status; he had no way to find out what they knew by using threats or pressure. For a whimsical moment, he thought that perhaps he could crush Marta by threatening to withhold his body from her, but he suspected that Marta could rapidly fill that void with any number of bodies, all of them better—and certainly in much finer tune—than his.

It would be very easy for him now just to lie around Berlin for a few days, sampling Marta and the life of the city, and then go home and tell Pardin he had found out nothing, zero, zip code, and let it all go at that. But somehow that seemed dishonest and unfair. Dishonest and unfair to whom? He didn't know. Certainly not to Mrs. Kohl and Marta, because if they wanted him to involve himself in the search for Anna Mueller, all they had to do was say so. And they hadn't.

But he knew the answer. It would be unfair to Professor Kohl. He had let the man be murdered; he owed his spirit the quest for the truth.

He stubbed out his cigarette, sat up in the bed and reached wearily for the knee brace.

Back in his own hotel room, Hooks looked up Mrs. Kohl's telephone number. When she answered, he could hear the sound of voices in the background. More friends and relatives offering their condolences, he presumed.

"*Wie gehts*," she said.

"Frau Kohl, this is Steve Hooks," he said slowly. It seemed to take the woman a moment to snap her mind from German to English, and then she said, "Hello, Mr. Hooks. It is nice of you to call."

"Thank you. I had a question, Mrs. Kohl, that I wanted to ask you."

"Yes?"

"Your husband's work? Will it continue?"

"I do not know. If enough persons want it to, I suppose it will, yes."

"Probably by the people at the Institute that your husband set up?"

"Set up?"

"Created," he explained.

"Yes. Probably by the Institute."

"Who is in charge of the Institute?" Hooks asked.

"Herr Bockler. Rudolph Bockler. He has been with my husband many years."

"Would it be all right if I talk with Herr Bockler?"

"Of course. He is as stricken by grief as we all are. You might make him feel better," Mrs. Kohl said. "If you wish, I will call him and tell him to expect you."

I'm sure you will, Hooks thought, but he said, "That would be most kind. Thank you, Mrs. Kohl."

"You are welcome," she responded, then added hesitantly, "My daughter . . . she returned you safely to your hotel?"

"Yes, she did, and we had a nice dinner together later. She was very kind to me, Frau Kohl."

"Marta is very kind to many people," the woman replied with a touch of asperity.

"Well . . . I—I appreciated her looking after me," Hooks stammered.

"I am sure she was pleased to do it," Mrs. Kohl said. Her voice was still biting and Hooks ended the conversation lamely, then called the Institute for Contemporary Historical Studies. Rudolph Bockler, who spoke English with a strong guttural accent, agreed to meet Hooks in an hour. The Institute was only three blocks away from his hotel, and Bockler's directions on how to walk there were very precise and accurate.

Rudolph Bockler, stout and pompous, was sitting behind his desk when the secretary ushered Hooks into his office. His face was that of a man in his late thirties, but his paunch and his slow gait, as he rose and walked across the room to meet the American, were those of a man much older. He was dressed in a three-piece black suit, his shirt collar tightly buttoned, his tie neatly in place. As he walked, a large penknife suspended from a chain across his chest clicked metallically against a medal of some sort and what must have been a watch in one of the vest pockets.

He greeted Hooks with stiff formality and a touch of condescension, but thawed when Hooks spoke feelingly of how greatly Professor Kohl had impressed him and how much respect he had for the work he had been doing.

"Ach, it is a terrible loss," Bockler said and shook his head mournfully. "It cannot be the same without the guidance of the professor. But his work will go on here at the Institute. The historical record of the madness that has infected and can again infect the world must be made public. We will carry on without him, as he would have wished."

Bockler firmed his jaw and struck a determined pose. Hooks wondered if he had already had cards printed up with his new title as managing director of the Institute.

The American quickly brought up the subject of Anna Mueller, but Bockler only frowned.

"I know nothing of any Anna Mueller."

"The professor never mentioned her to you?"

The portly German shook his head.

"Professor Kohl kept an office here, didn't he?" Hooks asked.

"That is correct. He sometimes worked here on his writing."

"Perhaps in his files there would be a reference to Anna Mueller."

Bockler shook his head. "The professor did not keep any files here. He kept them elsewhere."

"Where? Hooks asked.

Bockler answered with a shrug. "At his home, I would suppose."

"No files at all?" Hooks pressed.

"No."

"Perhaps in his desk. Maybe there were some notes, a phone number, a random scrap of paper."

"There is nothing," Bockler said.

"How can you be so sure without even looking?" Hooks snapped.

Bockler rose and motioned Hooks to follow him to a door. He pushed it open, and Hooks looked inside. A desk had been turned on its side, a chair was upended, a typewriter lay upside down in the corner of the room. The wastepaper basket was upended in the middle of the floor.

"I can be very sure, Mr. Hooks," Bockler said, "because last night a burglar broke into these offices. He came directly to this office where the professor sometimes worked. If there had been a piece of paper here, it is gone now. That is how I can be so very sure."

He turned from Hooks and walked back to his own desk, the jewelry on his watch chain clicking with each step. Hooks just stared at the looted office, then nodded to himself and came back to apologize for his bad temper. They spoke for a while longer but Hooks found out nothing about Anna Mueller.

Bockler might be lying too. He probably was, Hooks decided, and was just a better actor than Mrs. Kohl and her daughter.

He left the office disappointed. Apparently the only person who did not mind talking about Anna Mueller was Edward Kohl. And Edward Kohl was dead.

* * *

Hooks was eating a sidewalk lunch outside the Congress Hall, a strange American-designed structure that reminded him vaguely of a Roman centurion's helmet. The knockwurst was spicy and the seeded bread was thick and meaty.

At another sidewalk table across from him, he noticed a middle-aged man reading a newspaper, and it triggered a memory. Professor Kohl had thought a newspaper advertisement in America might help him find Anna Mueller. What would happen if Hooks ran the same ad over here in Berlin?

The memory of what had happened in Washington sent a cold finger of fear down Hooks's spine, but he put it aside, wolfed down the rest of his sandwich and walked to a nearby corner where he found a string of taxicabs, waiting for fares, all parked in a neat Germanic row.

He bought a copy of the newspaper at a stand on the corner, paying with an American dollar bill, and walking away before it was necessary to try to figure out his change.

He walked down the line of cabs.

"*Sprechen* English?" he asked hopefully.

"*Nein*," the first two drivers answered.

"Sure, boss," the third driver said. "I speak the English good. You are Englishman?"

"American," Hooks said.

"Good. I speak the American better."

"Good," said Hooks. He got into the backseat and handed the driver the newspaper he had just bought.

"I want to go to this newspaper. To its office."

"Sure, boss. Where?"

"To the newspaper office," Hooks said. He had a sinking feeling that his cabdriver's English was restricted to "Sure, boss," and seven other words whose meaning he did not know.

"Office?"

"Yes. Office of the newspaper. Headquarters." He paused and pronounced it again. "Newspaper. Head-qvarters. *Schnell*."

The driver snapped his head around toward the road. "*Ja*," he said and pulled out of the parking spot.

How he did it, Hooks never figured out, but fifteen minutes later the cab was depositing him outside the offices of the *Berlin Free Press*.

"For you, boss, eight dollars," the cabdriver said.

Hooks considered asking him to wait, then decided against it and gave the driver a ten-dollar bill.

"Thank you," he said.

"Sure, boss."

Placing the ad was easier than finding the newspaper office had been. A rail-thin redheaded woman worked behind the counter in the display advertising department and spoke excellent English. At his request, she gave Hooks a pencil and a piece of paper and he wrote:

I seek information
about Anna Mueller.
Last seen in Berlin in
the spring of 1945.
Age then, about 25.
Contact occupant,
Room 317
Excelsior Hotel.

He handed it to the woman.

"Can you translate this into German for me?" he asked.

She read it quickly and nodded. "A friend of the family?" she asked, even as she began to rewrite his message onto another piece of paper.

"Yes," said Hooks. "My mother's friend. She was just wondering if she was still alive."

"I hope you find her," the woman said. She showed

Hooks her translation and he looked at it, but German made no sense to him at all, and he said, "I'm sure it's fine."

"How large an ad do you want?" she asked.

Hooks hadn't considered that, but the woman showed him several sizes and he settled on a two-column, six-inch long ad that cost him $246 in American money. She assured him it would run in the next day's editions.

"Thank you," he said.

"Good luck," the woman said.

"Oh, one thing," said Hooks. "Can you tell me how to get back to the Excelsior Hotel? Is it walking distance?"

She smiled at him. "Out the door, across the street and walk one block. It's there."

From his room he telephoned the number that Burton Sellers had given him.

As he had expected, the telephone was answered with a brusque "*Guten Tag*," and nothing else—no explanation of what office it was he had reached. It made sense, he thought. It would hardly do to answer telephones, "Hello, this is your friendly Central Intelligence Agency."

"Please speak English," he said to the woman on the other end of the telephone. "My name is Steve Hooks. I'm calling for Burton Sellers."

"Just a moment, please," the woman said, and a few seconds later Sellers was on the line.

"Yeah, Hooks, what's up?"

"I want to talk to you."

"You're not in any trouble, are you?"

"Not yet."

"Okay."

They agreed to meet at the cocktail lounge in the

Excelsior Hotel at five P.M. Hooks looked at his watch, saw he had three hours until the meeting and lay down for a nap. His knee hurt from walking, and he felt a headache starting behind his eyes. He took three aspirins and removed his brace before lying on the bed.

Sellers's eyes were so light a blue that it almost seemed as if the irises faded off into the whites with no clear line of separation. Hooks found it somewhat disconcerting to make eye contact with the thin blond man, so he fussed with his martini glass while they sat in a booth in a far quiet corner of the hotel lounge.

"I don't like it," Sellers said.

"Why not? It seems like the only way I'll find anything out."

Sellers took a long sip from his Dewars on the rocks and waited until Hooks looked up and met his eyes.

"You know, Hooks, I think you misunderstand what I'm doing here," he said.

"Probably. Why don't you fill me in?"

"My thought exactly. One. I don't give a rat's ass about Anna Mueller. Who she was or where she is now. She could be the bearded lady in the Moscow Circus for all I care. Two. I'm sorry Professor Kohl got killed because the little I know about him says that he was probably doing some good by ringing the bell on old Nazis and new would-be Nazis. But as for who killed him, it's none of my business, and it's not my job."

"What is, then?" Hooks asked.

"I was coming to that. Three. Keep Steve Hooks alive. Let him get out of Germany without getting himself killed. That's my job. This newspaper ad might make that more difficult so I don't like this newspaper ad."

"When I met with Frank Casey in Washington, he

made me think you guys would be interested in finding out who killed the professor."

"Who's Frank Casey?" Sellers said blandly. He looked down at his drink, and this time Hooks waited for him to look up.

"Look, Sellers, why don't we clear the air between us? You're not with the Foreign Service, you're with the goddamn CIA. The CIA talked me into coming here, and they gave me to you to shepherd. I don't know exactly what Casey's title is, but he's some kind of a Washington contact man for your group here. We're not going to get anywhere if we're going to keep jerking each other around."

Sellers sipped his drink and finally said, with a disarming grin, "You're not as dumb as you look."

"Thanks," said Hooks.

"And you're not as smart as you think, either."

"How so?"

"All right. I'm with the company. Casey's on our German desk at Langley. But his instructions to me were to get you back safely. He didn't care about Kohl, not really care, anyway. Oh, sure, if you come up with something about some super-Nazi plot to take over the world, starting with Washington, D.C., I think he'd want to know about it, but Kohl's just another guy killed, probably by some idiot splinter group of some lunatic faction of some moronic little terrorist society."

"Then why'd Casey ask me to come here?"

"Truth?"

"If we're going to be friends, let's try it," Hooks said.

"I think maybe he was doing your friend, what's his name, Pardin, a favor. I think maybe Pardin was worried that Kohl's family was going to squawk about American security and that maybe your visit would help stop that, and maybe stop the Secret Service from getting some kind of mud thrown at them. Maybe Pardin didn't think you'd come over here, and so he had Casey—maybe Casey owes him a favor—he had Frank come to your room and fill you with patriotic zeal. Was Casey wearing a trench coat when he came to see you?"

"He was carrying one, and he was smoking a pipe," Hooks said.

"There you go, Steve," said Sellers. Hooks noticed it was the first time the young man had used his first name. "Casey always uses that pipe when he's being theatrical. I think he thinks it makes him look like Sherlock Holmes."

"So what I'm doing here is a charade?" Hooks asked.

Sellers shook his head. "No, I didn't say that. Hey, if you find out who nailed Kohl, terrific. If you find out anything about some terrorist group that's escalated into killing, terrific. But I think basically you were doing a public relations job here."

"I'd still like to know who Anna Mueller was," Hooks said.

"Well, if anybody who reads your ad knows, they're going to call you, that's for sure," Sellers replied, and another smile flashed across his youthful face. "Hey, maybe she'll have a daughter."

"Or two," said Hooks.

The two men ordered another round of drinks, then drifted into a casual good-humored conversation. Sellers was thirty-eight years old, from a wealthy mainline Philadelphia family. He had joined the CIA almost as a lark after graduating Harvard.

"I mean, what the hell else was there for me? I was surrounded by all these stuffy lawyers in my family, living off the interest on their interest, and I was sitting there at commencement thinking, When I die, what are they going to put on my gravestone? Here lies Burt Sellers. He clipped coupons with the best of them. And I thought, What a crock, and I remembered the name of the CIA recruiter who'd been on campus a little bit before, and I called him."

"No regrets?" Hooks asked.

"Just one. If I had had a French nanny instead of a German *hausfrau* taking care of me when I was growing up, hell, I'd probably be on duty in Paris, cutting through those French chippies like a hot knife through soft lard. Instead I speak German, so here I am. In the land of oompah-oompah."

"The German women I've seen don't look so bad," Hooks said.

"All the good-looking ones are Russian spies," said Sellers. "The Russians rent them from Finland and Norway 'cause there isn't much to choose from in the USSR. It's not bad duty here, though. A lot of things happen in West Berlin that I can't tell you about because you're a civilian now, but I got into this because I wanted to get the bad guys, and around here at least you know who the bad guys are." He waved his arm dramatically around his head in a swooping full circle. "West Berlin's surrounded by the bad guys."

They drank some more and went to dinner at one of the large dining rooms in the hotel. Hooks found himself relaxing more as the evening wore on. At first, when Sellers had told him that his visit to Germany was primarily for public relations purposes, he had felt hurt and used, but now it seemed to have taken the tension out of him and he found himself relaxing and enjoying the evening's drinking.

Sellers, had, of course, heard of the jury verdict that had acquitted the assassin who had shot Hooks's wife and forever changed his life. "It made me sick," Sellers said, "that anybody could turn that bastard loose."

"He's not loose," Hooks said. "He'll be in a nuthouse. If he ever gets out, I just may go and close the door on him."

"You let me know if you need an untraceable gun, Steve. I'll find you one."

"Thanks. I may hold you to that someday."

At the end of the long, sodden night, it was Burt and Steve, and Sellers had told Hooks he would be over in the morning to start answering Hooks's phone.

"Why?"

"This is Berlin, buddy. Anybody who calls answering your ad is going to speak German. What are you going to tell them? *Gesundheit?*"

"I guess you're right."

They parted in the lobby. "Go right upstairs now," Sellers said. "I'm responsible for you."

"Okay, Burt. I'm going to go read for a while."

"What are you going to read?"

"I don't know. Maybe *Rise and Fall of the Third Reich.*"

"Lousy plot. But a great ending," Sellers said.

CHAPTER THIRTEEN

SELLERS SHOWED UP AT FIVE MINUTES PAST TEN WITH A
tape recorder, a deck of cards, a copy of the newspaper
with Hooks's advertisement circled in red and a tray of
hot coffee and toast from room service.

If he was any the worse for wear from the previous
night's drinkathon, the youthful CIA agent didn't show
it. Hooks felt hungover, and it took a preliminary cup of
coffee and a long shower to restore him.

When he came back into the bedroom, Sellers was
hooking the tape recorder up to the telephone. Hooks
sat on the edge of the bed, and Sellers glanced over at
his surgically scarred left knee, the pale white skin
crisscrossed by puckered pink lines.

"Christ, Joe Namath has nothing on you," he said.

"Except sex appeal and a million dollars," replied
Hooks.

"True, true. All too true."

After Hooks dressed, the two men began a marathon
gin rummy game, interrupted only for lunch and for
Sellers to answer the telephone.

Most of the callers had limited English. Several calls
were from newspaper reporters, and Sellers told them
that Anna Mueller was his long-lost aunt but refused to
give them any facts for a story. Two calls were from life
insurance agents who wondered if Anna Mueller's old
age had been adequately provided for by her loved ones.

One call was from a Mrs. Gottlieb who said her husband knew where Anna Mueller was because he had been cheating with her for forty years. It turned out that she believed Mr. Gottlieb had also been cheating with every woman on the block. Sellers was convulsed with laughter after hanging up.

It was five o'clock, and even at half a cent a point, Hooks was down ninety-one dollars to Sellers, when Thelma Winkler called.

Although he couldn't understand what Sellers was saying in his rapid-fire German, Hooks knew the call was important from the intent expression on his face and the notes he was jotting down.

"We may have a live one," he told Hooks after he hung up. "She's an old lady, lives in a nursing home. But she's got her wits together. Her husband was a dentist before the war, and she says Anna Mueller was his patient. I made an appointment to meet her at eight o'clock tonight at her place. I'll get somebody over here to spell us. Might as well have somebody come over right now so we can grab some dinner first."

The somebody proved to be a disgruntled middle-aged man who'd apparently had other plans for the evening until he was given this assignment. Sellers briefed him on how to handle any calls, then said, "Smile, will you? You're giving spy work a bad name."

The man glanced warily at Hooks.

"Don't worry, he's on our side," Sellers said. "Listen. Cheer up. Order a bottle of booze. Have room service send up dinner. We'll be out till nine anyway. If you've got a floozie, invite her over. Bill it all to this guy. He's a rich American. They're all rich."

"Go on, get out of here," the other man said. "And don't be late."

* * *

Hooks guessed that Thelma Winkler was in her late seventies. Her English was limited and uncertain, so the conversation was carried on by Sellers in German with a quick running interpretation for Hooks's benefit.

She said that the Mueller family had been patients of her husband since shortly after he opened his practice, and that as her husband's receptionist, she had known Anna Mueller since she was a little girl. She had grown into a quiet, attractive young woman with blond hair. Her teeth were good and had needed little attention over the years, because she brushed after every meal and came in for regular checkups.

She would not even have remembered Anna Mueller when she noticed the advertisement in the newspaper that day, she added, except that Edward Kohl, the famous writer, had questioned her about the girl some years before. That was before she had moved to the nursing home. But when, at Kohl's request, she had looked for the girl's records in her husband's files, they had been missing. That was why the name Anna Mueller had caught her eye earlier today.

"Find out when Kohl spoke with her," Hooks suggested.

It had been about four years before. Her family was selling the house she had always lived in and were planning to put her in this nursing home. Kohl came to her house, and they talked in her living room, surrounded by piles of cardboard cartons. She said she surprised Kohl when she told him that she still had her husband's office records. They were stored neatly in the cellar. She prided herself on her record keeping. She kept very good records, she said. But Anna Mueller's dental record was missing.

When had she last seen Anna Mueller? Perhaps it was early in 1945. Anna had been working in a hospital.

She dropped in one day to have a small cavity filled, and at that time she did not seem to be disturbed in any way.

No, Anna had never expressed any political opinions other than that she did not believe nations ought to go to war. No, she did not know if Anna had belonged to any of the Nazi youth movement groups, but she did not think it likely.

Where was Thelma Winkler when Anna was last seen in May of 1945? In a hospital, but not the hospital where Anna worked. Frau Winkler had broken a leg when she'd tripped over some rubble in the street. She was still in traction when the Russians arrived, she added, then closed her eyes in pain.

Her husband? Dr. Winkler had died in 1945, she said curtly.

Sellers glanced at Hooks and pressed her on the point. With obvious reluctance, she said that all she knew was that her husband had been escorted from his office by several S.S. men, leaving a patient still in the chair. He had never been seen alive again, to her knowledge, but his body had been found later and identified. He had been killed by two shots in the back of the head.

She became agitated and began speaking rapidly and emphatically, shaking her finger at Sellers, who nodded sympathetically and patted the old woman's wrist. Then she folded her arms and stared away angrily, her lips quivering.

"She says that it was not right or fair for the S.S. to take her husband away and shoot him," Sellers explained quickly. "She says he himself had been a member of the party for many years—much longer than most—and had many high members of the party among his patients. Even Goebbels came to Dr. Winkler. And the good doctor had always urged all his younger patients, including Anna Mueller, to join the party's youth movement and support the *Führer's* efforts to save Germany from its enemies.

"In short, he was a good German. A *very* good German," Sellers said without expression.

"*Ja*," Frau Winkler agreed, nodding vigorously.

She had no idea why her husband had been taken away and shot, but she insisted it must have been some terrible mistake—some mixup of papers, perhaps, that would not have happened if good and smart people had been in charge of the paperwork.

A nephew had taken over her husband's dental practice after the war. Of course, he had kept all her husband's records, and she could not explain why Anna Mueller's charts were missing. Her nephew certainly would not have thrown them away. Suppose Anna Mueller had appeared and wanted some work done? It would be unthinkable not to be able to consult her previous records. That was not her way of doing things. Perhaps Frenchmen did things that way. Or Englishmen.

No, her nephew had never known Anna Mueller because he was from Leipzig. And she could not imagine what had happened to the records, and she had so told Professor Kohl, the famous writer.

Hooks didn't like Thelma Winkler and decided that her husband probably got what he deserved for being a good Nazi. But he couldn't help feeling sorry for the lonely old woman, who was waiting out her days in the crummy old folks' home, and on the way back to the hotel he told Sellers, "Buy the old lady a color television set. I'll pay for it."

Sellers shrugged. "I told you, just put everything on American Express. Counterpart funds cover a lot of sins."

"I wouldn't know how to buy a television set here. You do it and let me know what it costs."

"Okay. You think what she told us was worth it?"

"Probably not," Hooks said. "But she did raise one interesting point."

"What was that?"

"It was thirty-five years after Anna Mueller disappeared that Kohl got to Mrs. Winkler. What happened to prompt that? What was he looking for?"

"Who cares?" Sellers said.

"Burt, you lack the inquisitive mind of a great detective."

"Nonsense. What I've got is the Ensign Pulver mind of the great survivor. Hide in the laundry room until the admiral dies."

The remains of a giant steak were on a steel platter outside the door to Hooks's room. Inside, the agent that Sellers had put on duty was asleep on the bed.

He woke up, seemingly irritated at being disturbed, and said there had been only two more calls while they were away. He had them both on tape.

One was from a drunken man who said he had slept with Anna Mueller a week ago and wanted to know if there was a reward for it.

The other was from a Mrs. Gottlieb. She said to let Anna Mueller know she was going to scratch her eyes out.

CHAPTER FOURTEEN

THE TWO MEN HAD LEFT, AND HOOKS SAT ON THE BED peeling off his shirt. He thought about calling Patti and immediately felt guilty that he had not only not called her sooner, but that she had not been on his mind for the last twenty-four hours. Neither had Joanna.

"How quickly we forget," he mumbled to himself. He thought that Patti would probably be in her office, and he was reaching for the telephone when it startled him by ringing. He picked up the instrument, hoping that it wasn't Mrs. Gottlieb threatening to wreak vengeance on her husband for dallying with Anna Mueller, but a male voice spoke.

"Mr. Hooks?"

"Yes."

"This is the front desk. I'm sorry, but we had a message for you before and we couldn't get through. Your telephone line was busy. May I read the message to you?"

"Go ahead."

"The message reads: 'Steven. I will be in my car in the hotel parking lot at ten P.M.' It is signed Marta."

Hooks felt his pulse jump. "Thank you," he mumbled, and as he replaced the telephone he glanced at his watch. It was ten after ten. Marta must have called directly from the airport when her flight landed. He hoped that she was still waiting there.

He quickly put his shirt back on and hurried downstairs. In the dimly lit parking lot, he recognized her white Opel parked near the far wall. He approached from the passenger side and opened the door. As he did, the overhead courtesy light came on, and he was startled to see that Marta was wearing a black dress with a black veil pulled down over her face.

Marta's hand appeared holding a small black revolver that pointed steadily at his chest.

The voice that came from under the veil was low, hard and masculine. "Just stay there, Mr. Hooks. Make no disturbance, and you will not be shot." Hooks's stomach knotted as he realized it was a man dressed in women's clothing sitting behind the wheel.

He heard footsteps behind him. For a moment he thought it was a passerby and perhaps he could flee if the person behind the wheel tried to conceal the gun.

No such luck. He felt another gun barrel press into his back. One pair of hands pulled his hands behind him and fastened them with handcuffs. Another pair of hands put a blindfold across his eyes and tied it in a tight knot at the base of Hooks's skull.

He let himself be walked a dozen steps or so, where he was helped into the backseat of a car.

"Just remain silent, Mr. Hooks, and nothing will happen to you."

As if to emphasize the point, a gun barrel was pressed into his belly, and Hooks nodded.

"I won't try anything," he said. He wished he had stayed upstairs and telephoned Patti.

They must have moved into a residential area because the traffic sounds had lessened. From time to time, the gun held by the man next to him pushed into his ribs, as if to discourage even thoughts of escape.

What was he supposed to do? Detectives he had read

about were always hearing telltale sounds—a steamboat whistle, a railroad crossing—that let them know where they had been taken. All he heard was the occasional *whoosh* of a passing car. He tried to count the seconds to try to estimate the time of the drive.

He was up to twenty minutes when the car pulled off, and he heard the tires squeak as they rolled up against a curb. The car stopped. The motor was turned off.

"Mr. Hooks," hissed a soft voice. "We are leaving the car now. We did not think to bring tape for your mouth. Please do not think of calling for help, or we will be forced to silence you in a most unpleasant manner."

He nodded and heard the car door open. Someone grabbed his arm and helped him out. His knee almost buckled as he stood up. Not many feet away, he heard an overhead garage door being opened, and then a car passed close by him; it drove a few feet more and then stopped.

He was led up a sloping walk and then down a flight of stairs. Behind him he heard the garage door again creak and groan and then stop with a thud.

The floor was hard under his feet, and the room had the musty odor of a basement.

He was pushed down into a hard chair.

A voice hissed, "Please keep your eyes closed." He felt somebody fumbling with the knot at the back of his blindfold, and then it was off. Instantly he opened his eyes, but the room was completely dark, and he could see nothing. A moment later, something soft was pushed against his eyes, and then the blindfold was restored. Large pieces of fluffy cotton, he decided. To make sure that he could not see from under the blindfold.

He heard a click and had a faint sense that the room was now lighter, but he was effectively blinded.

"Now we can talk, Mr. Hooks," a new voice said.

He heard the shuffle of several pairs of feet, an odd

clicking sound, the scrape of chairs being moved across the floor, a man coughing. People were seating themselves in a row facing him, he thought.

How many?

He decided that there were at least four: the man with the low voice who had impersonated Marta; the man who hissed and whispered and had held the gun on him in the car; there would be the third man who had driven the car carrying Hooks, and the new voice he had just heard. Probably from someone who had been waiting here for them.

"We wish to talk about Professor Edward Kohl," the new voice informed him.

"I'm not a bit surprised," Hooks said. He was pleased that his voice seemed calm. He realized that if they had planned to kill him, he would have been dead by now. No, they wanted information of some sort, and he made an instant decision to answer every question truthfully and thoroughly. Let those who got paid for it be heroes.

The questions started. Step by step, he retraced everything he had done, almost minute by minute, from the time he had met Professor Kohl at Dulles Airport. Then a full accounting of his time in Berlin was demanded. He admitted having taken Marta Kohl to dinner and then seeing her to her apartment. He did not volunteer that he had spent the night and, to his surprise, they did not question him further about it.

The omission worried him. Did they know something about Marta that he didn't? Was she all right?

"Where is Marta, anyway?" he blurted out. "Is she safe?"

"She is, I believe, in Greece at this time and I presume she is quite safe, Mr. Hooks. Why are you concerned about her?"

"Because you're driving around in her car. I wondered where she was."

The other man hesitated. "You were seen to leave the Kohl home with her yesterday afternoon. We took the liberty of borrowing her car from its place at the airport, and we will return it there later tonight. It was . . . a convenience."

Hooks wondered why the man had bothered to explain.

"And now today," the voice asked. "You were in your room all day, Mr. Hooks, with another man. Who was that man?"

"His name is Sellers. He's with the American Embassy."

"And what was his business with you?"

"I was expecting some telephone calls. I asked him to translate the German for me. I speak no German."

"These would be the answers to your advertisement about Anna Mueller?" the other voice asked.

They knew about the ad. Of course, they would have. Why had he been thinking that he could omit that part of the story?

"That's correct," he said.

"Did you have many callers?"

"A large number. Most of them cranks."

"Tell us about the ones who were not cranks," the voice said.

"It was one. An old lady in a nursing home. She said that Anna Mueller was a dental patient of her husband's. Her husband was killed by the . . ." He hesitated. Should he say Nazis? Suppose they were Nazis? "By the S.S. toward the end of the war. She said Anna Mueller just turned up missing one day, and no one ever heard from her again."

"Yes," the voice said, as if it had heard the story before. There was only the one voice questioning him, an educated voice, fluent in English, and Hooks had the feeling it belonged to a man of at least middle age or older. At times it sounded almost familiar, but he could not think of where he had heard it before.

The questioning went back to how Hooks had come to be selected as Kohl's bodyguard. He had been able to hold back when Marta had asked him the same questions, but this time he told more. "A friend of mine in the Secret Service received the professor's request for protection. He knew it was nothing that the government could provide, but he also knew that I was looking for work, so he recommended me."

"I see. And who was this friend?"

"His name is Bob Pardin. He works for the director of the Secret Service." His voice was growing hoarse, and he was grateful when he was allowed to sip from a glass of water held to his lips. His wrists were chafing behind his back.

Eventually the questions slowed and finally halted. There was a mumbled consultation among several voices. Straining Hooks heard one voice whisper, "*Nein.*"

"*Nein*" what? he wondered. *Nein*, don't use the Luger, use the ice pick?

He heard chairs being pushed back, the sounds of feet, the familiar sounding metallic clicking, a heavy smoker's cough, and two large hands grasped his shoulders, lifting him to his feet.

"We are taking you from here now to another place to release you, Mr. Hooks," his interrogator informed him. "You should be back at your hotel within ninety minutes. It would be best, I think, if you said nothing of this happening to the police. You have been truthful with us tonight, Mr. Hooks. Will you continue to be truthful? Do you promise no police?"

"Of course I promise. No police. I won't say a word to them."

"And you will not make any foolish attempt to escape before you are released?"

"Not me. I don't argue anymore with people who have guns. If I never see another gun for the rest of my life, it would make me very happy," Hooks said fervently, wishing that he had a machine gun in his hands at that moment.

"This is good. I agree with you, guns are bad things, and the people who enjoy using them are bad people. I regret that we found it necessary to use force to bring you here tonight, but we could think of no other way to do it."

"I understand," said Hooks, who did not understand at all. "But would you mind telling me who you are and why you wanted to talk to me?"

"Yes, we would," the other man replied. "Good night, Mr. Hooks."

He was led toward the steps, but as his foot reached the first step, he could not restrain himself.

"One more question," he called out. "Who is Anna Mueller?"

There was only silence for a long moment, and then his questioner's voice said sadly, "Just another poor innocent who died in the war. Good night, Mr. Hooks. Return to the United States, to your family."

Hooks was placed back in the car, and another drive followed, but this time it seemed like they didn't try to confuse his sense of direction, because the drive took only about fifteen minutes before the car slowed to a stop.

He was guided out of the car and over an irregular grass surface for a distance of several hundred yards, he estimated. Fingers fumbled with the handcuffs on his wrists and finally his hands were free.

He should be in Hollywood, he thought. Now he could rip the blindfold from his face, spin around and

111

down his captors with karate thrusts, then march them all off to prison.

But this was Berlin. He stood stock-still as a voice intoned, "You will stand here, facing in this direction, for at least five minutes. Do not remove the blindfold from your eyes. A man will be watching you. If you disobey, he will shoot you. Do you understand?"

"I understand. I'll stand right here."

He began counting to sixty by thousands, slowly, very slowly. Before he reached it, he could hear the sound of a car door closing and a car driving off. He was sure nobody had remained behind to watch him, but he saw no sense in disobeying the orders, so he continued counting to sixty, repeating the procedure five times.

Then he did it once more, just in case.

Finally, he removed the cloth holding the cotton pads against his eyes. It was dark, and there was almost no moon, but he was able to make out trees and bushes. He was in some kind of park, he realized.

He turned slowly around and walked back the way he had come, as best as he could judge. He soon came to a blacktop road and began following it, and eventually it led him to an entrance to the park. He walked for some time along a city street, hoping to see a taxicab, but the first thing he saw was a tavern.

The bartender spoke no English, but a patron understood Hooks's request and cheerfully telephoned for a taxicab. Ten minutes later, he was riding back to his hotel. As soon as he arrived, he called the number Sellers had given him. He left a message with the woman who answered the telephone to have Sellers call him immediately. Urgent.

Before he had gotten his shirt off, the telephone rang.

"What's up, Steve?" asked Sellers.

"You're not the police, are you?" Hooks demanded.

"Not me. I'm Foreign Service. Ask anybody."

"Good, then I can tell you what just happened to me."

He succinctly outlined what had happened since Sellers had left the hotel room earlier that night, but he was careful not to mention any names, just in case his telephone line was tapped.

"I'll be damned," Sellers said when he was finished. "Christ, I'm glad nothing happened to you."

"Me too," Hooks said sincerely.

"Cause my ass'd be grass if you got hurt," Sellers said.

"I'm touched by your concern for my welfare, Burt," said Hooks.

"You going to report this?" Sellers asked.

"I just did. That's why I called you."

"I mean to the police."

"Hell, no. I promised I wouldn't, and I always keep my promises to people who carry guns," Hooks said.

"It's probably all for the best. Do you have any idea who might have done it?"

"No. Maybe I've got an idea who *didn't* do it."

"What do you mean?" Sellers snapped.

"I don't think they were pros. Not the cops, not the Russians, not even gangsters. These people were smart, but they were amateurs. This isn't their regular line of work."

"How do you know?"

"Because I'm still alive, for one thing. And little things. Taking me to a residential cellar. I don't think that's too smart. Forgetting a gag and improvising a blindfold. Giving me water when I got thirsty. Just not professional."

"I see."

"But what's interesting is using Marta's name and her car. How'd they know I'd respond to her message? They must have been following me to see me with her. Or else they were following her. I just don't—"

"Hold on," Sellers interrupted. "I want to get some guys out to the airport."

He was off the line for several minutes.

"It's probably too late, but it would be nice if we could see who delivers that car back to the airport," he explained when he returned.

"I thought about that, but it went right out of my mind when I started talking to you," Hooks confessed. "That's why they dumped me in the park, though. To give them time to get the car back to the airport, before I could bring the police in on it. I realized that while I was in the cab coming back to the hotel." Suddenly Hooks wavered on his feet for a moment, and sat back heavily on the bed.

"I'm bushed," he said. "I've got to get some sleep."

"Bolt your door," Sellers ordered.

"Believe it. And a chair jammed under the doorknob. Hey. Have your guys find out one thing for me, if they can."

"What's that?"

"Whether the Opel was broken into and the wires jumped, or whether a regular key was used."

"Interesting questions," Sellers allowed.

"And maybe what Marta's flight schedule from Athens is," Hooks added.

"I'll see what we can find out. Go to bed, Steve. And no more trips tonight, okay?"

"Pray God," Hooks answered.

CHAPTER FIFTEEN

SELLERS SOUNDED CHIPPER AND ALERT WHEN HIS TELE-phone call woke Hooks the next morning.

"How do you feel?" he asked.

"Ask me when I wake up," Hooks growled. "What'd you find out?"

"The girl's car was already at the airport when we got there. The hood was still warm so we didn't miss them by much, dammit. My guys finagled the door open and checked the ignition. It looked like the wires were jumped."

"How could they tell?" Hooks asked.

He could almost hear Sellers shrug over the phone.

"Hey, Steve, how could *I* tell? You know us cookie pushers in the Foreign Sevice don't know anything about things like that."

"Yeah. Well, I guess that means the girl wasn't involved. Maybe," Hooks said.

"Maybe," Sellers agreed.

"Did you find out when she's due back? From Greece?"

"Yeah. She arrived at about four A.M. She's back now. I've got a question."

"What is it?" Hooks asked.

"How long are you thinking of gracing Berlin with your presence?"

"I don't know. I thought about it before I fell asleep. I think I'll probably go back tomorrow. Why?"

"Don't forget my mission. To make sure that nothing happens to you. If you were going to stay around, I'd get you a gun and a bullet-proof vest."

Hooks chuckled and Sellers said, "I'm serious," and Hooks stopped chuckling.

"I guess you are. No, tomorrow I'll leave. Can you arrange a flight for me into Washington?"

"Nothing would give me more pleasure," Sellers said.

"All right, I'll talk to you later."

He hung up the telephone and realized he could have left today, and he tried to convince himself that he was staying the extra day so that he could sightsee and shop for souvenirs for Patti and Joanna. But he finally gave it up and admitted that he wanted to see Marta again.

He dialed her telephone number. The phone rang three times before a tape-recorded message in Marta's voice came on. The message was in German, and Hooks could not understand a word of it, but he understood the beep tone after the message, and when it sounded, he said, "This is Steve Hooks. I'll try to call you early this afternoon. If you're going to be out of town, please leave a message at my hotel. I'm leaving tomorrow."

After dressing and eating a large, lard-laden German breakfast, he wandered out into the business district.

He browsed for several hours through a string of tiny shops, then finally picked out two expensive silk scarves for Joanna and Patti as mementos of the trip. He briefly considered buying Marta a scarf, too, but rejected the idea. It seemed an act of disloyalty to his wife and his sister-in-law.

Carrying his small plastic shopping bag, he stopped in a cozy wood-paneled tavern and ordered a beer.

When it came, he thought about what had happened to him the night before and realized with a start that it was the first time he had thought of it since waking that morning. Maybe he had been in Berlin too long already, when kidnapping was regarded as just another of the day's events. Or maybe it was that he had known instinctively last night that he was somehow in no real danger from the men who had abducted him.

But it was time to go home. Time to wash his hands of Professor Kohl's death and the search for Anna Mueller. Time to tell Pardin everything he had and had not learned. Time to resume his life with Joanna and, yes, with Patti. It was time for that.

But first, there was Marta Kohl. One more time.

He called her again from his hotel room.

"I am so glad that you called me, Steven," she said, with a touch of sultriness in her husky voice. "I was afraid you would fly back to America and forget all about me."

"I was kidnapped last night, Marta," he said flatly.

"Oh, stop joking," she said.

"I was. In your car."

She was silent for a moment. "This is not a joke?"

"No. No joke."

"You . . . I don't understand. Kidnapped? In my car?"

"That's what happened."

"Are you all right?"

"I'm fine."

"I am all confused. I have my car with me. How did this happen?"

"It's too complicated for the telephone," he said, and as he had hoped she would, she invited him to come over to her apartment.

He was there in fifteen minutes.

Marta Kohl was wearing a red sweat suit, soaked burgundy by perspiration, when she opened the door for him. She inspected him sharply.

"They did not hurt you," she said, reaching for his arm and pulling him into the apartment.

"That's right. They let me go, safe and sound."

She led him to the sofa, then poured two cups of coffee into mugs that were waiting on the coffee table. She had made her bed, he noticed.

"Tell me about it," she said. "All about it."

Hooks briefly recounted the incident. "So when I got back to the hotel, I went to bed. I had promised that I wouldn't call the police and I didn't see what good calling them would do anyway, so I let it go at that."

"I do not understand this business of using my car," she said, wringing her hands nervously. "I left it at the airport, and it was there when I got back this morning. Are you sure it was my car? There are many similar cars here in Germany."

Hooks shook his head. "It was your car. It had those papers stuffed on top of the dashboard and that decal on the passenger's window."

Marta's mouth trembled, and Hooks patted her hand reassuringly.

"First my father . . . and now this," she said. "I do not understand it. What can I do?"

Hooks put his arm around her shoulder and pulled her toward him. She laid her head gratefully against his chest. He felt sorry for her, and he also felt his heart beating faster.

"Don't worry about it," he said. "I'm leaving tomorrow. With me gone, this trouble goes."

She turned to him. "Must you leave?"

He nodded and saw there were tears in the corners of her bright-green eyes, and then she reached up and put her lips to his.

"I will miss you," she said.

"And I you."

"You will make love to me one more time?"

"Well . . . all right," he said, and thought, God, what I do for my country.

Marta was in the shower.

She had apologized earlier because, she'd said, she'd been exercising and sweating like a pig and how could any man make love to a woman so unappetizing? She had peeled off her sweat suit as she'd made this apology and Hooks had been prepared to show her that her basic conclusion was wrong but she'd gotten up and padded quickly away, naked, across the floor to the bathroom.

Now he heard her call his name, and he walked to the bathroom door.

"Yes?"

"Come in here."

He opened the door and stepped inside. The small bathroom was filled with steam. Through a translucent plastic curtain, he could see Marta standing in the tub, under the shower spray, her body large and full and magnificent.

"Yes?" he said.

"Take off your clothes and come in here. I want you to wash my back."

"My brace," he began.

"And my front," she said.

He began to undress.

The long afternoon shadows were beginning to fade into evening's darkness as Hooks rode back in a cab to his hotel. He was having trouble sorting out his feelings about Marta. For some reason, he felt he ought to despise her, for the free-living *fräulein* was everything that Joanna was not—a wild, sex-obsessed floozie who would jump into bed with a man she barely knew. God only knew how many men she had slept with—or women, for that matter.

And yet she was attractive, vivacious and charming, and she had released some long-denied desires within him, desires he hadn't even suspected he had. He realized that he did not even feel guilty about having been unfaithful to Joanna for the first time in their life together, and he tried to make up for it by feeling guilty that he did not feel guilty.

His thoughts jumped, as lately they so often did, to Patti. She had always been wilder, more impulsive than her older sister—and more sensual, he had always suspected. Was her private life like Marta's? Were there a succession of men for casual bedroom calisthenics? Did she enjoy an exotic variety of positions and practices? Where once he had chided himself for picturing Patti making bland perfunctory love with some faceless man, now he had vivid mental images of her doing this . . . and that . . . and that . . . and all too often the man in the picture with her was himself.

And the images were more intense now. It was as if he had fantasized in black and white before, and was now daydreaming in lurid living color.

He wondered how he would be able to face her on his return, and he worried more about her reaction to his infidelity, if he should ever confess it, than he did about how Joanna would react. Sadly, he realized he had probably given up expecting Joanna ever to react again.

His own words came back to him.

"Till death do us part. . ."

But this time they had a hollow ring.

At the hotel there was a message to call Sellers.

"Best I could do," the CIA man told him. "I've got you on a flight leaving Tegel at seven forty-five A.M., by way of Hamburg and London. You'll get into Washington about two-thirty local time."

"I have to change planes twice?"

"No avoiding it, Steve. Not unless you want to stay here until Oktoberfest. I can probably get you something direct then."

"No thanks. No offense intended, but I want to get out of here."

"I can understand it," Sellers said.

"And I guess you'll be happy to be rid of me so you can get back to work."

"Not true," said Sellers. "I was supposed to keep you alive, and I kept you alive. Mission accomplished. If you live through the night."

"I'll try," Hooks promised earnestly.

"By the way, just for your information, you weren't really a company operation, so I didn't file any reports. All I did was a memo for Frank Casey about your kidnapping. Anything else you want to tell them, go ahead."

"Thanks. Listen, if you ever get finished with this German duty or you ever get back for a vacation, look me up. Least I can do is buy you a drink stateside."

"I'll take you up on that, Steve," Sellers promised. "Adios, partner. Your tickets will be left at the hotel desk."

"Thanks. Take care of yourself. And don't forget that television set for Mrs. Winkler."

"It's already there."

Hooks ate dinner alone in one of the hotel's small dining rooms, and later in the evening he called Professor Kohl's widow.

She sounded surprised and pleased to hear from him. "But I was worried," she said. "What is this thing that my daughter told me? Someone tried to hurt you? And they used her car?"

"It was nothing, Mrs. Kohl," Hooks assured her. "Might even have been a mistake. I don't want you to worry. I'm going back to the United States tomorrow, and I just wanted to say good-bye to you before I left. You were very kind to me."

"Ach, it was nothing. Would you like to come here for dinner tonight? I have baked a fresh strudel."

"That would be very nice, but I can't," he said. "If I ever come back to Berlin, I'll accept your offer."

"All right, Mr. Hooks. *Auf wiedersehen*. Get home safely."

"I will," he promised. "And I hope if we meet again, it will be under happier circumstances."

"Come back for strudel," she said.

He hung up with relief. Grieving widows made him nervous—especially when they were more concerned with strudels than with grief.

Later he went down to the hotel lobby store and bought a large box of chocolates and had it sent to Frau Kohl.

And he bought an expensive scarf for Marta. What the hell.

CHAPTER SIXTEEN

AFTER A RESTLESS NIGHT WITH LITTLE SLEEP, FOLLOWED by an early departure and nearly half a day of either flying in airplanes or waiting to change planes or obeying bureaucratic instructions, Hooks was totally exhausted when he finally reached Dulles Airport.

He had doggedly carried Joanna's copy of *Karamazov* with him and even more doggedly had forced himself to read it while waiting and flying. The book was slow and heavy going, but he was able to fill his mind with Dostoevski's tortured visions and so keep his mind off his kidnapping, the murder of Professor Kohl and the question of who was Anna Mueller. He would tell Pardin about his trip, and that would be that. His hands were clean.

When he got into a taxicab at Dulles, he gave the address of his apartment and sat back with a sigh. Home at last.

He wondered if he should call Patti at her office or wait until she got home after work. But she might not go straight home, he thought. Maybe she had a heavy date with some big ape.

She would be hurt if he didn't call her as soon as he could, he decided. He would call her from the apartment.

He wondered if she would be able to tell instantly from his voice that he was an adulterous son of a bitch.

If she did, she disguised it cleverly with a squeal of pleasure.

"Steve! Are you all right? Why didn't you call? Is everthing okay? Isn't the weather terrific? Was it this nice in Berlin? Tell me all about it. Are we going to have dinner tonight?"

"Slow down, slow down, slow down," he said. "It'll take me half the night to answer the questions you just asked."

"I've got half the night," she said. "I'll pick up steak and French fries, okay? Maybe you'd rather eat out. You could have sauerbraten or something. I'd cook sauerbraten for you, but I don't know what it is. I'm a lousy cook. You shouldn't expect me to make sauerbraten."

"Steak and fries sound good. Bring beer too," he said.

Hooks changed into slacks and a sweat shirt and went inside to clean up the kitchen. Patti must have been there during his trip to Berlin because the dishes were all washed and stacked in the drain rack. Idly he picked up one of the plates and saw a speck of dried egg on its surface. Oh well, nobody was perfect—except maybe Joanna.

He thought about that for a moment.

He had loved his wife with a strong unwavering love and had happily focused his life around her, but he had never thought of her as "perfect" before the . . . the accident. Was it wise to idealize her now, simply because she was dying a lingering death in that hospital bed?

Wasn't it because he had finally given up hope, had finally begun thinking of her as already being dead, that he was now picturing Joanna with a halo around her head?

No halos. Joanna was often cranky. She never bore pain or disappointment well. She wanted her way, and she could be hellishly stubborn, especially about small unimportant things. She started a lot of things and finished only a small fraction of them.

She was very human.

She loved being held in his arms and cuddling up against him in bed, but after their first few months of marriage, she had shown little interest in sex. Their lovemaking had been routine and unimaginative, and she had been dutiful rather than enthusiastic.

In fact, compared to Marta, she was lousy in bed.

The thought paralyzed Hooks. He felt as if he would be struck by lightning at any moment. He held his breath; his mind whirled.

Nothing happened.

A surge of pain and self-disgust swept over him. How could he compare his loving, honest, tender-hearted wife with that slut stewardess? How could he betray her so? . . . It was worse than the actual act of infidelity to put her on a level with Marta.

He wandered back into the living room and slumped onto the couch. He tried to picture the two women standing side by side. Joanna seemed to look at Marta with amazement and a touch of horror, while Marta smiled back, condescendingly, sure of herself and contemptuous of Joanna's determinedly naive opinion of her.

Was Marta really that bad, he wondered, to be looked upon with horror by Joanna? He had known her only a brief time but he found no evil in her.

The two women were still in his mind. Now Marta seemed to be looking at Joanna with sympathy, even sadness . . . and Joanna, the disdain still on her face, seemed to be fading . . . fading . . . while Marta remained vivid and distinct.

That was wrong. Marta was just a brief interlude in his life, while Joanna was his wife until death.

But she was dim, indistinct, fading out, while Marta glowed with vitality and life.

Glowing and vibrant. . . .

The ring of the doorbell snapped him from his daydream. Before he could move from the couch, Patti unlocked the door and bounced in.

"Welcome home," she cried exuberantly, tossing him a package. "I picked up a strudel for dessert."

With Patti pumping, Hooks found himself talking steadily throughout dinner and afterward, as they sat in the living room sipping red wine, which he had found under the sink. He had the radio tuned, with the volume down low, to a station that played big band numbers from the thirties and forties.

He had described in detail his conversation with Frau Kohl, noting that her daughter was there but had little to say. He also dwelt at length on Thelma Winkler's story, and he had given Patti a brief travelogue of Berlin, centering mostly on the zoo, which he remembered, and making up things that he did not.

"So finally, it was pretty clear I was wasting my time there 'cause I wasn't going to find anything out. So I came back. But not empty-handed."

He went into the bedroom and returned with the scarves he had bought for Patti and Joanna.

She berated him for spending so much money on souvenirs.

"It wasn't my money. If I didn't use it, thieving congressmen would."

"Well, then, that's all right. They're perfect, Steve. Perfect."

She looked silently at the gifts for a few moments more, then glanced sharply up at him.

"What's the matter, Steve? What happened in Berlin?"

His jaw dropped. Another witch woman. She was as

126

bad as her sister. Were all women born with the ability to look through him as if he were a pane of glass?

"What are you talking about?"

She shook her head. "I know you too well. I can tell when you're holding something back. What happened in Berlin that you don't want to tell me about?"

He hesitated, terribly tempted to blurt out, "I got laid by a gorgeous girl with the morals of a mink and a motor that moved in seven directions at once."

No, he couldn't say that. Not now. Probably not ever.

She looked down, an embarrassed flush darkening her face. "Steve, I . . . I'm sorry if I'm putting my nose in where it doesn't belong. Forget that I asked."

More damned mind reading. Maybe his thoughts were written in fiery letters on his forehead? If they could perfect this act, they could make a million in show business.

He sighed. "I didn't want to tell you, Patti, but I was kidnapped."

"Three gorgeous blondes, no doubt," she said.

"No, three men with guns."

Her eyes grew round with shock.

"It was right after Sellers—the guy from the Foreign Service—and I went to talk to that Mrs. Winkler," he said and launched once again into a description of his abduction. He could recite it by heart now.

When he was finished, she let out a long breath. "You could have been killed."

"Honest? It never occurred to me at the time, but after a while I could figure out that they didn't really intend to hurt me. They were just pumping for information. You sure you weren't one of them?"

"No joking matter," she snapped. "I'm probably going to have nightmares, and it's your fault."

"Remind me not to schedule any more kidnappings when I go on vacation," he said. "And you drink some warm milk before you got to bed. It puts them night-mares to sleep." He glanced at his watch. "And speaking of sleep . . . Come on, I'll walk you to your car. It's getting to be that time."

"I thought I'd stay here," she said.

"You'll be late for work," he warned.

"Tomorrow's Saturday."

"Oh." He had lost track of the days.

"Don't even know what day it is, you must have had a wonderful time in Germany. How was the weather?"

"Wonderful."

"Did you feed the animals?"

"What animals?"

"In the zoo," she said.

"I threw one kid to the lions. He wouldn't sing the 'Star Spangled Banner' when I told him to."

"I don't understand that part about the stolen car. Why did they steal that girl's car to kidnap you? It's a big city, right? It must be full of cars they could steal. Why hers?"

I'm dead, he decided.

"When I left Mrs. Kohl, she insisted that her daughter drive me back to the hotel because there aren't many cabs cruising that neighborhood. It's all small homes. So these guys must have been watching the house and followed us. Then the next night they stole the car while she was working, and left me a message that she wanted to see me. I fell for it. I figured maybe she had some information she wanted to give me, and I recognized the car so I walked right up to it and got a gun in my face, and that was that."

She frowned. "What's her name?"

"Err, Mary, I think. No. Marty? No. Marta, that's it, Marta." Patti stared at him silently.

He wished he wasn't trying to give up smoking. He could light a cigarette, set his hair on fire and run from the building. No. Too complicated. Something simple. A heart attack.

"Where does she work, this Marta?"

Definitely a heart attack.

"She's a stripper in a local burlesque house. I kept meaning to catch her act, but I forgot."

She still stared at him. "You're teasing, right? She's not a stripper, is she?"

"No. She works for an airline, I think. Something to do with travel." He thought of the burlesque houses he had visited as a teenager. Marta could have had star billing.

Patti shook her head. "I don't like it, Steve. You could have been killed."

"Not me. Can't keep a good man down."

That's right, he thought. Get clever, Hooks.

"I'd like to see anybody try to keep you down," she said loyally, and he smiled and yawned.

"Oh, you poor thing. You're up hours too late. You're jet lagging."

"Guilty, Your Honor."

"Go to bed. I'll get the dishes. Git, git, git," she said, shooing him from the room as if he were a trespassing chicken.

He went without argument, a reprieved man escaping from the shadow of the gallows. Thank you, God. I don't deserve it, but thanks anyway.

His body was overtired, and he slept fitfully through the night. He woke up with a start just about dawn, wondering what had awakened him. The apartment was silent. Vaguely, he could hear a car moving down the street. He decided that his internal alarm clock was malfunctioning, but as long as he was awake, he got up to go to the bathroom.

His unbraced leg almost collapsed under him as he

129

stood, and Hooks wondered how long it would be before the fact that his knee was permanently damaged totally registered on all levels of his mind, so that he would no longer try prancing out of bed like a teenager, but would automatically favor the leg.

Then he remembered Patti was sleeping in the living room. Perhaps she had made a sound that had awakened him. He tossed his robe over his naked body and limped carefully into the other room.

Patti was lying on her side on the couch, breathing deeply. Her blanket had slipped down almost to the swell of her hip. She was wearing one of Joanna's nightgowns, a sheer peach-colored silk garment with a tiny row of lace ruffles about the neckline. Her left breast had slipped from the gown and Hooks's eyes fixed on it, and he moved closer and knelt beside her, bowing his head until it was only inches from her flesh.

He wanted to reach out, to touch her, to kiss her, to fill her with the same flush of desire that was running through his body.

But he did not dare.

His gaze crept up her body, lingered on the shadowed loveliness of her throat and rested at last on her face, which grew ever clearer as the morning light grew stronger. Her lips were slightly parted, and he could just make out the edge of her upper teeth.

He had never in his life felt such a desire to kiss someone as he did at that moment. He had no thought of Joanna or Marta; they might have never existed. Nothing had existed in the world or in his life until now except that face and those lips. He could feel his head inclining toward hers as if some giant hand were pushing him down . . . down . . . down.

He squeezed his eyes shut and clenched his jaws so tightly that he felt his teeth would shatter. Then, slowly, as if bowed under a tremendous weight, he forced himself to lean away from her and stood up.

He took one last, loving look, and walked silently back to the bedroom. From there he glanced once again toward Patti. She was sleepily fumbling with the blanket, her eyes still shut in sleep. She pulled it back up over her bare breast and shoulder and gave a sigh of contentment.

Hooks went back to bed, thinking that what he really needed was an ice-cold shower.

And that what he didn't need was an empty bed.

CHAPTER SEVENTEEN

HOOKS HAD OPENED JOANNA'S RIGHT HAND AND PUT THE scarf across her palm. Her fingers remained open.

Gently, he closed the fingers of her hand around the piece of rad-and-white silk. The fingers remained closed.

Her eyes were shut. Her chest rose and fell slightly with her shallow breathing. Her ash-blond hair had been combed and lay evenly on the pillow framing her smooth-featured, pretty face.

Hooks looked at her face for a long moment, then sat in the chair at the side of the bed.

"I hope you like the scarf, Jo. It's red and white, and it's got little gold threads running through it. When I saw it I said, 'That's just the thing for Joanna.' So I hope you like it. Patti said you would.

"Berlin was all right. Nothing really happened there except I did a lot of sight-seeing. I missed you. I wish you had been able to take the trip with me. It's a shame we didn't do more traveling when we had the . . . when we had more time to do it.

"I've been reading your book every chance I get. I thought if I'm going to read it to you, I'd better start practicing up on all those Russian names. I'll start now, okay?

"'Alexey Fyodorovitch Karamazov was the third son

of Fyodor Pavlovitch Karamazov, a landowner well-known in our district in . . ."

Hooks stopped reading ten minutes later when Mrs. Bordino, the day nurse, came into the room.

She smiled when she saw him, and he stood and put the paperback book into his pocket.

"I thought you were out of the country, Mr. Hooks," she said.

"I just got back. Any change?"

"Well, she hasn't improved," the woman said carefully.

"Has she gotten worse?"

"Not really, but . . ."

"But what, Mrs. Bordino?" He stopped. "Let's not talk here, as if Joanna can't hear us. We don't know that, do we?"

They stepped outside the door of the room.

"I'm sorry, Mr. Hooks," the nurse said. "It's just that Joanna's condition, well, it's just a strain on all of us. There's just never any change. If there is, it may be just a slow, gradual deterioration, but it's so slow and so gradual that there's just nothing for us to fight against. All we can do is wait. I know how hard it is on you, Mr. Hooks. I just . . . well, it's hard on us too."

"I know, Mrs. Bordino. You've been awfully good to both of us. Just give me a moment. I wanted to say good-bye."

He stood alongside the bed.

"Sleep well, Jo. Get your rest. I'll be back as soon as I can. You can count on that."

And she could, he told himself fiercely as he left the room.

CHAPTER EIGHTEEN

"SO I GAVE UP ON IT AND CAME HOME," HOOKS CON-
cluded.

Robert Pardin produced a long, thin aluminum tube
from an inside coat pocket, removed a fresh cigar,
inspected it carefully and lit it. He puffed the smoke
courteously to one side, then studied the glowing tip of
the slender cigar as if surprised at what he saw there.
Then he looked on Hooks's cluttered desk for an ashtray.

"That's all Mrs. Winkler had to say?" Pardin asked.

Hooks rose heavily, walked to the file cabinet and
removed an ashtray. He put it on the desk.

"Sorry. I'm trying to quit and it helps to hide the
ashtray. Yeah, Mrs. Winkler said Anna Mueller vanished. That's all she knew."

"Not very helpful," Pardin said.

"No, but at least it tells you there was an Anna
Mueller. I didn't think Professor Kohl invented the girl.
He might have been a little crazy, but he wasn't nuts."

"You think he was crazy?" Pardin asked.

"I don't know. He was obsessed anyway with Nazis.
But that's a good thing to be obsessed by, I guess. He did
the world some good with his work."

"A Nazi under every bed?" Pardin said with a slight
frown. "I don't know that that's good."

"It is if there *is* a Nazi under every bed," Hooks
replied.

"You're a crusader now?" said Pardin. "I didn't think you were the type."

"I'm a small businessman, trying to make a living," Hooks corrected. "Crusades are for those who can afford them."

"You've got no idea who those kidnappers were?" Pardin asked. "No familiar voice, nothing?"

"No," Hooks said. "Oh. Your name came up, by the way."

Pardin put his cigar down on the ashtray. "My name? How?"

"They wanted me to be very specific about how I was hired as Kohl's guard. I told them the job came from you, because you knew I was out of work."

Pardin nodded slowly. "I wish you hadn't told them that."

"Why not?"

"It kind of involves our government in this whole mess."

"Hey, they knew the government was involved. I told them that the government sent me over to bring regrets to Mrs. Kohl."

"You really chitchatted away, didn't you?"

"Sometime when you have a gun next to your ear, you can give me lessons on being the strong silent type," Hooks snapped.

"Easy, easy," Pardin said casually. "I'm sure you did what you had to do."

"Damn right," said Hooks. "And while we're on the subject, you never expected me to find out anything over there, did you?"

"What are you talking about?" Pardin said. His face was a mask of innocent curiosity.

"I kind of got the impression from the local CIA people that there was no investigation going on into Kohl's death. Basically, I was there as a public relations gesture, just to keep the family quiet, so they didn't go dumping on the United States *and* the good old Secret Service."

"Truth is it was a little of both," Pardin conceded. "But I hoped you'd come up with something about who killed Kohl."

"Cops here in D.C. didn't come up with anything?"

"Zilch," Pardin said. "It's already in the unsolved crimes register. That must be the biggest file cabinet in the world. Unsolved crimes in Washington, D.C."

"I imagine."

"Do you believe that Mrs. Kohl and the daughter, what's her name . . ."

"Marta."

"You believe that they didn't know what Kohl was working on?"

"I couldn't crack them," Hooks said. "Not them or that Bockler who runs the Institute. Oh, that's right. He said there was a burglary there the night before I showed up. Somebody looted Professor Kohl's old office. If there were any notes, they were gone by then. But he said he didn't know anything about Anna Mueller. Him, I might believe was lying. The two women, I'm not so sure."

"He's not one of your favorites?" said Pardin.

"A little too stuffy. A little too ambitious. A little too much college pin and penknife and watch clicking around on his vest. He just gave me a bad feeling."

Pardin nodded and flicked some ash delicately from the cigar. "So what are your plans now?"

"This afternoon I'll check the layout on a tastefully designed brochure that relates in quiet yet authoritative terms the qualifications of Steven J. Hooks, personal security consultant to corporations and wealthy but terror-stricken individuals. It will not, I'm afraid, contain a glowing personal endorsement from the late Professor Edward Kohl."

"Don't be too hard on yourself, Steve. There's no way one man can protect someone if someone else has made up his mind to get him. You know that."

"Sure I know that. But logic doesn't make him any less dead. It was my job, and I blew it."

"You want some advice from a friend?"

"Go ahead."

"Forget that Kohl ever existed and forget about Anna Mueller too. It's all ancient history now. Do you have any other business lined up?"

"Not yet. That's why I need the brochure."

"I may have a client for you," Pardin said, again flicking ash neatly in the center of the ashtray.

"If it's another visiting celebrity from Germany, I don't want it," Hooks replied.

"This one's as American as apple pie. You know Congressman Jack Kinderman from California?"

"Heard about him but never met him. Isn't he the golden boy who's going to be our next president?"

"Keep talking that way. I love to hear it," Pardin said. "I think we're going to have to wait a few more years, though, before we make him President."

Hooks arched his eyebrows in surprise. "We? I never heard you say a kind word yet about a politician. This guy must be a friend of yours."

"I've known him for a long time, since I was stationed out in California. Jack is something special, not like most of these creeps who come to Washington to take the money and live it up, and the country be damned."

"No argument there," Hooks said. "What's Kinderman's problem?"

"The more his name's in the papers, the more nuts come out of the woodwork. Now he's been getting hate mail and some threatening phone calls. He's got his own security people. Did I tell you he was loaded?"

"No, but it's nice to hear," said Hooks.

"Yeah, he's loaded. But he's worried about his wife and kids. They've got this big ranch in Southern California. It's out of his district but that's where the family stays. The wife doesn't like Washington. Jack wants someone to look over the ranch and figure out how it can be made airtight. I told him you'd be perfect."

"Why not you, Bob? You're obviously high on this guy."

"You forget, Steve. I'm a bureaucrat these days. Things change so fast in this field, and I'm hopelessly behind times. You're still up-to-date."

"Well, you've been here an hour, and you can tell my phone's not exactly ringing off the hook. Sure. I need the work."

"Jack'd like to have dinner with you to talk about it. Can you make it tonight? He's off to South America tomorrow on a fact-finding mission or something."

"I don't have anything planned," Hooks said. "Too bad that brochure isn't ready."

Pardin waved a hand in dismissal. "That doesn't matter. He probably wouldn't read it anyway. He's satisfied with your background and experience; he just wants to meet you to see what you're like as a person."

"If I don't have to promise to vote for him," Hooks said.

"Good. How about eight o'clock at the Golden Circle? That's the new restaurant off Dupont Circle."

"Better there than here. I made a mistake on this office. It looks like something out of Sam Spade. Maybe I'll get a Maltese falcon for the file cabinet."

"With the fee Jack can pay, you can lease the whole floor and hire hot and cold running secretaries."

"You know me, Bob. I'll be fair. Thanks to this bum knee, I won't starve, and Joanna's all covered up by our major medical, and I'm just not hungry enough to gouge anybody."

"Kinderman wants the best. He'll be willing to pay for it. Don't undersell yourself. This is the big time, buddy."

The two men shook hands, and Pardin strolled out of the office, closing the door quietly behind him. His cigar still burned in the ashtray.

Hooks jabbed it out and threw open a window, then waved a magazine energetically to chase some of the smoke out of the room. When the air was clean again, he lit a cigarette—his first of the day, he noted with some pride.

He sat back with his feet on the desk to enjoy the cigarette. He tried to think of Jack Kinderman, but for some reason the image of Rudolph Bockler in Berlin kept jumping, unbidden, into his mind.

He was supposed to meet Patti for dinner at six o'clock, and he was a few minutes early, but Patti was already sitting at the bar when he walked into Charlie's Place, an inexpensive Italian restaurant on M Street. She was laughing as she talked amiably with a conservatively dressed young man sporting a full, luxuriant mustache. He smiled down at her possessively; his smile displayed the dimples in his strong face to good advantage.

Hooks paused, just inside the door, hesitant to interrupt them. He had begun thinking about carrying a cane on days when his leg was really bad, and he wished he were carrying it right now—a good strong cane that could take a guy out with one swing. The mustached man looked like a middle-echelon government attorney. With few exceptions, they all deserved caning, he decided.

Maybe a sword cane would be better.

Patti glanced over, saw him, waved gaily and jumped from her bar stool. The younger man's face fell. Patti said something to him, patted his hand, picked up her drink and came over to Hooks. She put her free arm through his.

"They're holding a table for us in back," she told him.

"Good," Hooks said. He was glad she hadn't made him come over to the bar and join in the conversation with Dudley Do-Right. He always felt tongue-tied in those kinds of situations. While other people sparkled, he felt he just fizzed a little before going totally flat.

He wondered if the younger man had asked Patti for a date. He was a damn fool if he hadn't. He wondered if she had accepted. He wondered if she would wind up in bed with the young man. He looked as if he were used to going to bed with girls he met in bars. He was probably very good at it.

He wondered how Patti was in bed.

"Who's the guy?" he asked mildly, feeling twenty years older than when he had walked in.

"Isn't he gorgeous?" she said enthusiastically. "His name is Joe something. He's a computer salesman, and he says he models too. I believe him. With dimples like that, everybody should be a model. Why do you ask? Are you jealous?"

"Yes. He makes me feel old and homely."

"Just another pretty face," she said. "This town is full of them. I always went for the weather-beaten, character-filled faces, like yours."

"Is that just a nice way of telling me that I'm older than coal?" he asked.

"No. It's a nice way of telling you that your face is weather-beaten and filled with character. Don't knock it. Anybody can be pretty," she said.

He helped her into her chair, then walked around the table to his own.

She must have noticed his limp because she said, "Knee hurts pretty bad?"

"It has its moments. I guess my dancing days are over."

"I've danced with you," she said. "Your dancing days were over before they even started."

"Liar. We've never danced," he said.

"Sure we did. At your wedding. Once to 'Sentimental Journey' and the other one was . . ." She thought a moment. "'Everything Happens to Me.'"

"God, I remember," he said. "I was high as a kite, and I spun you into a table. No wonder I put it out of my mind."

"You weren't *that* bad."

"Bad enough. I can't remember the last time Jo and I danced. No loss, I guess."

Patti looked at him steadily for a moment, her large dark eyes fixed on his. "I don't like that," she said. "Steve, I want you to take me dancing some night."

"My days as Disco Danny are over. You've seen the last of my Fred Astaire knee-drops," he replied.

"Slow touch-dancing," she said. "Some night when your knee feels okay."

"Well . . ."

"Good. That's a promise. Don't try to back out of it."

"Listen," he said. "I'm going to have to leave early tonight. I've got a business dinner at eight o'clock. So why don't you order up? Maybe I'll just pick at your dessert or something?"

"Who's the business meeting with?"

"Some rich Californian. Wants his ranch secured."

"Good. We'll celebrate. Short but sweet," she said.

She waved for the waiter and ordered another Manhattan. Hooks ordered a beer, and before the waiter left Patti ordered chicken parmigiana and a salad, but no dessert.

"Damn. I was counting on that dessert," said Hooks.

"I'm getting too fat. A girl has to stay skinny if she wants men to invite her out to dinner to fatten her up."

"Somewhere, I'm sure there's logic in that statement," Hooks said, "but I'm damned if I know where. But with your looks, you'd never have to pay for a meal as long as you live."

"I wish," she replied with a snort. "Half the guys I know are gay; the other half are married. Not that a little thing like that stops them from asking you out."

"Don't be bitter. Not everybody's like your soon-to-be-ex, Lawrence."

"Most are," she said gloomily. "No, what gets me is that they are so damned dishonest about it. Always pretending they're not married or saying they're separated or they don't get along with their wives. The day some guy looks me in the eye and says, 'Hey, honey, I love my wife and we get along great, but I'd like to jump in bed with you for a one-night stand,' I'll give him an award."

"What kind of an award? Or shouldn't I ask?"

She laughed. "A kiss on the cheek. Tell me about your rich California friend. You going to build a moat around his ranch? Fill it with sharks and alligators?"

"It never seemed to stop Errol Flynn," he said.

"That was Hollywood. Nothing works right in Hollywood. Is this guy a Hollywood producer? Ask him if he knows Clint Eastwood."

"As it happens, he's a congressman."

"He still might know Clint Eastwood," she said. "Who is he?"

He told her what he knew about Jack Kinderman, including Pardin's comments about the young man's political future.

Patti was unimpressed. "I met a congressman once at a party. He pinched my fanny."

"What'd you do?"

"I told him I'd never vote for him again."

"Did you ever vote for him before?" Hooks asked.

"No. But it shook him up anyway. Mention votes or money, and congressmen tremble. He apologized all night long. Finally he offered to take me out to dinner the next night. I said I'd meet him at L'Escargot."

"Did he behave himself at dinner?"

She looked at him in surprise. "What do you take me for, anyway? I never went near the place."

Hooks laughed aloud. "You're a dangerous woman, Patti."

"I have my moments. I was tempted to go and scream at him for getting me pregnant. I would have, except I didn't trust the son of a bitch. Suppose I had showed up and he hadn't? You watch yourself with this Kinderman guy, Steve. Make sure you get a contract. You're too trusting. You believe everything people tell you."

"Only you," Hooks said. "I believe everything you tell me."

"See? That's proof. I just wish you had told me about this job before. I could have worn that pretty scarf you brought me. I'm saving it for a celebration."

"Maybe after I'm sure I get this job," he suggested.

"Maybe." Then she was off on another subject. He wondered how much she had had to drink; she was really flying high tonight, and he hoped she would leave with him when he left. He didn't like the idea of leaving her in this place, with that male-model shark hanging around the bar.

He put the thought out of his mind. Patti's personal life was not really his business.

They laughed their way through her dinner. She had to remind him when it was time to go meet Kinderman.

CHAPTER NINETEEN

HOOKS WALKED PATTI PART OF THE WAY TO HER APART-
ment, then put her in a cab and cut north to get to the
Golden Circle. The weather had turned chilly and
damp, and his knee was paining even more. He hoped
that it was not going to turn into a prosthetic barometer.
He hated the vision of himself, aged and toothless,
sitting in a rocking chair on the porch of an old folks'
home, boring everybody by telling them that snow was
in the air, he could tell it from his knee. A hell of a finish
for someone who'd been an all-county basketball player
in high school and county swim champion.

A tail-coated headwaiter with an apparent French
accent and a Levantine complexion glanced at him
disdainfully with lizard-lidded eyes.

"Monsieur has a reservation?" he inquired with
bored condescension.

"I'm having din-din with Congressman Kinderman,"
Hooks said. Yes. A sword cane would be nice.

The maître d' blinked skeptically. "Your name, monsieur?"

"Monsieur Hooks." A knout might come in handy
too.

"Hooks," the man repeated, looking nauseated. He
consulted a large notebook, nodded dubiously and
snapped his fingers imperiously at a waiter hovering
nearby. "The Aragon Suite," he ordered, as if glad to
wash his hands of the whole filthy business.

"*Merci,*" Hooks murmured.

The maître d' bowed slightly, one hand moving a few inches away from his body for the expected gratuity. Hooks wished he were smoking because he would have ground out his cigarette on the poseur's palm. Instead, he stared at him with cold contempt. Maybe he would start carrying around a cat-o'-nine-tails. He could start a craze that might sweep the nation, flogging unctuous headwaiters. He smiled at the thought and followed the waiter the length of the main dining room and up a short flight of steps to one of several private dining rooms.

Bob Pardin answered the discreet knock on the door and nodded for Hooks to enter.

"Hello, Steve. Congressman, this is Steve Hooks. Steve, Jack Kinderman."

The man who rose from the sofa and advanced on him, hand outstretched, was in his late thirties, of average height, with dark-blond hair and a fair, slightly ruddy complexion.

"Glad to meet you, Steve," he said in a voice that could have carried to the back row of a theater. "Bob's told me a lot about you."

Kinderman had the politician's practiced handshake, Hooks noted: a firm grasp, a good squeeze, a quick double-pump, accompanied by a slap on the shoulder with the free hand.

"This is Fred Maier, one of my most valuable people," he added, gesturing to the third man in the room.

Maier strode forward and his huge hand swallowed up Hooks's with a surprisingly delicate touch, as if he were afraid he might break a bone. Maier was as tall as Hooks and a good forty pounds heavier. He had the build and the look of a football linebacker, complete with an unfashionable crew cut and the controlled yet energetic movements of an athlete.

"Hi there, Hooks," he said in a soft tenor voice.

"Pleased to meet you." He seemed both flustered and pleased by his employer's introduction, and at first glance, he did not look like either the legalistic or bureaucratic type to Hooks. He looked like a bodyguard.

All three men were wearing plain dark business suits.

Kinderman gestured toward a small service bar in the corner. "What'll you have?"

"Bourbon and water," said Hooks.

The waiter, still hovering in the doorway, started for the bar, but Kinderman waved him off. "I'll take care of it," he said. "We'll ring when we need you."

The waiter nodded and backed out. Hooks glanced around the room. There was a glass of white wine in front of Kinderman's seat. Pardin was holding a whiskey on the rocks. Maier had no glass. Hooks would bet that he didn't smoke, either.

Kinderman, his back to Hooks as he mixed the drink, said, "Bob says he's filled you in on why I need you."

"Generally. I was just wondering, have you ever called the police about any of the threats?"

Kinderman turned, holding Hooks's drink. He smiled and his eyes burned into Hooks. His eyes were dark-blue, but they were deep-set and gave the impression that by staring into them long enough, one could see into the soul of the man behind them. They were hypnotist's eyes.

He handed Hooks his drink and said, "Crank letters. You know that, everybody in politics get them. All I do is ship them over to Bob so that the Service can file them and keep track of the nuts rolling loose around the country. Sit down." He gestured Hooks toward a chair and sat facing him on the couch. "But the ranch is a different thing. California can get scary. You know, Charles Manson and all that. And my wife and daughters are there. So I really want the place as tight as a drum. I think you can do it. You want the job?"

"I'm not in the business to turn down jobs," Hooks replied. "You understand though, Congressman—"

"Jack," Kinderman interrupted. Hooks thought, One of the virtues of being a civilian again. You get to call congressmen by their first names.

"Okay. You understand, Jack, that the total costs involved depend on how elaborate a system you want. If you want good locks on the doors, that's one thing. If you want a moat filled with alligators dug around the ranch, that's something else." Bless you, Patti, he thought.

Kinderman laughed. "Scratch the moat, I'm afraid. I doubt the voters would approve, and my ranch is pretty big. It's about five hundred acres, north of San Diego. I think a moat might be impractical."

"Okay, no moat. Too bad. I was looking forward to designing the drawbridge."

Kinderman chuckled and so did Maier. Hooks told himself to watch that, to see if Maier ever laughed without first checking to see if his boss was amused. You could tell a lot about people by the way their employees acted.

"Maybe when you're done at the ranch, you can build a moat around my office here in Washington. You can't believe some of the people who wander in. But I want you to understand, Steve. I'm not talking about cut-rate. I want the best that's available at whatever it costs. I want a system that's second to none."

He reached over and pressed a button for the waiter, who appeared within seconds.

They sat at the oblong dining table, elaborately set, and after the other three men had ordered, Hooks choked back an impulse to ask for a hamburger, personally prepared by the maître d'. He ordered filet mignon instead.

Kinderman leaned slightly across the table toward Hooks, his gaze again disconcertingly direct. "I noticed your limp when you came in. Is your leg bothering you?"

147

"It acts up once in a while," Hooks said.

"I remember when that nut case shot the President. The doctors were talking for a while about amputating your leg."

"I told them they'd better amputate my hands, too, or I'd choke them to death," he said, scowling at the memory. "But it's okay now. I get around all right most of the time. It's only once in a while that it feels like there's a rusty screw rolling around inside, and today's one of those days."

Kinderman shook his head respectfully, his eyes never leaving Hooks's. "I guess you've heard this until it's coming out your ears, Steve, but our society owes a lot to people like you," he said.

Hooks flushed and moved uneasily. "Well . . . I was just doing my job," he mumbled. He glanced over at Pardin, expecting the man to have his usual tight-lipped smile, but Pardin was nodding his head solemnly, his eyes fixed on Kinderman.

"Just doing your job," Kinderman repeated. "What a world we'd have if everybody could say that and mean it. But it's not that way. We all know it. All across the country, they know it too. You should see my mail, Steve." His voice was rising, now almost too loud for the small room.

"I see it all the time. People want a return to principles. They're tired of us drifting every which way, every time a different breeze blows."

Hooks nodded, completely at a loss for words. Kinderman's eyes were boring into his with fanatical intensity, making it impossible for him to look away.

Kinderman nodded. "They want a country again where people will 'just do their jobs.' I'm sorry, Steve. Sometimes I get carried away. But I know the price you paid for doing your job. I know what you must think about a system of justice that lets the lunatics go free so they can kill again."

He repeated again softly, "Just doing my job. Thank God for you and men like you, Steve Hooks."

Kinderman bowed his head respectfully to Hooks, who flushed and looked down at his plate, confused. He had not expected anything like that. The other two men were silent. Glancing at them, Hooks saw they were both still staring at Kinderman, as if mesmerized.

Kinderman slowly raised his wineglass. "To those who just do their job."

"I'll drink to that, by God," Pardin said. "Right," said Maier. Hooks nodded and raised his glass and the four men clinked glasses in the middle of the table.

Hooks was almost glad when the conversation got around to his Berlin trip. At first he glanced at Pardin, but the Secret Service man smiled and said, "Jack's on the House Intelligence Committee. He knows more about what's going on than I do."

In Hooks's opinion, most politicians were egotistical, conniving bullshit artists, but as he felt himself being pumped by Kinderman, he began to realize that the California congressman had a quick, trained mind.

He was especially interested in Hooks's interview with Thelma Winkler and seemed disappointed that the old woman had not remembered more about Anna Mueller. He led Hooks, step by step, over the often-covered ground, and prompted Hooks to remember that he had been followed from the church at Kohl's funeral service by a man in a white trench coat.

"You didn't tell me that," Pardin said.

Hooks shrugged. "Slipped my mind. I might just have been imagining it."

"I doubt it," said Kinderman. Hooks noticed how quickly he regained control of the conversation, and just moments later Kinderman was leading him through his first meeting with Mrs. Kohl and Marta.

Hooks did not remember how it happened, but there came a moment in the questioning when he realized that somehow he had made it very plain that he had spent the night with Marta Kohl.

Kinderman didn't comment and just kept moving along, through his meeting with Bockler, through his kidnapping, picking and pulling at Hooks to remember everything that had registered in any way in his mind.

He felt like a butterfly pinned to a board, but despite that, he was impressed. Kinderman would have made a furious prosecutor, and he found himself wishing that the man had represented the government in the case of the would-be presidential assassin. The bastard would have burned by now.

Eventually, Kinderman glanced at his watch.

"Oh, Steve, we could talk all night," he said. "But it's getting late, and I've got papers and committee business, and I've got to grab an early plane. Fred here will draw up some kind of contract and have it to you tomorrow morning. I'm hoping you can get out to the ranch right away and get started."

"This week?" Hooks asked.

"Tomorrow, if you can. The sooner the better."

"We haven't talked price," Hooks said.

"All right. How's this? Ten thousand dollars for you to inspect the ranch, make specific recommendations and provide me with a written report and plan of action to secure the place. Full details."

"That's more than I would have asked," Hooks replied honestly.

"Good. I'll work you harder than you expected," Kinderman said with an ingratiating smile.

He reached out to shake Hooks's hand. "I know, Steve, that you'll just do your job. And do it right."

He turned toward the door and left with no more ceremony. Maier hurriedly scrambled to his feet to follow. At the doorway, Kinderman said, "Bob, can I talk to you for a moment?"

Pardin followed the other two men outside and closed the door behind them.

Hooks lit a cigarette and sipped at his brandy. He felt drained, as if he had just finished running a marathon.

He finished the cigarette and was lighting a second one when Pardin came back in. He had a smile on his face as he sat down, produced one of his long thin cigars and lit it carefully.

"Well, what do you think of our congressman?" he asked.

"He's something else. Mind if I ask you what he wanted to talk about?"

"No. He just wanted to tell me how happy he was that you were going to do the job."

And he took seven minutes to do it, Hooks thought. Thanks, but no thanks. However, he let the subject drop.

"He could sell sand to Saudi Arabia," he said.

"But only if sand were what Saudi Arabia needed," Pardin said quickly. "This guy's no blowhard, Steve. He's a special man. A very special man."

"You don't have to convince me, Bob," said Hooks with a small smile. "I already agreed to take his money."

But Pardin seemed not to have heard. He was looking off as he said, "He's going to the top."

Hooks noted the ring of almost religious fervor in Pardin's voice and the look of devotion on his face. This wasn't the Bob Pardin he thought he knew—the skilled bureaucrat and cool, detached, amused observer of other men's passions and enthusiasms.

He felt he had to say something. "You're right, Bob. He could go all the way."

"He will," Pardin said with enormous satisfaction. "He will. Because nothing will stop him."

CHAPTER TWENTY

AT HIS OFFICE THE NEXT MORNING, HOOKS FOUND THAT
the mailman had already delivered the first load of junk
mail and fund-raising solicitation letters, along with a
catalog from a local electronics firm.

There was also a brief message from Patti on his
telephone answering machine: "About time you got to
work, you slug. Buy me a drink after work and tell me
how everything went last night. *Ciao.*"

He leafed through the electronics catalog, noting half
a dozen items that might be put to good use in setting up
the security system on Kinderman's ranch. He was glad
now that he had been an engineering major in college,
even though he had promptly left the field on passing his
Civil Service examination and being accepted by the
Treasury Department for Secret Service training.

Not that he could even dream of becoming an
engineer again. Every branch of the profession, and
certainly electronics, had taken immense strides during
the nearly two decades he had been chasing counterfei-
ters and protecting top government officials. But his
background had allowed him to maintain at least a
sketchy knowledge of developments in electronics, and
he had received special training in the use of mechanical
devices for investigative and protection purposes.

Some of his fellow agents had even started calling
him "Bugsy" for a while, after he had successfully

planted one especially elaborate set of taps in the offices and shop of a small printing plant under investigation for counterfeiting.

Even the FBI had requested him several times as a guest lecturer at training sessions—perhaps for some ulterior interdepartmental political reason, but nevertheless a satisfying nod of recognition of his skills.

Now he was trying to make those shredded skills the foundation of a second career.

It helped, of course, that he really didn't need the work. His disability pension and the income from the prudent investments he had made with his and Joanna's savings gave him more than enough money for his simple needs. And Joanna's hospital bills were covered by the comprehensive insurance policies he had carried on their health.

If they had had any children, his economic situation would be significantly worse, he thought with a subdued pang. But it would have been worth it, he thought, wondering if he would ever fully reconcile himself to never being a father.

The telephone interrupted his musings. It was Frank Maier, Kinderman's burly assistant.

"The congressman's already left the country," Maier told him, "but I've got a contract drawn. Can you stop by the office and sign it?"

"Sure. Right after lunch?"

"I'll be here," Maier said.

The contract was brief and clear, setting forth what was required of Hooks and obligating Lady Lauren Enterprises, Inc. to pay him $10,000 and appropriate expenses for the work.

"Lady Lauren Enterprises?"

"That's a holding company that has title to the ranch," Maier explained. "The congressman's wife is named Lauren."

"Don't tell me a lawyer drew up this contract," Hooks said. "I can understand every word of it."

Maier giggled. It was strange to hear such a high, childish laugh from such a big, muscular man. "The congressman likes things simple," he said.

Hooks signed the contract, and Maier handed him an envelope with an advance payment of four thousand dollars and detailed instructions for getting to the ranch.

"When do you think you'll be able to go?" he asked.

"I'm going to try for tomorrow," Hooks said.

"Good. I'll be there Friday night, but Mr. Mack can show you around in the meantime. He and Mike Read, the foreman, can answer any questions for you."

"Who's Mr. Mack?"

"That's Henry Mack, the congressman's stepfather. He's the retired chairman of Great Central Western Industries. He spends most of his time at the ranch."

Hooks nodded. The name was familiar to him. The owner of a modest regional beer company, Mack had assembled one of the biggest conglomerates in the country during the sixties and had become one of the wealthiest men in the nation. He was notorious for his antiunion practices and Hooks realized where Kinderman had received some of his law-and-order political orientation.

Before going back to his office, Hooks stopped at the offices of the electronics firm. As he thought, they had a special limited-circulation catalog listing the latest in bugging devices, wiretap equipment and security systems. Just glancing through it made him feel better about the job at Kinderman's ranch. Everything he could possibly need was in the catalog.

There were two messages waiting for him at the office.

The first was from Bob Pardin.

"Just thought I'd let you know that a couple of

agencies have run a very thorough check on your Anna Mueller and can't find any evidence of her coming to the United States. No records of her at all. So put it away and forget it, kid. It's ancient history. Glad you're taking the job at Jack's ranch. I'll see you when you get back."

Well, that's that, Hooks thought. He wasn't really surprised. He was glad Pardin had passed along the information. It would help him to forget forever about that mystery woman.

He forgot about her the instant he heard the next voice on his tape recorder. It was Marta Kohl.

"Shame on you, Steven," she chided. "I fly all this way just to see you, and you are not in your office. I am at the Capital Hilton Hotel. Please call me. I am in Room four eighteen."

Her voice stopped, and he gaped at the tape machine. He had presumed that he would never see Marta Kohl again. He didn't expect ever to return to Berlin, and it had never occurred to him that Marta might come to Washington and seek him out.

The blood began pounding in his veins. He looked up the number for her hotel and called. Her room telephone rang six times, and he was beginning to think that she had gone out, when the telephone was picked up.

"Ja?"

"Hello, Marta. It's Steve."

"Steven. I was just running the water to take a nice bath. Would you like to join me? It's a big tub."

"Whoa. Hold on. What are you doing in Washington? How long have you been here?"

"I just arrived this morning. I have a few days' vacation, and it is easy for me to fly anywhere to spend it. I came here to see you. Are you happy?"

"Yes, I am," he said.

"Good. Come over and wash my back."

"I can't right now. I have work to do this afternoon."

"Then we will have dinner?"

He hesitated. "I wish I had known you were coming. I'm going to be tied up for dinner."

"Tied up? It sounds like fun," she said. "After dinner, then?"

"All right," he said. "How about nine o'clock?"

"Good. We will meet at the bar downstairs."

"I'm sorry about beating you out of dinner," he said.

She laughed. "I'm a big girl, Steven. I can eat by myself, if I have to, but as it happens, I don't. One of the passengers invited me to dinner tonight, and I said maybe. Now I will say yes."

"Lucky him," Hooks said.

"It is a her, not a him. I think she will be disappointed when I do not stay for dessert."

"Why won't you stay for dessert?" he asked.

"Because I think I would be the dessert," Marta replied. "Nine o'clock," she said.

When she hung up, Hooks wiped his brow. He hoped Patti would leave her magic crystal ball in the office.

He started to dial her office number, then replaced the telephone. He had not been sure he would go to San Diego, but Marta had made him sure. He was going to get out of Washington just as rapidly as possible. While he hoped to enjoy the German woman's pleasures tonight, trying to juggle between her and Patti was more than he wanted to deal with.

He called a travel agent and arranged a flight to San Diego for the next afternoon, then called Patti at her office.

"You still there?"

"No," she said. "I left five minutes ago. I'm standing on the corner hustling sailors while I wait for you. Of course I'm still here."

"Don't get sassy," he warned, "or I won't tell you what happened last night. The glitter, the glamour, the hushed coversations, they'll all remain a mystery to you forever."

"Listen," she said. "All I want to know is did you get the job?"

"Yes."

"Good. Then you can spring for dinner. Charley's Place. Five-thirty. I'll let you feed me."

"Exactly what I had in mind," he said.

Charlie's Place was even more crowded than usual.

"This place is getting too popular to suit me," Patti complained. "Isn't that always the way? Every time you find a halfway decent place that nobody else knows about, everybody finds out about it and brings all their friends and relatives. Let's go to my place. I'll fix some spaghetti and meat sauce."

"I remember your last spaghetti and meat sauce," said Hooks. "One enormous lump of pasta covered with catsup."

"I thought it was a pretty good improvisation," she said. "Anyway, this time I bought real sauce. And the next time I'll remember to turn off the spaghetti."

"Next time, maybe," he said. "I'm in the mood for Chinese food."

There was a small Chinese restaurant only half a block away, and it was almost empty.

They sat at a table in the back and Patti said, "Now tell me everything."

"Everything," he promised.

He told her about the dinner in great detail, including the snobbish elegance of the Golden Circle and the arrogance of the maître d'.

"I hate people like that," she said. "They make me

157

want to spit. Take me there some night and point him out, and I'll make a scene he'll never forget."

"Hold that thought. Now don't interrupt. I'm coming to the good part."

She listened to his meeting with Kinderman and clapped aloud when he mentioned that his fee was ten thousand dollars. She munched silently through his summary of the congressman's flag-waving monologue and stole part of his egg roll while he was describing his visit to Kinderman's office that morning.

"I read about that Henry Mack somewhere," she said. "The stepfather. He doesn't sound like a very nice man. You're not going to let him push you around, are you?"

"I don't plan to. If he gives me any snot, I'll tell him I'll sic my sister-in-law on him. That'll put the fear of God into him."

"This Kinderman really made an impression on you, didn't he?" she said shrewdly.

"Yeah. He's a very unusual young man. He's amazingly forceful, like one of those evangelists you see on television, except he's better."

"You don't like him, though. Why's that?" she asked.

"I didn't say I didn't like him."

"You didn't have to. Why don't you like him?"

Hooks rubbed his chin and finished chewing a mouthful of rice. "I don't know. Maybe I just flinch from people who are that sure of themselves. Maybe I don't trust him because he's a politician and wants to be the President of the United States. Maybe I'm just jealous because he's got two tons of personality, and I have maybe six ounces on a good day."

"Oh, bullshit," she said with a snort. "There you go sniveling and whining again. You've got plenty of personality. You always get respect from people who know you. Why do you keep putting yourself down?"

"That headwaiter last night didn't gimme no respect," he said.

"Headwaiters. For two dollars they kiss your feet; for five, they'll kiss . . . well, anything you want kissed. You didn't really say anything about why you don't like this Kinderman."

"He just comes on too strong, that's all. He had me nodding my head like I was hypnotized, and that scares me. He's the kind of guy that people will jump off buildings for if he told them to, like that Jim Jones guy down in South America. It's the strongest kind of power, and I don't think many men can be trusted with it. Add that to the fact that he's got money, and the combination frightens the hell out of me. He's got Pardin twisted around his finger. If he wanted to really work on me, I think he'd have me jumping through hoops."

"Not you, Steve. You're not a hoop-jumper-through."

"I jumped through a lot of hoops for Joanna," he said.

Her expression softened. "That's different. You love her."

"I'd jump through hoops for you if you'd stop stealing my egg rolls."

"You're out of luck, fella," she said with a small smile. "Your torment has barely begun."

The odd turn of phrase reminded him of Marta. He glanced at his watch. *Oh, God. Eight-thirty already.*

He hurried through paying the check and walked Patti the seven blocks to her apartment building.

"Patti, I won't have time to see Jo tomorrow. Will you tell her what's been happening for me?"

Her lips tightened. "Do you really think she'll hear me, Steve?"

"I don't think so, but I don't know that she isn't hearing every word we say to her. It may be the only thing that's keeping her sane, keeping her alive, even."

Patti sighed and nodded. "I'll tell her, Steve, as soon as I can."

He bent down and kissed her lightly on the forehead.

She grabbed the lapels of his jacket and shook him gently. "You look out for yourself in California. Don't take any nonsense from that Mack character. And watch out for the congressman's wife. There's something funny about her staying on the ranch all the time while he's running around the world. She may make a play for you. Be careful. And give a girl a call once in a while, will you?" She kissed him hard on the lips, then whirled and vanished inside.

Hooks waited until the door had closed behind her before heading for the corner. He gave a long sigh of relief. Either his acting ability was improving or Patti's mind-reading ability was slipping. He had been sure that sometime during the evening she was going to ask him what was the big rush and who was the floozy he was in such a hurry to meet. But he'd gotten away with it; still, his heart was pounding, and he guessed that he was just never going to be the sort who could cheat casually in a relationship.

Marta was sitting alone at a small table in the dimly lit cocktail lounge. Two men standing by the bar were eyeing her appreciatively, Hooks noticed. He didn't blame them. She looked slim and elegant in a midnight-blue sheath dress and a simple strand of pearls. A short silver-gray fur coat was draped on the chair beside her.

She smiled when she saw him approach but frowned when she noticed his limp.

She rose and kissed him strongly and said, "Your leg is bothering you?"

"Comes and goes," he replied, sitting beside her with a sigh.

"Like many other things," she said with a smile. She

put her hand on his. "I'm so glad to see you, Steven. Already this vacation has been made wonderful for me. I like you, and I'm happy to see you again."

"My feelings exactly," he said.

"How is your business?" she asked. "Are you going to be able to sneak away from your office so you can make a sightseer of me?"

He shook his head. "Oh, Marta, I'm afraid not. I've got to go out of town tomorrow on business."

"Oh? That's too bad. Where are you going?"

"To San Diego."

"See. Already you are becoming a nationwide firm. Tell me all about what you are going to do in San Diego."

"There's a congressman out there. He wants his ranch security checked, and he picked me for the job."

"Wonderful," she said. "Your reputation must really be good that you should be picked for such an important job."

"Well, I wish that were the case," he said. "But a friend recommended me."

"Let me guess. I know. That friend of yours from where you used to work. His name was . . ."

"Bob Pardin," Hooks supplied.

"That's right. I always think it is a high honor when the people you work with recommend your work to others. You must be very good at your job."

Hooks was confused. Why so much talk about work? He wanted the woman to grab him and order him to take her to her room. He wanted to exhaust his body on her. He was tired of talking about business.

It was almost as if she had read his mind. Under the table, she put her hand on his upper thigh.

She whispered softly in his ear. "You are leaving tomorrow, but we have tonight, don't we?"

"Yes," he said thickly.

"Steven, you sound as if you are afraid of me. Please

do not be. Right now, I am having a crush on you, but it will pass away in time. Let us enjoy it for now." She squeezed his leg, and he nodded.

"Will you come up to my room with me? I will make you forget your painful leg," she said.

The elevator was empty riding upstairs and Marta asked casually, "Who is this congressman? I want to know so I can watch for his name in the newspapers."

"Kinderman. Jack Kinderman," he said.

He thought he saw a faint, satisfied smile cross her face, just for a flickering instant, before it vanished.

She wasted not a moment when they entered the room. The door had just closed behind them, and Hooks had turned to speak to Marta and saw her sliding her dress down off her shoulders and stepping out of it. She was naked, and she extended her arms to him and then crushed him against her body.

Their lovemaking was as rich and imaginative as Hooks had remembered it, and when he dressed to leave at three A.M., he was exhausted, but it was a pleasant, fulfilling kind of exhaustion.

She kissed him good-bye without getting up from the bed, but when he reached the door, she called his name.

"Steven?"

"Yes."

"Be very careful in California," she said.

CHAPTER TWENTY-ONE

HOOKS ENVIED PEOPLE WHO BOUNDED OFF AIRPLANES, charged by the excitement of hours aloft and ready for new adventures.

He hated flying. It seemed sometimes that he had spent years of his life flying from one place to another, and the more he had done it the more he had hated it.

He hated the takeoffs and would clutch his armrests grimly and try to force out of his mind the memory of all the planes that had crashed on takeoff. He would close his eyes and silently concentrate on using some undiscovered mental power to lift the plane up, up, and away.

Thus far it had worked, but it was exhausting.

He found the flights themselves ultimate refinements in boredom. He derived little pleasure from the music he could listen to through little plastic earphones that fit badly and kept slipping from his head. Their main benefit was serving as a defense against jabbering seatmates.

He never saw a movie on a plane that he wanted to see. Usually he had seen it at least once before and hadn't liked it the first time.

He always brought a book and tried to read, but he found it hard to forget his surroundings and to concentrate on what he was reading.

Airplane meals usually varied from poor to disgusting. Fortunately, they were always much better in first class, but for that much extra money it should have been lobster all the way. He was always strongly tempted to drink himself blind on flights, but he was now making a concerted effort to control his drinking. Patti's concern had shamed him, because he remembered the sorry spectacle her father had made of himself in the last years of his life. He had no wish to become an alcoholic; the thought frightened him. So, there could be no blotting out his fear of flying by climbing into a bottle.

Finally, there was the landing to endure. Hooks had never prayed as fervently in a church as he prayed when landing in an airplane. Again, headlines announcing previous plane crashes would flash through his mind. He would try to keep from wondering frantically if they were running out of fuel, if the landing gear had properly locked in place, if the pilot and copilot were not both blind drunk and crawling around the floor of the cockpit with acute cases of delirium tremens. Maybe both pilots had bailed out hours ago and the plane, on automatic controls, was heading inexorably out to sea and a watery grave.

Each time he promised himself that the next time he would take a train. Or he would drive. Or bicycle, like some of those nutty teenagers . . . or walk the whole way.

Next time.

When he left the huge jetliner after the almost six-hour flight from Washington, he felt completely worn and exhausted, as if the stewardesses had taken turns beating him the entire way with a wooden club. He had tried to doze off but had failed miserably. He had tried to read, but the words had quickly become meaningless. He had listened grimly to symphonic swing rather than endure the babblings of the elderly woman beside him, her purse bulging with out-of-focus snapshots of incredibly ugly grandchildren.

The good news was that he had made it, safe and reasonably sound.

The bad news was that, inevitably, he would have to travel the entire way back again.

Maybe next time by train.

A helicopter with the name Lady Lauren painted on her nose was waiting for him at the airport, and Hooks found to his surprise that the flight was pleasant and interesting. The plane flew low enough so that he could enjoy California's immensely varied scenery.

The pilot said nothing to Hooks during the flight; then, after about thirty minutes, he tapped Hooks on the shoulder and pointed down.

"That's the ranch," he said.

Hooks looked but could only see more rolling green in a sea of rolling green. A few miles off he saw a small mountain. The land was dotted below with lakes and long stretches of sand, apparently a border between California's greenery and the state's deserts.

"Where are we?" he asked the pilot.

"Little town called Cahuilla. About fifty miles northeast of San Diego."

Hooks nodded. The helicopter gently set down in a large open field, and when Hooks stepped down he saw a station wagon coming toward him from a large house a quarter of a mile away.

A young man in a checked shirt and jeans leaned out of the car. "You Hooks?"

"That's right."

"Come on in. I'll take you up to the house."

The man turned him over to a Chinese servant who showed him to his room in the sprawling adobe ranch house. Dinner would be served in two hours, he was told.

That was another thing wrong with flying, Hooks

thought. His reset watch told him it was five o'clock California time but his stomach told him it was eight o'clock, and it was hungry.

There were apples on a small end table in his large high-ceilinged bedroom, and he wolfed one down as he looked out onto a patio and large swimming pool.

A woman sat in a chair by the pool, reading a magazine, her face shaded by an enormous straw hat. That might be Kinderman's wife, whom Patti had warned him about. Hooks again felt a twinge of guilt, remembering how he had left Patti to hurry to his meeting with Marta. The guilt was quickly forgotten in the memory of the German woman's unabashed and inventive sensuality.

No wonder he was feeling so weary.

He put his clothes away, showered and changed into slacks and a sport shirt. He would locate and present himself to his hostess. But first he would lie down on the bed and relax for a few minutes.

He was awakened by a rapping on the door. Dinner was being served.

Henry Mack might have been in his early seventies. He was a bald, paunchy man of average height with craggy, weathered features and a loud booming voice. He was dressed in baggy slacks and a loud sport shirt that hung outside his pants, which were tucked into scuffed cowboy boots. He spoke in a twangy western drawl—whether natural or put on, Hooks wasn't sure—and was completely uninhibited about expressing his opinions on any subject that occurred to him, accenting his comments with a variety of forceful and occasionally colorful obscenities. Hooks quickly learned that those opinions included an astonishing array of racial prejudices.

Hooks had found Mack busily dispatching a tall

highball in a large room with a raftered ceiling. Hooks was received with convivial enthusiasm by Mack, who bellowed at a passing servant to fetch the guest a drink. Hooks settled for a beer.

Nodding curtly at the silent manservant, Mack informed Hooks that almost all the ranch's house servants were Chinese. "They're sneaky, thieving little devils, but at least they know their place and don't mind a little hard work. You can't say that about most of the others." Most of the others, Hooks found out, included blacks, Mexicans, Indians, Latins, Italians, mackerel-snappers, Turks, Arabs and Greeks. The sexual proclivities of most of them were described and condemned, and the role of the pope in weakening the fabric of Western civilization was noted in passing.

These were kind-hearted warm-ups for Henry Mack's soliloquy on Jews.

According to Mack, they controlled all the world's financial resources and owned all the newspapers and television stations, which explained why all the crap they reported was vicious left-wing propaganda lies. Mack confided that for many years he was sure that Jews were also the mind and heart of international Communism, but of late he had been swinging around to the opinion held by some of his closest friends.

The clear evidence of continuing Russian anti-Semitism, he conceded reluctantly, indicated that perhaps the Kremlin was not under the direct control of the masterminds behind the Jewish plot to take over the world.

"But that don't make no difference 'cause they're helping the Commies to ruin America," he explained, flecking Hooks's shirt with sprays of saliva. "They know that once they get this country so weak that the Commies take it over without firing a shot, then they can knock off the Commies because those Russians are so damn stupid they can't count to three without using both hands. But you know all this. You're a law enforcement man."

"I *used* to be a law enforcement man," Hooks said, "and I don't know any of that."

They were the first words Hooks had spoken since meeting the old man. He hoped he never had to say another word to him as long as he lived. He guessed that his host was drunk or senile, or both.

Dinner in the next room consisted of hearty servings of basic American foods, including a thick, painfully hot chili. They were well into the meal when Lauren Kinderman and her two daughters made their appearance.

Lauren was a tall, painfully thin woman, probably an inch or two taller than her husband. She had large gray eyes and thick blond hair. Her daughters dutifully kissed their grandfather while Lauren slipped quietly into her seat. When Mack loudly identified Hooks as "the Secret Service guy Jack sent to fix our fences," she looked at him shyly, murmured something inaudible and flushed when Hooks half bowed to her from his seat. She dropped her eyes quickly to her plate and began picking slowly at her food.

Mack was totally unaware of her reaction. He kept babbling. "Laurie's pa and me, we raised a lot of hell together when we was young. Hank made his pile in oil and gas, and he backed me when I took over that little brewery. Them was good times, goddammit."

Neither Lauren nor her two daughters, blond-haired twins named Eva and Francesca, appeared to notice the old man's profanities, and Hooks thought they had probably been hearing them all their lives.

The girls, seated opposite Hooks at the long table, seemed normal, lively and mischievous, but their mother seemed cowed by life. She spoke only when directly addressed, answering questions briefly in a hesitant voice, almost a whisper. She seemed frightened of Henry Mack, of Hooks, even of her own servants.

Hooks found the meal totally unpleasant. He tried making some remarks to the woman but soon gave up out of a feeling of pity, since the strain of answering questions was obviously painful for her.

The children ate quickly and scampered off at the end of the meal and, to Hooks's relief, Henry Mack left also. "Got to see a man about some horses," he announced, favoring Hooks with a large wink. "I'll be back late, Laurie."

"All right, Uncle Henry," she agreed meekly.

Hooks wondered whether he should excuse himself but decided to have another cup of coffee and was surprised when Lauren remained at the table with him. She flavored her own coffee with a large slug of brandy, then offered the bottle to him.

He put a token amount in his own drink, more from politeness that from a desire for alcohol.

"Your home's really beautiful, Mrs. Kinderman. I hadn't realized that it would be so large."

"Well, we've added onto the original ranch several times," she explained apologetically. "It just grew. It's really bigger than we need."

"Your husband told me you prefer staying here to being in Washington."

"I don't like cities. I love the desert and the open air, and I don't like being around too many people. They make me feel . . . well, sort of cringy. Like I might get stepped on?"

He nodded. She ended many of her statements in an uncertain, inquiring manner, he noted.

"I know the feeling," he said. "One of the things I really disliked when I was with the Secret Service was that so much of the time I was in big rooms with big crowds, or airports with mobs. I always had a secret worry in the back of my head that someday a crowd would just go crazy and go stomping all over me."

She flinched visibly at the image he painted and nodded in agreement with the thought.

"Jack had me see a doctor when we were both living in our Washington house," she confided timidly. "He said I had a kind of claustrophobia. I didn't like it at first; it made it seem like I was crazy or something, and now I don't mind because it got me out of Washington and back here. I don't think Washington is a good place to bring up children, either. It's not safe, you know. You always have to be afraid of kidnappers and crazies with guns and fanatics?"

"I know," he said simply.

"Oh . . . I'm sorry. I was forgetting about your—" She broke off in confusion.

"My wife?"

"Yes," she said softly, looking down.

"If we had had any children, I think I would have preferred to bring them up outside of Washington too," he told her. "Joanna felt that way too. We were both from small towns in the Midwest. We liked Washington, but we were adults. If we had had children . . ."

He let the remark trail off, noticing that once again he was speaking of his wife as if she were dead. It was getting to be a bad habit.

She looked at him sympathetically with a touch of real interest. Hooks sat quietly, aware that silence would probably impel Lauren Kinderman to talk some more. He had long ago learned that he had a knack, apparently an inherent talent, for inspiring people to talk to him. Something about his quiet manner seemed to draw conversation and confidences from people. As a lawman, he had proved to be an effective interrogator, not by asking a stream of cleverly worded questions, but simply by chatting for a while with people and then waiting for them to assume the burden of conversation.

Patti had once accused him of "sucking words out of people, like a sponge."

Shyly at first and then with increasing self-confidence, Lauren Kinderman began talking with him. She said little of substance, commenting mostly on the beauty of the surrounding country and the serenity of life on the ranch, but she talked.

She was also drinking steadily, he noticed, now sipping the brandy directly from a glass that she refilled several times.

"I enjoy sitting on the patio at this hour," she said. "I like watching the moon reflected in the pool and sometimes you can hear the coyotes yipping off in the hills. The dogs hear them, too, and start barking back at them."

"Would you like to go out there now?" Hooks asked. "Unless you'd rather be alone?"

"No, no," she said, flushing. She rose when he stood and took her brandy bottle and glass with her, past sliding doors where they sat at a small metal table beside the pool. The sky was beautiful, ablaze with myriad stars, so different from the spotty view through the light-hazed and soot-laden air over Washington.

"Beautiful," he said, then remained silent, content to sip his coffee whether she spoke further or remained mute. He wondered idly how much she knew about him. Obviously she had been told about his wife.

Lauren sipped steadily at her brandy, occasionally saying a few words about the ranch or her children. She did not mention either her husband or her father-in-law, Hooks noticed.

He wondered what it must be like for her, caught between the powerful personalities of the two men, as if between a rock and a hard place. No wonder she drank.

Stronger people than she was could be crushed between those two strong men. Perhaps her drinking was the reason that Jack Kinderman did not want her in Washington.

He saw she was sitting with her eyes closed, half her face shadowed by the light of the moon. Even though gaunt, she was an attractive woman, he thought, and then wondered if he could seduce her.

The thought astonished him. He often admired attractive women and wondered idly what it would be like to go to bed with them, but never since his marriage had he seriously considered inducing a woman to sleep with him. Not even Marta Kohl. That had been strictly on her own initiative.

Recently his growing physical desire for Patti had dismayed and even frightened him; it filled him with guilt about his betrayal of his wife's confidence in his loyalty.

What sea change had Marta brought about in him that he could now wonder calmly about seducing a woman he barely knew, a woman whose looks did not excite him, whose personality was so weak and tenuous? He felt no lust for Lauren Kinderman, just an almost abstract curiosity as to whether he could get her into bed. Not even whether he or she would enjoy it; just whether it could be done.

How the hell could he be wondering about getting a woman into bed when he wasn't interested in being in bed with her?

It wasn't her timidity. The two women who now inspired surges of lust in him were both strong, vivid women.

And Lauren's wealth was no aphrodisiac.

Was it a reaction to the uncertainty and confusion in his life? He did not think so. Did he think he would be doing Lauren a favor by brightening her existence with the sunburst of his radiant personality? Surely he was not that juvenile.

Then why?

An ugly misshapen thought was lurking in the shadows in the back of his mind, and he seized it and dragged it squirming into the light, examined it and shook his head sadly.

Seducing Lauren would simply be his way of thumbing his nose at Jack Kinderman, he realized—a nasty act of vandalism to revenge himself for having been so impressed by the wealthy, powerful congressman that it had shaken his self-esteem.

Lauren's eyes snapped open, and she looked startled. "Gotta go inside," she said in a slurred, anxious voice. "Gettin' late."

She swayed upright, and Hooks caught her upper arm and held it firmly, guiding her toward the sliding doors.

"Where is your room?" he asked when they were inside.

"Upstairs," she said, indicating the way. "Slippery. Don' fall."

"We won't," he replied, hoping his knee would not collapse under the strain of the woman's almost dead weight.

He got her up the stairs, and she led him unresistingly to a room at the end of the hall. It would be so easy, a voice was whispering from beneath a rock in the back of his mind. She'd never resist. She probably wouldn't even know what was happening.

But I would, he told himself.

He opened the door for her. "Will you be all right, Lauren? Should I call a maid for you?"

"No, don' do that," she protested weakly. "No maid. They talk. I'm all right now," she said.

"Good night," he said and closed the door behind her. He hoped she wouldn't pass out on the floor.

Poor little rich girl, he thought again sadly. A young woman and look what life had already done to her.

He wondered how much of the damage had been done by her husband and father-in-law. Henry Mack was certainly enough to drive anyone to drink.

CHAPTER TWENTY-TWO

THE NEXT MORNING, HENRY MACK INTRODUCED HOOKS to Mike Read, the general foreman of the ranch. Read was a short, chucky man of about fifty with a weathered complexion and an air of quiet competence.

"Mike here is one of them Mormons from Utah. He says he's only got one wife, but I'm not too sure," Mack brayed, slapping his thigh.

Read bared his teeth briefly in a wintry smile, and Hooks suspected he had long ago gotten tired of that particular pleasantry from the old lunatic.

Read led Hooks on an inspection tour of the down-stairs portion of the sprawling house. Hooks shook his head when he inspected the door locks. Those on the sturdy front door were strong, but several other points of access had flimsy doors with locks that could be forced with a credit card. He made notes in a spiral-bound notebook he had bought at the airport.

The windows also had cheap dimestore catches, most of which were unfastened.

There were three doors at the end of one of the house's corridors, and Read walked him by without entering.

"What's in there?" Hooks asked.

"Congressman's private offices," said Read.

"We ought to take a look at them."

"Ain't nobody allowed in there," Read said stubbornly.

"We want to make sure that nobody gets in there that doesn't belong in there," said Hooks.

"I ain't got the keys. You have to talk to the congressman when he gets back."

Hooks nodded and jotted some more notes in his book.

They went outside with Henry Mack still trailing along, offering a steady stream of comments and suggestions. Hooks noted approvingly that the main house and a few small outbuildings were well sited on a slight rise of ground. A low, double-strand barbed-wire fence sealed off a two-hundred-yard square, inside which the buildings were located. The fence might serve its primary function of keeping cattle from straying too close to the buildings, but it would never stop any human intruders, and the road that went through an opening in the fence to approach the house had no gate.

"What kind of ranching do you do here?" Hooks asked Read.

"Not a real ranch," Read said. "We ain't got but a hundred head of cattle and some horses. Me and two other guys take care of everything. We live over there in the bunkhouse."

He pointed to a small adobe house, fifty yards from the main living complex. There was another identical house on the other side of the main building. When Read saw Hooks looking at it, he said simply, "Servants' quarters there."

There was a three-foot-diameter aboveground pipe that ran from out near the main public road in the distance to a small blockhouse next to the main building.

"What's that?" Hooks asked.

"We had well problems," Read said. "Had to dig a

new well out near the road to get clean water. We run a line in through that pipe."

Hooks started to make a note in his book, but was interrupted by Mack braying, "Doberman pinschers. That's what we need. That and good German shepherds. Let them run around at night and bite the asses off anybody what sneaks in here."

Hooks nodded reluctantly. "Might be some help," he admitted.

"Laurie's afraid they'll chew up on the kids," Mack told him.

"Well, we'll think about it," said Hooks.

Mack suggested that Read take Hooks on a jeep trip around the rest of the ranch, but Hooks noticed the foreman's frown and guessed that he had other work planned.

"Truth is," Hooks said, "I'd just as soon borrow the jeep and make the trip myself. It'll give me a better chance to think. I kind of like to work alone."

Mack snorted and Read nodded. "I'll bring the jeep around. We got five hundred acres and you'll know it 'cause we got a single-strand wire fence around it. Signs posted. Otherwise you get people in trying to shoot birds. Damn fools."

Read left, and when Hooks made a show of drawing a diagram in his notebook, Mack wandered off too. "I'll see you later, Hooks," he said. "Careful. There's an Indian reservation near here. Those loafers'll try to sell you a rug. Buy the damn rugs in Hong Kong. Chinamen can't make a rug no better than damned Indians can."

When Read brought him the jeep, Hooks drove out to the main entrance of the ranch property. It was on a small paved spur road that peeled off from the main highway, Route 371, which paralleled the spur, perhaps fifty yards away. Again, there was no gate in the fence, and Hooks made a note to check on how the two girls, Eva and Francesca, got to school every day.

From the entrance, a single-strand wire fence moved off in both directions, and Hooks started to trail along inside the fence.

An hour later, with the sun high in the sky and the day turning unseasonably hot, Hooks realized he had lived in the city for too long. When Kinderman had said his ranch was small, only five hundred acres, Hooks had accepted "small" at face value.

But five hundred acres, he started to realize, was a pretty big chunk of real estate, about the size of five hundred square city blocks. He tried to remember how many acres made up one square mile, and he thought it was six hundred forty. So Kinderman's ranch was almost a mile square. Hell, there were a lot of American towns that weren't that big.

Despite the sun, Hooks found the work pleasurable. He stopped often and drew diagrams on sight lines to the house, but most of the time the main structure was not visible because of trees blocking his view or because of the rough up-and-down nature of the terrain.

The shabby wire fence, although in good repair, was absolutely no barrier at all. It could be vaulted or climbed under or just cut and walked through by anybody who wanted to get onto the property and approach the house. He kept making notes of sight lines at different spots along the fence, as it trailed its way through trees, then across sandy desert patches. Occasionally, he ran across some stray steers grazing contentedly on patches of scrub grass. They looked at him with curiosity, and he was surprised, as he almost always was with livestock, at how tall and heavy the creatures were.

When he had finished his giant circle of the ranch and returned to the main entrance near the road, he glanced at his watch and saw it was lunchtime. The prospect of having to eat another meal with Henry Mack and listen to his outpouring hatred of everybody did not sit well with him, so he drove out of the ranch property and onto the road to go find the town of Cahuilla.

In the center of the small town, he stopped at a friendly-looking pub and had a cheeseburger and a bottle of beer. He realized that he had gotten a pretty good sunburn driving around in the open-topped vehicle without wearing a hat.

He had another blessedly cold beer before deciding to go back to the ranch. When he noticed that the gas gauge on the jeep read almost empty, he stopped in a gas station to fill it up.

"How much do I owe you?" he asked the attendant after he finished pumping the gas.

"That's the congressman's jeep, isn't it?"

Hooks didn't answer. A black Ford had just driven past the gas station, and he thought he recognized the driver. At the next corner, the Ford made a left turn. Behind the wheel was a dark-haired woman.

Was it? He realized the attendant was talking to him.

"That Kinderman's jeep?" the attendant asked.

"Yeah, that's right."

"Okay. No charge. I'll just put it on his bill."

"Thanks," Hooks said and drove out of the gas station.

He turned at the next corner, but the Ford was not to be seen. He drove around the small town for the next ten minutes before giving up the search and heading back toward the ranch.

He thought he had seen Marta Kohl driving that car.

Back in his room, Hooks was changing into his bathing suit when he noticed something. The electronics supply catalog he had brought with him was atop the small desk near the window. But he would have sworn

179

that he had put it inside the desk drawer before leaving on his tour of the ranch that morning.

He looked into his dresser drawers but could not tell if anything had been disturbed.

But one of his jackets in the clothes closet was hanging crookedly from its wire hanger, and he was too neat about hanging up his clothes to have done that himself.

Somebody had searched his room.

What the hell for? He sat on the bed for a moment to think about it, but the best he could come up with was that that old cuckoo, Henry Mack, had done it. Maybe Mack thought that Hooks was hiding a Mexican immigrant in his luggage, he thought with a wry smile.

He tried to shrug it off, took a towel from the small bathroom that was part of his room and walked barefoot down the steps and through a door leading to the patio. At poolside, he carefully unstrapped his knee brace and slid into the water.

It was cooler than he had expected, but it was invigorating after a day in the sun, and he steadily swam ten laps back and forth before pulling himself up onto the stone deck to catch his breath and rest.

He waited for ten minutes, then slid back into the water again and resumed swimming. Only grim determination permitted him to finish another ten laps before he collapsed, lungs heaving and gasping, his arm and leg muscles trembling. He was badly out of condition, he realized. Just a year ago, he could have swum fifty laps with no great effort. As a young athlete in training, he had swum miles each day.

Lauren Kinderman came out of the house and sat down at one of the tables beside the pool. A servant followed her, carrying a tray with a cup and coffee service. For a moment, Hooks thought that maybe one of the servants had gone through his things, but he quickly rejected that thought. Who would risk a job for an adventure like that? He had been around Henry Mack too long, he thought.

"Would you like some coffee?" Lauren called out.

"Very much." He climbed out of the pool and began drying himself with the small towel, aware that Lauren was looking at his ugly, scarred knee.

"I'm sorry," she said. "We didn't give you the proper supplies. Lee. Another cup for Mr. Hooks and bring him a robe and scuffs," she called to the servant as he was entering the house. He nodded and returned in a few minutes with the supplies.

Hooks limped heavily over to the table with Lauren and sat down.

"You swim much?" she asked.

"I used to do a fair amount, but I'm afraid those days are gone. I'm just out of shape. It'd be worse, I guess, if I hadn't quit smoking. Now I just have an occasional cigarette." He eyed her pack longingly. She smiled and pushed the cigarettes toward him, and he lit up gratefully.

"I'm afraid I wasn't a very good hostess last night," she said.

"You were fine. I don't know what you mean."

She flushed and looked down at her coffee. "I think perhaps I drank a little too much?"

"I didn't notice," he lied politely. "You seemed fine to me."

"My husband has been scolding me about my drinking," she confided in a low voice.

Embarrassed for her, he studied his cigarette. "I wouldn't know," he said. "You seemed all right last night."

"You . . . you won't say anything about last night to him or Uncle Henry, will you?"

He frowned and looked at her directly. "Mrs. Kinderman, I'm not here to spy on you. I'm here to figure out how to make your house safe. I have no intention of talking to anybody about anything."

She smiled timidly. "I wish everybody thought the way you do," she said with a sigh, and then added, almost as an afterthought, "Fred Maier will be here tonight. He called."

"Good. I'll want to talk to him about the ranch."

"Did you enjoy your tour?"

"Your place is beautiful," Hooks said honestly. "I can understand why you prefer this to Washington."

She nodded, but when he finished his coffee and got up to return to his room, she shyly touched his hand and said softly, "Thank you for not saying anything."

After showering and dressing, Hooks prowled the house and the nearby grounds again. He also measured the windows and inspected the grounds alongside the house. There were several shrubs that would have to be removed. He found himself outside the windows that would belong to Kinderman's office, and when he was sure that no one was watching he tried to peer inside, but the shades and drapes were tightly drawn and he could see nothing.

He busied himself in his room and transcribed his notes, until a servant called him for dinner.

Dinner was a reprise of the previous night's with Henry Mack except that Fred Maier was there, seated opposite Hooks. Henry Mack launched into a lengthy and detailed analysis of the biological and social genealogy of the nation's Supreme Court over the past several decades, ending with his magnum opus: a carefully constructed case in which Earl Warren turned out to have been the illegitimate son of Josef Stalin by Eleanor Roosevelt. He pronounced the name "Rosenfelt."

Hooks glanced toward Maier and hoped to win a

coconspiratorial wink, but instead he found that Maier was listening in rapt attention to the old man rant. He looked around the table and was pleased to get a wink from Lauren Kinderman. Perhaps he had made a friend, he thought.

He concentrated on his meal as Mack and Maier spent the rest of the dinner loudly discussing a senator known for his hard-line stance on the cold war and his support for higher defense spending. They agreed he was a lily-livered wimp and a disgrace to the state he had represented for twenty years. This confused Hooks until he found out that the senator did not support the National Rifle Association and believed in legalized abortion.

After dinner, Hooks excused himself to Lauren and joined Mack and Maier in the billiard room/bar. He turned down a highball but had a bottle of beer. Something about California's heat brought out the beer thirst in him.

"I haven't wanted to discuss one subject in front of Mrs. Kinderman," he said. "But what precautions do you take to prevent any attempt to kidnap the children?"

Both men looked blank. "One of the hands drives them to the road, and they catch the school bus," Mack said. "I guess we could have him carry a gun."

Hooks shook his head. "That wouldn't do any good unless he really knew how to use it. Anyway, what would stop someone from flagging down the school bus and grabbing the girls?"

"Shit, who'd do a crazy thing like that?" Mack demanded.

"A crazy person, maybe," Hooks said flatly. "You want some examples?"

The old man muttered but reluctantly nodded agreement and looked worried.

"I'm not saying anything like that is likely to happen

in a thousand years," Hooks said. "But the congressman wanted things made secure around here. The children could be a weak link."

Maier said, "When the congressman gets more national exposure, somebody could take a crack at the kids. What do you suggest?"

"Well, I'm going to work tomorrow on a full report," Hooks said. "But I think maybe the kids should be taken from the ranch directly to school by a trained man in a properly equipped van. And I mean trained and I mean properly equipped."

"Bullet-proof? Stuff like that?" the old man asked.

"Not just that. Heavy-duty suspensions. Special tires. A double radiator so it can't be disabled. And most important of all, reliable radio equipment. I'll put this all in my report."

"You're going to be doing it tomorrow?" Maier asked.

"Yeah."

"Pretty fast," said the young man. He giggled slightly, and Hooks again thought how discomfiting it was to hear that girlish sound emanate from that football player's body.

"I told you I was being overpaid."

Maier nodded. It was obvious he agreed with that proposition. He said, "The congressman's coming back the day after tomorrow. I hope you'll be here to talk to him."

"I hope so," Hooks said. "And then I want to get back home."

In only a few minutes, the two men had resumed their discussion of the world's political sins, and Hooks excused himself and drifted out to the patio.

Lauren Kinderman was there. She had a coffee cup in front of her and this time she had not brought her brandy bottle, Hooks noted with relief.

He joined her, and they chatted quietly. Hooks

guided her into describing her background. The only child of a boom-and-bust wildcatter, she had had a nomadic upbringing throughout the southwest, never staying anyplace long enough to establish roots or form long friendships.

Her marriage to Jack Kinderman had been almost an arranged affair, Hooks gathered, but she expressed no regrets. On the contrary, she seemed to marvel that a man as intelligent, as handsome, as forceful as Jack Kinderman would have married her. The only touch of resentment he could note in her voice came when she mentioned the twin girls.

"Jack loves Eva and Francesca, but I wish he would spend a little more time with them. He's so busy, you know. Sometimes I think he's a little uncomfortable around them. It might be different if they were boys."

"You think Jack would like to have a son?" Hooks asked, thinking that he would give his good right leg to have two daughters like Eva and Francesca.

"We did have a son," she replied, "but he died right after birth." She fell silent.

"I'm sorry," he murmured. "I'm going to steal another one of your cigarettes," he said to change the subject.

"Go ahead."

"Tell me, does Fred visit the ranch often?"

"He's here a lot," she said and she took another sip from her cup. Her coffee must have gotten cold a long time ago, he thought.

"I've never really been able to figure out just what he does," said Hooks.

"He's a little of everything. He's been with Jack for four or five years. He worships my husband. I guess really he's sort of a bodyguard. He was a green beret in Vietnam. He'd do anything for Jack."

She sipped again from her cup, and Hooks realized he could detect the faint smell of brandy.

"You don't like him, do you?" he said.

She was startled at first, then looked down. "I guess I don't trust him. I always think he's spying on me when he's here. I don't like the way he looks at me. I always feel like my hair is mussed?"

A few minutes later, Maier appeared in the door to the patio.

"Hi, folks," he said in his high-pitched voice. "Am I intruding?"

Hooks saw the startled look on Lauren's face.

"No," Hooks said. "Come on out. I was just finishing my brandy before turning in."

With his body shielding him from Maier, Hooks reached across the table and pulled Lauren's coffee cup over in front of him, then turned toward Maier, and made a large show of draining the drink.

Maier glanced at the table.

"It's been a long day," he said agreeably. "I think I'll go to bed too."

Hooks rose as Maier turned and went back inside the house. Before he left the table, Lauren reached over and touched Hooks's hand.

"Thank you," she said softly.

Hooks nodded. She was safe from her husband's bloodhound for the moment, at least.

In his room, Hooks picked up the telephone. He was going to call Patti, but when he looked at his watch he realized it was early morning back east.

She would either be asleep or out. If she was asleep, he didn't want to wake her.

If she was out, he didn't want to know it.

186

CHAPTER TWENTY-THREE

ONE OF THE SERVANTS BROUGHT A TYPEWRITER TO Hooks's room the next morning after breakfast, and he began putting his observations and recommendations on paper.

Frequently checking the catalog of electronic supplies he had brought with him, he came up with a plan that he was sure would make the Kinderman ranch as secure as the Pentagon.

He felt good doing the work. He was out of his element traipsing around Germany playing detective, and listening to Henry Mack discourse on politics was both boring and distasteful, but this was work he understood and did well.

He recommended replacing the single-strand outside fence that crawled around the perimeter of the ranch with a stronger, higher fence to discourage garden-variety trespassers. The inside of that fence could be supplemented with electric-eye-type detectors that would set off an alarm if anyone broke through their beams.

He had worked out the sight lines for the detectors all around the ranch, and the number of devices that would be needed was surprisingly small.

He recommended a high hurricane-style fence around the large living compound. The fence could be topped with barbed wire and various kinds of ivy and plants could be grown to cover it and make it less of an eyesore. Inside that fence, he recommended another fence be erected, creating a small ringed corridor, and that guard dogs be freed there to patrol the grounds at night.

Of course, both the outside and inside fences should have electrically controlled locking gates.

He recommended four special nighttime video cameras to sweep the compound grounds and be monitored in a special guard station that could be set up in the bunkhouse.

He recommended an auxiliary-power system be built for the ranch. He had noticed that power came in on a few bare sets of overhead wires, and anyone planning a real assault on the ranch could cut off the power with no effort at all. He recommended that a strong citizens' band radio hookup be set up, also, in case telephone service was ever cut off.

When he glanced at his watch, it was almost noon. He decided it was time for a break, and he called Patti in her Washington office.

"Hi, stranger," he said.

"Steve," she squealed. "Where are you?"

"Still in la-la land."

"All right. Don't tell me, let me guess. You're sunburned, and your eyes are all squinched up from looking into the sun."

"How'd you know that?" Hooks demanded.

"Because you left your sunglasses home," she said. "I found them when I was going through your closet and taking your suits to the dry cleaners. How can you go to California without your sunglasses? How's anybody going to mistake you for Robert Redford?"

"Patti, I don't own sunglasses," he told her, puzzled.

"Brown ones," she said.

"Not mine."

"They were in your jacket pocket," she said.

"Not mine. Maybe Jo's?"

"Men's glasses. She wouldn't wear them," Patti said.

"And they're sunglasses," he said.

"Right. I looked through them. Sunglasses."

"Add it to the list of life's great mysteries," he said. "I didn't really call to talk about imaginary sunglasses."

"When are you coming home?" she asked. "You fall in love yet with any of those big California blondes?"

"No. I'm still as pure as the driven snow," he said. "And there's a chance I might get home tomorrow night. If not the next day."

"Good," she said. "I miss you. I want to try out a new spaghetti recipe on you."

"I miss you, too, but not your spaghetti," he said.

"Can we talk on this line?" she asked.

It hadn't occurred to him. He glanced at the telephone receiver. There were no buttons for other lines, but that still did not mean that there was not an extension to this phone somewhere else in the house.

"I'm not sure," he said. "Be discreet."

"Okay. Discretion's my middle name. Did that congressman's wife take a run at you yet?"

He laughed despite himself. "I'd hate to see you when you're indiscreet," he said. "No, everybody's been very nice here. They've got two beautiful little twin daughters, and I've been working hard. I'm doing my preliminary report right now."

"No son?" she said.

"What?"

"They have daughters but no son?" she asked.

"That's right."

"I wonder how the future President of the United States feels about that?" she said. The woman was uncanny, Hooks thought for the thousandth time. Often

189

she acted as if she had a head full of butterflies, and then she would come up with an incisive thought like that.

"Well, we'll talk about it when I come home," he said. "Did you see Jo?"

"I did. I told her where you were."

"And?"

"She's the same, Steve. No change."

"Okay," he said. "Listen, this call is costing me more than I'm making. I'll call you when I get back."

"Good. I'll start cooking the pasta now. I miss you, Steve."

"Same here."

Hooks went down to the kitchen where the cook rustled him up a plate of sandwiches and a pot of coffee, and he brought them back to his room and went back to work on the report.

Somehow he had the sense that he had forgotten something, but he couldn't wring it out of his mind. He made recommendations for security inside the main house itself; he also specified the type and style of window and door locks that should be used and wrote a long section on ways to make sure that nothing happened to Eva and Francesca on their way to and from school.

Squeals of laughter distracted him. It must be late afternoon, he realized. The twins were back from school, and he walked to the window to watch them. They were enjoying themselves in the pool with some other youngsters, Mexican-American children, he noted approvingly.

Lauren was acting as lifeguard, sitting by the pool in her bathing suit and a huge straw hat. She eventually joined them and paddled sedately back and forth a few times, but she avoided the children's roughhouse. She was on terms of easy familiarity with the Latin children, Hooks was pleased to see.

He went back to his desk, still with the nagging suspicion that he had forgotten something. Carefully, he reread his report. It was not bad for a preliminary document. A few extra points would probably come to mind, and he'd insert them, but he felt good about having something to give Kinderman when the congressman arrived the next day.

There was a knock on the door.

Lee, the Chinese servant, stood there. He pushed forward a slip of paper to Hooks.

"There was a telephone call for you, Mr. Hooks. The woman said to give you this."

"Thank you," Hooks said as he took the paper. The message was brief—"Steven. Call M"—and it gave a telephone number. He felt his pulse quicken.

"It was a woman?" he asked Lee.

"Yes."

"And she called me Steven?"

"Yes, sir."

"Thank you," Hooks said. He closed the door. He hadn't been dreaming yesterday. He had seen Marta Kohl in town. No one else that he knew called him Steven.

Why was she here? What did she want?

He pushed his report aside on the desk and dialed the telephone number she had given him.

She answered on the first ring.

"Hello," she said.

"This is Steven."

"Steven, this is Marta. I must see you tonight."

"Well, I—"

"Please, Steven, it is very important."

He hesitated. "All right. Tonight. Maybe we could

get dinner." He thought it might be a pleasure to get away from Henry Mack's raving for one evening.

"Yes. That would be fine. What time?"

"Eight o'clock?"

"I will be in the bar at the Valley Motel at eight o'clock," she said.

"Is everything all right?" he asked. His voice, he noticed, had a curiously hollow sound on the phone.

"It will be," she said cryptically and hung up.

Hooks started to replace the phone, then hesitated. He listened carefully and heard a faint click. Someone had been listening in to his call.

CHAPTER TWENTY-FOUR

WHEN HOOKS ASKED LAUREN KINDERMAN IF HE COULD borrow a car for the evening, she told him that there was a string of cars in the garage behind the house; all of the cars had their keys in them, and he could help himself.

He passed up two blue station wagons and a long Cadillac and settled on a black Volvo sedan.

He arrived a few minutes after eight and found Marta sitting at the bar in the motel; she was sipping a glass of wine and being pestered by some fat businessman who had ignored a long bank of empty bar stools to plop himself down next to her.

Hooks squeezed in between the two of them, and the fat man grudgingly gave way.

She greeted him with a kiss.

"It's nice to see you again, Marta. I didn't expect to so soon."

"I had business out here," she said. "Have you eaten yet?"

"No, I'm starved," he said.

"Let's get out of this place, then. There is a restaurant down the road."

The restaurant was noisy and crowded. Hooks had tried asking Marta questions in the car on the way there but she had deflected them, preferring to talk instead about how much she liked California's weather and how she would like to live on the oceanfront.

They got a table in a far corner of the restaurant, but still too close to other diners to suit Hooks.

"I don't know how I'm supposed to act," said Hooks. "I'd like to enjoy this dinner and make believe it's a date, but your telephone call sounded anything but pleasant."

"Let's just enjoy this dinner," she said with a large smile. "And maybe later, if you have some questions, I can answer them." She was truly beautiful, he thought. He had never noticed it before, but her sparkling green eyes had almost an Oriental cast to them that, with her jet-black hair, gave her an exotic look. Somehow he had expected a German woman, no matter how lovely, to look like a milkmaid, but Marta would have been more at home in an elegant international casino.

"I'll ask one question, and then I won't ask any questions," he said.

"That's fair."

"Did you really have business in California? Or did you come here to see me?"

"Both," she replied. "I had a very important thing to do here. I remembered that congressman's name that you told me, and I looked up where he lived. That is how I called you."

"I'm flattered," he said.

"I'm really happy to see you well," she said.

They spent dinner in small talk, but Hooks noticed that whenever he strayed too far from the subject of the ranch or his security work, Marta reined him in and brought him back.

He mentioned how he had been working on his report that afternoon when she'd called and how he had not known it was late until he'd heard the children's voices in the pool.

"Children? Are there children?"

"Yes. The congressman has two children."

"I did not read that," she said. "What are they? Boys or girls?"

"A pair of girl twins. The prettiest little girls you could imagine."

"And their names are? . . ."

"Eva and Francesca," he said. She had a forkful of food on the way to her mouth, but her arm froze in its motion.

"Please tell me their names again," she requested.

"Eva and Francesca. Ten-year-old twins," he said.

There was a strange look in her eyes. It was wild, as if she were a jungle animal that had just stirred. And it was something else too. It was a triumphant look.

"What's going on?" he said.

"Why do you ask?"

"Because of that look on you face."

"I must learn to control my looks." She put down her fork and touched his hand. "Soon, Steven, soon. But first our dinner."

He noticed, though, that she seemed to have lost her appetite. Instead of eating, she merely pushed the food around the plate; she was absorbed in her own thoughts.

Finally, she looked up and smiled brightly. "You will take me back to my room," she said, "and we will talk there. I have something to show you. And I have some large truths to tell you."

"Will we still be friends afterward?"

"Hopefully, more than ever," she said.

He parked the Volvo in front of the door to her motel room.

"Steven," she said, "I think tonight calls for a celebration."

"Good," he said.

"So walk over to the bar and bring us back a bottle of wine. I'll wait for you."

He helped her out of the car and walked away while she was fumbling with the key to her room.

Apparently the bartender did not get many calls for packaged goods because he had to confer with the owner before he brought a half-gallon jug of Gallo from beneath the bar.

"Ten dollars," he said.

"You got it," said Hooks.

He walked back to the room and tapped on the door. He waited about ten seconds, then tapped again.

He thought he heard a sound inside, so he rapped louder. "Marta," he called.

There was no answer.

Then he heard a thud and the sound of a window opening. He set down the jug of wine and slammed his shoulder against the door. It shuddered but didn't open. He slammed again, and the door flew open, hit the wall and rebounded toward his face. He pushed it aside and stepped into the room.

Then he ran forward.

Marta Kohl was lying on her back on the floor at the foot of the bed. The front of her white blouse was soaked with a spreading stain of blood. He ran to her and knelt alongside her. He felt for a pulse in her throat, but could find none.

He started to rise, to call for help, when her eyes opened. They rolled wildly around, then fixed on him.

"Steven." Her voice was a soft strangled hiss.

"Don't talk. I'm calling for help."

"No. Tell them . . ."

"Don't. Please . . ." he began.

"Tell them . . ." He leaned forward to hear her words.

"Tell them he is the beast." She forced out the words, and then her eyes rolled back up into her head, and she went limp in his arms. A faint trickle of blood rolled from the corner of her mouth, and Hooks knew he was no longer holding Marta Kohl in his arms. He was holding a dead body.

He set her down gently, then quickly closed the front door to the room.

A back window was open, and he ran to it and peered out. It opened onto a parking lot, but he could see no one there. When he looked around the room again, he noticed that Marta's dresser drawers had been ransacked and her single piece of luggage had been looted; its contents were spilled onto the floor.

His mind was reeling. The inevitable questions, who, what, why, jumped into his thoughts and seemed to stand there, like little soldiers, shouting for attention and for answers. But he had no answers. Only more questions. "Tell them he is the beast." Tell who? Who is the beast? What does the beast mean?

And out of all the questions, one clear answer came into his head.

He had to get out of there. Marta Kohl was dead, and nothing he did was going to change that. Maybe, somehow, he might find out who had killed her.

But that would never happen if he called the police and waited there for them and went through their inevitable questioning which would inevitably turn up the fact that he had also been in a hotel room with Marta's father when he, too, had been killed by an unknown assailant.

Sure, Hooks, it's a wonderful story, so go to jail for twenty years while we think about it.

He looked carefully around the room. He had touched nothing. Except the rear windowsill, looking out. He went to the window and rubbed the sill with his handkerchief, knowing that he was quite possibly also erasing the only fingerprints the murderer might have left behind.

He looked around again. He had touched nothing else. He walked toward the front door, but as he passed Marta's body he looked down at the dead young woman. She lay there, her body twisted, agonized, her eyes open and sightless, and he wanted to cover her with a blanket, to do something to make her final moment less obscene. But instead, he just asked her quietly for forgiveness, and walked to the front door.

He used his handkerchief to open it, and peered out in both directions. No one was in sight, and he stepped outside, closed the door and wiped the knob with his handkerchief. The door, its frame splintered by the impact of his shoulder, was no longer locked, but at least it appeared to be tightly closed. His jug of wine was still on the walk outside the door, and he took it quickly to his car, started it and drove out of the lot.

He drove around to the lot on the other side of the motel. Only three cars were parked there and all seemed empty. He did not want to chance stopping and looking carefully into each car. He might be seen; his car's license plates might later be remembered.

He turned around and drove from the lot and out onto the road, heading out of town, toward the Kinderman ranch.

Could anyone connect him with Marta? He had met her in the motel bar, but had not even stayed for one drink. Any description given by the bartender or the fat businessman who was next to him at the bar would be sketchy at best.

In the restaurant where they'd eaten dinner, they had sat at a back table, he with his back to the rest of the restaurant. Probably few had seen him; and none had a reason to remember what he looked like. He had paid for the meal in cash so there was no credit card number with his name on it.

He had bought wine when they went back to Marta's

room. But he hadn't said anything to the bartender, who was different from the one who had been working the cocktail hour. There was no reason to remember Hooks. Especially since the jug of wine he had bought was on the seat next to him. It would not be found in Marta's room.

Anything else?

She had called the ranch.

But she had not left her name. Just a telephone number and her initial. M. No one would connect that up. Not unless . . . He groaned. What if Marta had his name or the ranch's telephone number written down inside her purse? The trail would lead right to him, and then his flight from her room would seem like an admission of guilt.

He slowed down and thought of driving back. No. It was too dangerous. He'd have to take his chances. Why would she write down his name? She knew his name. She didn't have to remind herself of it when she called the ranch.

He was off the main road now, driving, almost without looking, toward the entrance to the ranch. And then a thought struck him, a thought so odd but so logical that it sent a chill through his body.

He had called Marta back, and had thought someone had been listening in.

Had that someone been the killer?

And then another thought, even more chilling, hammered itself into his mind. Suppose the killer had known he was with Marta. Suppose he had followed them. And suppose, then, he had not been surprised by Marta in her motel room. Suppose, instead, he had been waiting for them, for both of them.

Had Hooks escaped being murdered only because Marta, on a whim, had decided he should buy a bottle of wine? To celebrate. To celebrate what?

Just too many possibilities, too many questions.

He parked the car in the garage behind the main house and was stepping out when he remembered the bottle of wine on the seat. He picked it up, then saw a home-sized garbage dumpster in a corner next to the garage entrance. He opened the bottle and poured the wine on the ground outside the garage, then tossed the empty bottle into the dumpster.

He was walking toward the house, but an idea suddenly came to mind, and he walked back to the garage. The Cadillac and two blue station wagons were still parked there.

He felt their hoods, but all of them were cool. None of them had been driven in the last hour or so.

The house was silent as he walked upstairs to his bedroom. He closed and locked the door behind him, and then propped a chair up, under the doorknob.

He sat in the room's easy chair and tried to think, logically, step by step; he tried to make some sense out of what had happened. But the thoughts would not come, just bits and impressions flashing into his mind, and before he could focus on them they were gone. He saw the shadowy figure of Anna Mueller running down a street in terror, with a black-cloaked figure after her, and then he saw Marta Kohl running, with the same figure after her, too. Was it the beast? What beast?

The thoughts would not come, but the emotions did, and his first flush of fear gave way to something stronger and more elemental.

Anger.

Someone was going to pay for Marta Kohl's death. Pay in full.

CHAPTER TWENTY-FIVE

DURING THE NIGHT, HOOKS HAD PACKED. AT SEVEN A.M., he called the San Diego Airport and made a reservation to New York on the earliest flight available, leaving at one P.M.

Then he showered and changed, and at eight A.M. went downstairs to breakfast. He gave his breakfast order to the cook in the kitchen, then walked out onto the patio where Lauren Kinderman and Henry Mack were sitting. Their breakfast dishes were in front of them, and Mack was reading a newspaper.

"Morning, Mr. Hooks," Lauren said politely. "Are you ready for breakfast?"

"I just stopped in the kitchen. Lee is fixing me something." The woman smiled, and Hooks thought, So far, so good. If they'd been told to watch out for me as a murderer, I don't think Lauren would be handling this with such aplomb.

Hooks sat down, and Henry Mack put the paper down.

"Hey, boy," he said. "Look at this."

He handed the newspaper over, and Hooks looked at page one.

Taking up four columns in the center of page one was a photograph of Jack Kinderman, speaking in El Salvador. His fist was raised above his head in a power salute, and the headline on the story read:

TOURING KINDERMAN RAPS LEFTISTS;
CALLS FOR NEW WORLD ORDER

The story under the headline was a glowing account
of a giant rally in El Salvador at which Kinderman, the
main speaker, had first shouted down a group of hecklers, and then told the crowd that "everwhere, in every
country that values freedom, in the heart of every man
who cherishes liberty, a struggle is being waged . . .
waged by the forces of freedom against the leftists, the
Communists, and the secret powers that fund them and
support them.

"It is a great struggle and a perilous one, but it is a
struggle we will win. We will win because we must win,
because to lose the struggle is to lose all that we hold
dear and precious . . . to lose all that makes life
worthwhile.

"But we will not win by sitting on our hands while
our enemies' depredations go unchecked. We will win
only by joining the battle, by meting out the full
measure to them that they would mete out to us. We will
win when all good men and all good governments
everywhere come together in a New World Order,
prepared to meet on the battlefields of the mind and on
other battlefields, if need be, the forces that would
enslave us all."

The report said that Kinderman was greeted with
riotous cheers by a jubilant crowd and chants of "Kinderman for President" resounded through the public
square.

Hooks looked at the picture of Kinderman again. His
arm raised over his head, reminding Hooks somehow of
a Roman legionnaire. And the look on Kinderman face
was that of a conqueror, triumphant and fearless, a
Caesar ready to lead. It was the face of a man who could
lead the world to heaven. Or to hell.

And then another story caught his eye. It was just a brief item in the corner of page one.

WOMAN FOUND DEAD IN MOTEL

The body of a young woman was found early this morning in a room at the Valley Motel. Police said she had been stabbed through the heart sometime during the evening, and had apparently died instantly.

The woman had carried no identification but she had rented the room under the name of Marta Taubman of Berlin, Germany. Police said a back window to the room was open, and they are looking for a man who was seen with the woman in the motel cocktail lounge earlier in the evening.

That was all. Marta Kohl's life, and murder. Two paragraphs in a small California newspaper.

Henry Mack was speaking to him.

"What's that?" Hooks said as he handed the paper back.

"What do you think of that, boy?"

"Strong stuff," said Hooks.

"From a strong man," Mack said. "Dammit, someday he's going to be President."

"Of what country?" Hooks asked with a smile. "It sounds like he's running for President of El Salvador."

"This country. But Jack knows it's going to take the whole world to beat the Commies. And it's going to take a leader. You don't know it, but he was born to be a leader. It's in his blood."

"His folks in politics?" Hooks asked casually.

"No. They worked for me. Nice couple, but they got killed in a car crash. Jack was only three, and I'd be damned if I'd let him go to some orphanage somewhere. So I adopted him."

"Oh. I thought you were his stepfather," Hooks said.

"Yeah. I kinda say that 'cause it's easier to handle.

He's my boy, though, and he just may be the biggest man this country, maybe the world, ever saw. I hope I live long enough to see it happen."

"I hope so too," Hooks said, for lack of any other polite response. He smiled and turned away from Mack and asked Lauren, "Where's Fred Maier today?"

"Oh, you don't know. Jack is coming in today, and he was arriving in San Diego on an early plane, so Fred went down there last night to spend the night so he could pick him up early and drive him back."

"No helicopter?"

Lauren shrugged. "Fred said he needed the time with Jack to talk business. Only place he can capture his ear and not be interrupted is in a car."

"Well, I hope they get back soon," said Hooks. "I'm leaving today."

Mack said, "So soon?" He seemed annoyed.

"Yes. I think my wife's taken a turn for the worse. But I did want to see the congressman before I leave."

"Well, he should be here soon," Mack told him. He finished his coffee and rose from the table. "Excuse me. Got some things to do."

After he had gone, Lauren asked Hooks, "Have you finished your report and recommendations?"

"Pretty thoroughly," Hooks replied. "I wanted to give the congressman the rough copy. I'll polish it when I get back to my office and send him the finished report later on."

Lauren nodded, then said, "Then I guess you should leave as soon as you can."

He looked at her searchingly. "Why do you say that?"

She flushed and looked away toward the pool. "Oh. Because of your wife and all."

He took the woman's hand. "Lauren. That's not what you meant. What did you mean?"

As if he were electrically charged, she pulled her

hand away from his and stood up. Without looking at him, she said, "Steve. Just leave. Right away."

Then she walked quickly away into the house. And an odd thought occurred to him. It was the first time she had ever called him by his first name.

Hooks was ready to go. He carried his bag downstairs, left it in the hall and found Henry Mack in the billiard room, playing a solitary game of pool with a large glass of liquor near his hand.

He looked up as Hooks came in and handed him a sealed envelope.

"That's my report for the congressman," Hooks said. "I didn't want to give it to Mrs. Kinderman. She might read it and get alarmed by some of the possibilities I raise."

"I'll see Jack gets it. You're going now, huh?"

"Yeah. I want to get home."

"Jack wanted to talk to you before you left," the old man said sullenly.

"I'm sure I'll see him back in Washington," Hooks replied. He tried to smile. "We're hometown neighbors, remember?"

Mack nodded curtly.

"Is it okay, Mr. Mack, if I borrow one of the station wagons to drive in to the airport?"

"Yeah, go ahead. I'd have one of the hands take you in, but they're all working the cattle today. You can just leave it in the parking lot and lock it up with the keys inside. We got extra keys to all them cars."

"Thanks, then," said Hooks. "I'll be on my way." He extended his hand and after a momentary hesitation, Mack took it. The old man's grip was surprisingly weak, Hooks thought. "Give my regards to Mrs. Kinderman and the girls," he said.

"Yeah. I'll do that." He turned back to the pool table.

* * *

Hooks had to stop just before turning onto the roadway because a car pulled off the road, through the fence opening and onto the ranch property.

He saw Fred Maier at the wheel and Jack Kinderman in the passenger's seat.

Kinderman waved to him over the top of the car, then stepped out and walked over to him. He was wearing a neat blue suit, but his white shirt was open and he wore no tie.

"Hi, Hooks. Hear you're leaving," Kinderman said. There was a strange little hesitation in his voice, as if he were not quite sure of his audience.

Hooks nodded. "Yeah, I've got to get back. I gave the report to Mr. Mack, and I'll be sending you another one in a couple of days."

"I was hoping you were going to stay for a while. Is everything all right?"

"I think my wife's taken a turn for the worse," Hooks told him.

"Oh. I'm sorry to hear that," Kinderman said. Hooks noticed that Maier was staring at him. It gave him the impression of a marksman looking down the barrel of a gun at his target.

Kinderman said, "I was thinking that maybe Henry was a little much for you to take and that's why you were leaving."

Hooks shook his head. "No. We got along just fine."

Kinderman nodded. "Well, I want to thank you. I'm looking forward to reading that report. I guess I'll be seeing you back in Washington."

"Sure thing."

"And next time you get out this way, maybe you can spend some time. I bet you didn't even get a chance to go riding."

"Next time," Hooks promised. The two men looked

at each other wordlessly for a few seconds, then Kinder-man nodded and walked back to his car. Hooks drove off. In the rearview mirror, he saw that their car continued up the road toward the main ranch house.

Kinderman had seemed not quite himself, but he was a few miles down the road before he recognized it. The congressman had been nervous about talking to him.

Why?

He wanted to sleep. His body ached and cried out for sleep. It would have to wait, he told himself.

He was an engineer. He was trained to think logically, and that was what he had to do now.

Hooks was in the first-class compartment in a window seat. The seat next to him was empty, and he spread several magazines and a pillow from the rack overhead on it to discourage seat-switchers from pouncing on it.

He put the stereo earphones in his ears to discourage anyone who might want to stop and chitchat with him, then turned the volume off so the sound wouldn't disturb him. Then, with pen and notebook, he began to write down everything he could remember about his meetings with Marta Kohl. And Anna Mueller, because he had the sense that somehow that long-dead German woman had led to last night's brutal murder.

Long dead? Why did he think Anna Mueller had been long dead? Because the kidnappers in Berlin had told him that. What had the man with the soft cultured voice said? That Anna Mueller was just another poor innocent who had died in the war.

But Professor Kohl had come to America to look for Anna Mueller. Why hadn't he thought of that before? Was is possible that Kohl had been wrong, that the woman he had been seeking had died almost forty years before? Or could there be two Anna Muellers?

His mind wrestled with that proposition for a while, writing it on the paper of his notebook as a possibility, then rejecting it and crossing it out.

It made no sense, but it was the only thing that made any sense. He had not seen the kidnapper's face, but when the man had told him that Anna Mueller was dead, Hooks had believed him. The man had not been lying. But Professor Kohl had not been lying, either. He had spent hours with the man talking about how to launch a search for the missing German woman. If Kohl had been lying, he felt sure he would have been able to tell.

He put that thought aside and began to think about the kidnappers. They had lured him to Marta's car with a phony message from her. The message. What had it said? "Steven. I will be in my car in the hotel parking lot at ten P.M. Marta."

Steven. The message had called him Steven, just as Marta always had.

But how had the kidnappers known that she called him Steven?

Unless she had told them herself.

She had lied to him when she professed ignorance of the kidnapping. She had not only known about it; she had helped set it up.

But why?

He had told her everything he knew about the professor's death. He had added nothing to the account he gave the kidnappers.

Nothing.

Nothing . . . except Robert Pardin. He had told the kidnappers that Pardin had recommended him for the job to guard Professor Kohl.

Pardin. And Pardin had been upset when Hooks had told him that he had been forced to mention that to the kidnap team.

And when Marta had come to Washington—God,

was it only three days before?—she had mentioned that Pardin probably had gotten him the job at Kinderman's ranch.

Pardin.

But what was his connection with any of this? And what did any of it mean?

Marta had lied in Germany when she and her mother had said that they knew nothing about Anna Mueller. She had as much as admitted that at dinner last night when he'd asked her, Is this about Anna Mueller? She had said, Yes.

But what was it? What did it all mean?

Why had she pumped him so hard about the Kinderman job? Why had she followed him to California?

What explained that look of exultation when he'd told her the names of Kinderman's twin girls?

Why had she been killed?

"Tell them he is the beast."

Who, Marta, who?

Someone had waited for her in her room. Was it someone from the ranch who had listened in on his telephone call to her?

Her room had been looted; even her purse had been emptied. Any papers or documents she might have had were gone.

Had the burglar been surprised by Marta coming back and killed her in panic? No. That would have been too much of a coincidence. He had looted her room and then waited to murder.

Why?

Because of something she knew.

And because Hooks had been with her, it would have been logical to assume that Hooks knew it, too, whatever "it" was.

He closed his notebook in weariness. He understood two things.

One. Marta's impulsive decision to send him to buy wine had saved him from being killed.

Two. Whoever the killer was would try again.

Hooks was now a target.

He closed his eyes to rest for a moment, and he thought to himself, Good. Two decent people have died because of something they tried to find out or something they knew.

The killer would be coming after him next. So first, Hooks would find out the answers to his puzzle. And then, he would even the score.

CHAPTER TWENTY-SIX

HOOKS RETRIEVED HIS ONE LIGHT BAG FROM THE LUGgage carousel, and then went crisscrossing through the air terminal, wandering in and out of shops, until he was sure that he was not being followed.

He went outside and climbed into a cab and put his suitcase on the seat.

"Where to, Mac?" the driver asked.

"We're going into the city. I'll figure out where as we go."

The driver grunted, but Hooks ignored him. As the cab pulled away, he saw a figure in a trench coat get into the next cab in line, and it pulled quickly away from the curb behind him.

Hooks leaned forward so the driver could hear him through the protective screen that separated the front and rear seats.

"Listen to me," he said. "I want you to pull up in front of that terminal and let me off at the center door."

"What the hell kind of a fare is that? For this, I lost my place in line?"

"Just do what I tell you. Let me off at the center door, then drive down and stop in front of the end door. I'll be back out right away."

"That's stupid."

"It's what I want to do."

"You're gonna skip on the fare, ain't you?"

211

"I'll leave you my luggage. Just do what I say, will you? There's a good tip in it for you."

"Well . . . all right," the driver said grudgingly.

The driver stopped, and Hooks got out and moved as quickly as he could into the small terminal building. He immediately turned to his left and began walking through the building.

Over his shoulder he could see another cab stop where his had stopped. Good, he thought. If it's a tail, let them squabble for a while over the fare.

He was at the end of the terminal now, and he walked quickly outside and got back into his waiting cab. He saw that the second cab had just pulled away from the terminal entrance. It carried only a driver, no passenger.

"All right," Hooks said. "Let's get the hell out of here as fast as we can."

"Is this like something for the cops?" the driver asked.

"Spy stuff," Hooks said. "Let's hit it."

Ten minutes later, they were on a broad freeway barreling in toward downtown Washington.

Hooks leaned forward again.

"Now here's what I want you to do," he said. "I want you to get off at the next exit and go someplace where I can make a phone call. A bar or a diner, whatever."

"You going to have the money to pay for all this?" the driver asked.

"You'll be able to retire," said Hooks.

"All right."

From a pay telephone outside an all-night diner, Hooks dialed Patti's phone number. He let the phone ring four times and then hung up. God, let her be home, he thought. He repeated the procedure. The third time, he let the telephone keep ringing. He hoped that annoyance or curiosity would finally force her to answer.

"Hello?" she said sleepily.

"Patti, this is Steve."

"Oh. Steve. Where are you?" ⋅

"Long story. Can I stay there tonight?"

"Sure. You in town?"

"Yeah. I'll be there in a little while. Make sure it's me before you open the door."

"Is everything all right?" she asked anxiously.

"Everything's fine," he said.

He got back into the cab and told the driver to take him into the city. But a few blocks later they passed another diner, and alongside it was an all-night cab stand with one tired-looking cab parked in front of it.

"Never mind," Hooks said. "You can let me off here. I'm going to stop and see my mother."

"Mister, I'll be glad to let you off anywhere."

The meter read $9.40. Hooks gave the driver thirty dollars.

"For all the trouble," he said.

The driver looked at the tip and said, "Hey, what trouble? If you're in a service business, you gotta give service, I always say."

Hooks got out and waited until the cab had driven away before walking back toward the cab stand. The owner-operator-driver was asleep inside the little booth and Hooks woke him up and hired him to go into the city. On the way in, he gave him Patti's address.

Not perfect, he thought, but it'd do. If someone was following him, they'd be a long time picking up his trail. Unless of course they already knew where Patti lived and had her apartment under surveillance.

He had the cabdriver go twice around the block, and when he saw no one, he paid the driver, got off in front of Patti's apartment building and walked quickly inside.

Her soft voice over the speaker system immediately answered his quick jab at her doorbell.

"Yes?"

"It's Steve."

She rang and let him inside, and he rode the elevator up to her fifth-floor apartment.

She was waiting for him in the doorway. She pulled him inside, pushed the door shut, slapped the suitcase from his hands and threw her arms around him.

"Oh, Steve. I was so worried. You sounded so—"

"Easy, kid," he said. "I'm all right."

He pushed her back from him. Tears glistened in the corners of her dark eyes. She wiped them with the sleeve of her velvet robe, then shook her head. "No, you're not all right. What's the matter? Something's wrong. I know it."

Because he didn't know any other way to say it, Hooks said: "I think somebody's trying to kill me."

Her jaw dropped open. He had often read about people doing that when surprised or shocked, but he had never seen it happen before.

Finally, she said, "Steve, take off your jacket and sit down on the couch. I'll make you a drink, and then you can tell me about it."

The idea sounded just right. He walked toward the sofa and behind him he heard Patti double-lock the door and slip the antiburglar chain into place.

He told her the whole story and omitted only the fact that he and Marta Kohl had slept together. Patti sat on a chair facing her, her arms wrapped around herself as if she were chilled to the bone. Her huge dark eyes were fixed on his face, as if memorizing it. She looked utterly terrified.

"Maybe I don't have any reason to think it, but I think I was a target last night. I think the killer meant to get me too. And I don't know, but I think if I had stayed at that ranch, I never would have left alive." He sipped his drink and stared at her. "That's probably stupid," he said.

"No, it's not. It's why Mrs. Kinderman told you to leave. She must have known something."

"But why me? Why would someone want to kill me?"

"Because Marta Kohl knew something. Because they think you know it too," Patti said. "That's obvious."

"But what?" he asked. "What? I've thought it through, I've turned it upside down and inside out, and I don't know a damned thing. And who's 'they'? Kinderman? Pardin? Henry Mack? Or Maier? I don't know."

He finished his drink with an angry gulp and put the glass on the tile-topped coffee table.

"I know one thing," he said. "I can't hang around here. If somebody's after me, I can't take a chance of involving you."

"Horseshit," she snapped ferociously. "Dammit, Steve, this is where you belong. You've got to be careful of your apartment, maybe even your office. But you're safe here. Who knows me?"

He shrugged. "If they want me bad enough, they'll find out about you."

"Right. And if they find out about me, they're going to find out about whether you're here or not, so I'd just as soon have you here."

It made him uncomfortable, but it was logical. Through no fault of her own, Patti was involved, and his only chance of protecting her—if protection was really needed—was by being near her.

He nodded grudgingly.

Patti had opened the sofa into a bed and insisted that he sleep in it. Before he could ask the obvious question, she had turned a lumpy, angular foam-rubber chair into a low single bed for herself.

The lights were out in the apartment, but now, an

hour later, Hooks still could not sleep. He heard Patti's regular breathing from across the room.

His body, he thought, must be overtired, and he could not get Marta Kohl out of his mind. The thought that the woman might be lying in some California morgue and that her mother might not know of the tragedy filled him with disgust. Tomorrow he would have to do something about that. But he didn't know what.

"Steve?"

"Yeah?"

"Can't sleep?"

"No. Overtired, I guess."

He heard her moving across the room toward him, and then she lifted the light blanket and slid into the bed next to him.

"Patti . . ." he began.

"Shut up. Turn over," she said, her voice soft, in a way it had never been soft before; close to his ear in a way it had never been close before.

Dutifully, he rolled onto his side and Patti snuggled up against his back, insinuating her body against every bend of his. She reached her right arm under his and around his body to hold his chest. He was suddenly painfully aware that he was not wearing pajamas, only his briefs.

"I'll hold you until you sleep," Patti said in his ear. Her warm breath sent a tingle through his body, and he shuddered.

"Are you cold?" she asked.

"No. Patti, this is no good."

"Why not?"

"You're a woman, for Christ's sake. I can't make believe that you're a hot water bottle."

"Use your imagination."

"I can't," he said.

He felt her body move back from his a little for a

moment, and then she pressed against him again. She had opened her pajama top and her bare breasts rubbed against his back. Her right arm slid down from his chest, and her fingers reached inside his shorts.

"That help?" she said.

His answer was a sudden sharp sip of air. She giggled and stroked his aroused body. He wanted to pull her hand away but couldn't.

"Patti, you're like a sister to me."

"Incest is the poor man's polo."

"Like a sister," he insisted.

"No, I'm not, Steve Hooks. Not like a sister. I'm a woman, and I've always loved you, and I've wanted to make love to you every day for the last twelve months. Just like you've wanted to make love to me for the last twelve months. Now do it."

"But . . ."

"No buts," she snapped, and then pulled her hands away from him. "Okay. You want to talk, we'll talk." She pulled him over onto his back and sat next to him, her legs pulled up underneath her. In the dim light filtering into the room he was painfully aware that her bare breasts were only a few inches from his face.

"In all the time you were married to Jo, did you ever cheat on her?"

"No. Not once."

"Since the accident . . . since she's been in that hospital, have you had another woman?"

He hesitated. "Just one," he admitted.

"Marta Kohl," she said flatly.

"Yes."

"Steve, I hate to hurt your male ego but you had nothing to do with that. I know it. I know that woman came after you because somebody wanted to find out something."

"I know that, too."

"Do you feel guilty about it?"

"I did," he said.

"You shouldn't. You've got nothing to feel guilty about. Steve, Jo isn't with us anymore, and it's time we face up to it. I would never have done anything to hurt your marriage, but it's over, Steve. It's over. And I want you too badly, too desperately . . ."

He felt her slipping his shorts down his legs, and then her own satin pajamas were off and she pressed against his body. He felt her warm and wet, and he touched her.

"You can't say no to me, Steve. This is the start of our lives. I love you."

"And I love you too," he said.

And then her lips were biting his, her tongue was searching and finding his own, her belly pressed against him and his arms were crushing her against him with a desperate intensity.

He rolled her over onto her back, and she yielded with a joyous gasp, her legs encircling his body and pulling him closer to her. Flesh met flesh; there was a momentary searching, a yielding, and he was buried deeply inside her.

She received him with joy and abandon, holding him tightly, until all the world and time forever exploded within him, and she cried out in exultation, and he sank down upon her, limp and lifeless.

He fell deep into sleep, still on top of her, and she held him gently with a radiant smile on her face.

CHAPTER TWENTY-SEVEN

HOOKS AWOKE DISORIENTED AND CONFUSED, UNTIL HE realized he was lying in Patti's arms. It was Saturday, and they made love again, slowly and tenderly, without the frenzied intensity of the night before.

Then he showered and dressed quickly, gave Patti instructions and left the apartment.

He went out through a basement service door, through a courtyard and alley that let him out on a side street. He walked four blocks to a small hotel, where from a pay phone in the lobby, using a credit card, he called the Berlin telephone number of Burt Sellers's office.

The same woman answered the phone. "Hello."

"Is Burt Sellers there, please?"

"Who's calling, please?"

"My name is Hooks."

"Mr. Sellers is not here."

"All right. Please contact him. My name is Hooks. Tell him I will call him again on this same number in exactly ninety minutes. It's very important."

"Yes, Mr. Hooks."

Hooks took a taxi from the hotel to his apartment, and ordered the driver to circle the block twice before getting out a block away. He had seen no one obviously loitering or seated in a parked car. He strolled back up the block on the side opposite his apartment building and walked past to the end of the block. He still saw nothing suspicious.

Taking a deep breath, he crossed the street and came back down the block and into the entrance of his garden apartment building. His apartment was on the top floor, and even though it pained his leg, he walked up the steps to the third floor with every nerve tense, ready at the slightest sound to make a mad dash for safety.

Still nothing.

He edged his head slowly out of the stairwell. The corridor was empty. He waited cautiously but heard nothing to indicate that anyone else was waiting for him.

Finally, he walked quickly down the hall to his apartment, slid his key into the lock and opened the door a crack. He waited a moment, then opened the door wide, again prepared to limp for his life.

The apartment seemed empty.

He edged cautiously inside, leaving the door open in case he had to make a panic exit. Moving slowly and placing his feet carefully to avoid making noise, he sidled through the living room, peered cautiously into the bedroom and finally reached his destination—the bedroom. The door was closed.

If someone were waiting inside with a gun, Hooks knew it was highly unlikely that he could escape from the apartment before being shot down. But he had to get to the bedroom closet.

He took another deep breath, then jumped into the bedroom. His bad knee buckled, and he fell on to the floor.

He rolled over and sat up, but no one was standing there pointing a revolver at him. Wiping sweat from his brow, he got to his feet and walked to the closet. It wasn't until he had recovered the small box from the top shelf and had his snub-nosed .38 caliber Chief's Special in his hand that he began to feel safe.

He quickly loaded the weapon, put it into his jacket pocket and reached for the shoulder holster he had left hanging from a hook in the corner of the closet.

He had hoped, even expected, that he would never wear it again, but now he could hardly wait to put it on. Nothing like a couple of murders to change one's outlook on life, he thought bitterly. Better armed than harmed.

He went back into the living room and closed and locked the apartment door.

He had clothes at Patti's, in the suitcase he had brought back from California.

He took a smaller bag from the closet to the desk in the living room and began to dump the desk's contents into it. It was his life's paperwork. Checkbooks, address books, letters, bills, insurance contracts, a copy of his will. His life, he thought, fit neatly into one small vinyl suitcase.

Before leaving, he gave the apartment a cursory inspection, but saw nothing out of place.

Except there was a pair of brown eyeglasses on the living room table. Whose? Then he remembered. They were the sunglasses Patti mentioned to him on the telephone that she had found in one of his suit pockets.

He picked up the glasses and studied them. They were Professor Kohl's. How had he gotten them? He puzzled and then vaguely remembered that after he had awakened from being slugged in the professor's hotel room he had found the glasses on the floor. He must have stuck them in his pocket and forgotten to tell anyone.

He held them up to his eyes. The tinted lenses were nonprescription glass. Sunglasses. Well, maybe they would come in handy, he thought, and he stuck them in his pocket.

At the door, he thought for a moment, then came back into the apartment. He wedged a tiny piece of paper into his telephone in the seam where the earpiece screwed onto the receiver. If anyone picked up the handset to make a call, the paper would be dislodged.

When he had closed the apartment door behind him, he poked another tiny piece of paper in the crack beside the hinges. Hardly foolproof burglar alarms, but there was a reasonable chance they would not be noticed by an intruder, and he could tell if his apartment had been entered in his absence.

He entered his office warily but with greater assurance than he had shown going to his apartment. For one thing, his hand was cradled around the gun in his shoulder holster. For another, even though it was Saturday, there were still enough people in the office building to make an ambush unattractive.

He locked the door behind him and glanced at his watch. Ten minutes before he would call Sellers again.

He dumped out the contents of his center desk drawer into his suitcase, then glanced at his telephone answering machine. The monitor showed that he had received six calls while he was away in California.

The first five were calls for storm windows, public television, magazine subscriptions, life insurance and making a million, with no risk and hardly any money, in the fast-paced and exciting options market. The sixth call was from Bob Pardin.

"Hey, old buddy, I hear you're back in town. I also heard great things about your work in California. So give me a call right away. I may have another job for you, but it won't keep. And this is a big one. Call as soon as you hear this."

Not on your life, Hooks thought. Or mine.

Sellers was there when Hooks called the Berlin office.

"Burt, this is Steve Hooks."

"How's it going?"

222

"Not too well," Hooks said. "Listen, I've got a piece of news for you."

"All right."

"Marta Kohl, the professor's daughter?"

"Yeah?"

"She's dead."

There was just silence on the other end of the teleplone for a full three seconds.

"When? How?"

"Two nights ago in California. She was murdered."

"Who did it?"

"I don't know. He got away."

"Did you talk to her? Did she say anything?"

"Yeah. She said something strange."

"What?"

"She said, 'Tell them he is the beast.'"

"Who?"

"I don't know," Hooks said.

There was another long pause.

"Why'd you call me, Steve?"

"I don't know. I couldn't stand thinking of that poor girl's body in a morgue somewhere, but I didn't have the heart to call her mother."

"But why me?"

"I don't know. I don't have any friends here. I thought maybe you could tell the mother or something. Just privately, maybe anonymously, I don't know."

"Are you in trouble, Steve?"

"I think somebody's trying to kill me. I think I was just lucky to get away the other night."

Another pause.

"Steve, we've got to talk."

"We are talking."

"No. Face-to-face. If I fly to Washington, can I meet with you?"

Alarm bells rang in Hooks's mind. He delayed answering directly. "When could you come?" he asked.

"Let me think. I could be there tomorrow night. Could we meet?"

"Do we have anything to talk about?"

"Yes. A lot of things," Sellers said.

"Such as?"

"Anna Mueller. Why somebody's trying to kill you."

"You can give me the answers?" Hooks asked.

"Yes."

"All right. You fly into Washington. Rent a room at the Airport Motel. I'll call you there."

"Okay. I can understand your being cautious."

"I wouldn't care even if you took offense," Hooks said.

"My coming is unofficial. Don't say anything."

"I won't," Hooks promised.

"And Steve. Be careful. Stay alive until tomorrow night. It's important."

"To whom?"

"To the whole world," Sellers said.

"I'll call you tomorrow night."

Patti picked him up outside a downtown hotel.

As he had instructed, she had parked his distinctive black Porsche in a garage and had rented a nondescript brown Ford sedan.

The backseat of the rented car was taken up by luggage. He squeezed the small bag he was carrying in alongside the larger suitcases.

He kissed her as he got into the car.

"Mmmmm," she said. "My first kiss as a single woman."

"What's that?"

"The mail came. The divorce was in it. Lawrence and I are splitto."

"Good going," he said.

"Where to?" she asked as she pulled away from the curb. "We leaving town?"

"One stop first," he replied.

CHAPTER TWENTY-EIGHT

"HELLO, JOANNA. IT'S YOUR WANDERING HUSBAND, BACK from a thrill-filled trip to the Golden West.

"It's beautiful weather outside, Jo. The leaves are starting to turn. Remember that trip we made down Skyline Drive a couple of years ago? It's starting to look like that now. Maybe someday, when you're out of here, we'll do that again.

"A lot of strange things have been happening in the past couple of weeks, Jo. Don't you worry about them; I'm going to be all right. It's just that . . . well, I'm going to have to be away a lot for the next little while. So I guess I'll have to put off reading *Karamazov* to you until later. What'd we get up to, anyway? Page ten? A lot of help I am.

"So I'm going to be away, but I don't want you to think I've forgotten you. I'll never forget you, Jo, no matter what happens. And I'll always love you.

"And I'll always come back to you. You can count on that."

Steve Hooks looked down at the body in the hospital bed, a sleeping princess with only faint lines of weariness to mar her expressionless face. He patted her hand softly, leaned forward and kissed her lips. It was a long, slow kiss, without passion, but a vow and a benediction and a wordless plea that she understand and trust him, even though he no longer understood or trusted himself.

"Good-bye, Jo. I have to go now. But I'll be back."

* * *

There had been no one waiting for him at the hospital and Patti, in the parking lot, said she had seen no one loitering around.

As they drove away, Hooks wondered if he were not the victim of a murder plot, but only of an overactive imagination. Was it possible? Had he just succumbed to a chance word here, a phrase there, and somehow had woven it into a totally fictitious tapestry of intrigue and murder?

Ten miles south of the city, he told Patti to pull off the road into a highway rest stop, and from a telephone inside the urine-scented block building, he called Bob Pardin's home in Washington.

"Hello, Bob. This is Steve Hooks."

"Steve, where the hell are you? What happened in California?"

"I don't know. What happened?" Hooks asked.

"I don't know. I heard about some woman who was murdered or something, and you, and I don't know really what to make of it all. We've got to get together."

"I don't know anything about any of that, Bob," Hooks said mildly.

"We've got to meet to talk. I'd feel lousy if you got into trouble on a job I recommended you for. Where are you? I'll come right over."

"Sorry, Bob. I can't do that. I'm going out of town till next Wednesday or so."

"Steve. I think this is important enough for you to postpone your trip. I could meet you right away."

"No, 'fraid not. I've had this Cape Cod trip planned for weeks, and I'm running late now. I'll call you when I get back."

"Steve, no, we've got to—"

"I'll call you when I get back," Hook said as he hung up the telephone.

227

Back in the car, Patti asked, "Who'd you call?"

"Bob Pardin," Hooks said, as he moved her over and slid behind the wheel.

"And?"

"He wants to kill me," Hooks said.

CHAPTER TWENTY-NINE

UNDER OTHER CIRCUMSTANCES, IT MIGHT HAVE BEEN THE start of a honeymoon. They stopped in a motel in the Virginia countryside, eighty miles from Washington, and they spent the afternoon in the swimming pool, the evening in the motel's cocktail lounge and the night making love; but although they both tried, it was no good. There were too many ghosts in the motel with them. The ghost of Joanna. Patti had said they had to consider her as dead and get on with their lives, but she wasn't dead, and every time Hooks looked into Patti's dark eyes, in their deep wells he saw the image of his wife—his wife for life—lying unconscious in a hospital bed.

There were other ghosts. Their relationship as brother-in-law and sister-in-law. Patti's divorce. Even though she regarded it as a cause for celebration, it reminded both of them that each was still carrying around a lot of baggage from the past. And there was one chilling specter that hovered over everything: the grim thought that not one hundred miles away, someone might actively be planning to murder Steve Hooks. And Patti, too, if the killer should decide that she also was a threat.

The next morning, they lay side by side in bed, smoking.

"I wish we could stay here forever," Patti said.

"I know," replied Hooks. "Maybe someday."

"What's next?" she said.

"We can't make any plans until I talk to Sellers and find out what this is all about. We just can't go back and make believe nothing ever happened; that maybe somebody wants to kill me, but that was last week and this is a new week. Or ignore the possibility that you might be in danger, too, through no fault of your own. Sellers is the key to this. I've got to hear what he knows."

"You know, I remember you telling me about him. That he was, well, almost annoyed because he had to watch out for you in Berlin. That he couldn't care less abut you, or Anna Mueller, for that matter."

"That was the impression he gave," said Hooks. "I guess he was just a better actor than I thought he was."

"Exactly," she said.

"What do you mean?" Hooks asked.

"He fooled you once, Steve. Don't let him fool you again."

"Not this time," Hooks said. "Not this time."

They drove back to Washington in the late afternoon. The road snaked its way through the Virginia countryside, and the late sun stabbed Hooks's eyes and almost blinded him. He felt in his pocket and took out the pair of brown sunglasses that Patti had found and put them on.

The nose bridge was a little narrow for him so the glasses were perched up higher than they should have been, but they helped.

Professor Kohl's glasses.

"You know," Hooks said, "these are really sunglasses."

"Well, of course they are," said Patti.

"But, you know, Professor Kohl's eyes were failing. He was going blind. A couple of people told me that."

"Yeah," Patti said. He glanced to his side and saw she was chewing her lower lip as she often did when wrestling with a problem. After a few seconds, she said, "Maybe he just wore these to rest his eyes, like when he wasn't working. Some people with bad eyes do that."

"Yeah," he said. "That's probably it."

Patti rented a room on the second floor of the Airport Motel under a false name.

"What do we do now?" she asked Hooks after they arrived in the room.

"We wait for Sellers to show up," Hooks said.

Sellers checked in at nine P.M.. Patti had been calling the hotel operator every half hour since ariving there, and after six phone calls over three hours she had struck up a friendship with the operator. So when she called again, the operator knew that she wanted to surprise her brother, Mr. Sellers, and instead of just connecting Patti with Sellers's room, she violated rules and told her that her brother was in Room 423.

"Thanks. You're a dear," Patti said as she hung up the phone. "Room four twenty-three," she told Hooks.

"You're a dear too. You know what to do now?"

"Yes, I know, I know, I know, I know."

"Good. Do it right, right, right, right."

She left the room and five minutes later his telephone rang.

"Yeah."

"He turns right," she said.

"Good. Be careful."

Hooks waited five minutes more, then dialed Room 423. Sellers answered.

"This is Hooks. You alone?"

"Yes."

"All right. I want you to come out of your room and

walk down the stairs to the lobby. Use the stairway to your right. I'll be waiting for you near the lobby door."

He hung up before waiting for a reply.

Hooks left his room and walked down the hallway to the fire door leading to the stairwell.

He waited only a minute before he heard steps coming down the stairs. He waited until the footsteps passed him, then opened the fire door. Sellers was just beginning to go down the steps toward the lobby level.

"Sellers," Hooks called.

The young blond man turned around. His vivid blue eyes seemed to light up with honest pleasure, but it faded as he saw the snub-nosed pistol in Hooks's hand.

"Come in here," ordered Hooks.

"No arguments from me," Sellers said.

He came to the door, brushed past Hooks with no comment and walked down the hall. Hooks unlocked the door, and had Sellers walk in first, then told him to sit in a chair across the room.

"Please keep your hands on top of your head," Hooks said.

"Sure," Sellers replied with an easy grin, even as he put his hands on his head. "Mind telling me what we're doing?"

"We're going to wait for a moment."

"For your lookout to call?" Sellers asked.

Hooks said nothing.

"Was it the pretty black-haired girl I passed in the hall? You're traveling in good-looking company," Sellers said.

The telephone rang, and Hooks picked up the receiver.

"Yes?"

"No one followed him," Patti said.

"Okay. You know where to go. Wait for me there."

Hooks replaced the telephone and said to Sellers, "You weren't followed. How'd you know I had a lookout?"

Sellers shrugged. "I guessed. It's the way I would have done it, and I always figured you had at least as much sense as I have."

They looked at each other across the room for a moment, then Hooks said, "Where do we start?"

"First thing, maybe, you come over here and take the gun I've got under my coat," Sellers suggested.

Puzzled, Hooks came across the room, stood behind Sellers and took a small pistol from his shoulder holster.

"All right," he said. "Why'd you tell me to do that?"

"Couple of reasons," replied Sellers. "One, I want to put my hands down because my fingers are falling asleep."

"Go ahead," Hooks said. He sat on the bed facing Sellers.

"Two, I didn't want you to panic or do anything dopey when I told you I wasn't telling the truth."

Hooks had let his gun hand lower toward the floor, but now he snapped the barrel up so it was again pointing at Sellers.

"See?" Sellers said. "That's just what I meant. Easy with the gun, will you?"

"What truth weren't you telling me?" Hooks asked.

"When I told you I was alone. I'm not. There's somebody in my room."

"Who is it?" Hooks said.

"Somebody you ought to meet."

"Who is it?" Hooks snapped again.

"Professor Edward Kohl," Sellers said.

Hooks nodded slowly and handed Sellers back his gun.

Kohl was shorter than the man Hooks had been hired to guard, and his face was a little rounder. But the similarity of their features was striking, even to the dark-brown eyeglasses Kohl wore. Up close now, Hooks could see that the professor's eyeglass lenses were sharply curved, indicating a very strong correction. The other man had worn simple brown sunglasses.

Sellers had taken Hooks back to his room and introduced the two men.

As they shook hands, Hooks said, "I heard a rumor somewhere that you were dead."

"I am sorry for all the trouble that that caused you," said Kohl. His English was soft and precise and familiar. It was the voice of the man who had questioned Hooks in that Berlin cellar, his kidnapper's voice.

"You will tell me about Marta?" the professor said.

"Yes," replied Hooks. "I'm sorry. She was murdered."

"By whom?"

"I don't know, not for sure," Hooks said. He didn't want to answer questions now; he wanted to hear answers. And he could wait no longer.

"Who was it who was killed in the hotel room? Who was the man I thought was you?" he asked suddenly.

"It was my brother, Otto," said the professor. "We knew there was some risk attached to what we were doing, and Otto insisted that he go in my place. We were only a year apart in age and looked much alike."

"He looked older," Hooks said.

"He was dying," Kohl told him. "Cancer. He died here rather than a month later at home. He thought it worthwhile."

Hooks shook his head. "Thought what worthwhile? What?"

Sellers said, "Whoa. Professor, I think we ought to take this right from the top, so that Steve knows what's going on." The professor nodded, lit a cigarette and turned toward Hooks, who was sitting in the chair on the opposite side of the motel table.

He paused, marshaled his thoughts, and his manner became a touch more pedantic, more the college lecturer.

"You are familiar, Mr. Hooks, with how I earn . . . earned my living?"

"Yes. You write books about Nazis, past and present."

Kohl nodded. "We can do little about Nazis past. It is Nazis present who have come to concern me more and more in recent years. In many countries, not just mine but many including your own, there are people who still embrace the madness that was Hitler. Even some of the regimes in South America, governments that your government considers leftists and Communist, are mere shams. They are Nazis, ready to come forward at the proper time, their so-called people's revolutions financed for them by Nazi money amassed during the war and still used for its purposes around the world."

"What does it all have to do with me?" Hooks asked.

"Yes. It was necessary first to give you the historical background. I and those of my institute have devoted our lives to tracking down and exposing this Nazi menace." Kohl cleared his throat, puffed deeply on his cigarette and coughed. "You are familiar with what happened in the last days of the war in Berlin?"

Hooks shrugged. "The Russians were coming. The war was lost. Hitler committed suicide, and the Nazis burned his body."

"Early in the morning of April twenty-eight, 1945, Hitler married his mistress, Eva Braun," Kohl said. "Soon after that, he handwrote a will. He left all his possessions to the Nazi party and appointed as executor of that will, Martin Bormann. He also said that he and Eva would choose death to avoid the disgrace of defeat, and it was his wish to be cremated immediately. On

April thirtieth, in the afternoon, a small group gathered outside Hitler's apartment in the bunker in Berlin where he had been staying.

"They heard a shot from inside the apartment. All had been waiting for this moment. Goebbels, and Bormann went into the apartment and came out a moment later. '*Der Führer* is dead,' Goebbels said. He took cyanide and then shot himself. Eva—'Frau Hitler,' he called her—was also dead of poison. He opened the door a crack and allowed those standing there to peer inside. Hitler was sprawled at one end of the blue-and-white couch. Blood ran down his face from a bullet wound in his head. Eva Braun, her back to the door, lay on the other end of the couch as if sleeping. The people at the door could see her carefully waved blond hair. Goebbels closed the door and ordered the people to flee to save themselves; the Russians were only a thousand yards away. He, his wife and their six children would, he said, join *Der Führer* in death.

"The few mourners left. Goebbels called two S.S. men, who carried Hitler's body up the emergency stairway and deposited it in a shallow shell hole in the garden. Bormann himself carried Eva Braun's body; he carried it oddly—facedown across his arms—and then placed it still face down, in the shell hole next to Hitler. They filled the hole with gasoline from cans that had been brought by Hitler's chauffeur, and then ignited it. The two bodies were engulfed in flames. For hours, Goebbels and Bormann and the S.S. men kept refilling the shell hole with gasoline, to keep the fire going. By evening, there was nothing left of Hitler and Eva but their blackened skeletons. An S.S. detail then moved the skeletons to a larger shell hole and covered them with earth."

Professor Kohl lit another cigarette from the stub of the one in his hand. He coughed again.

"Soon after, Bormann fled. Eventually, he escaped to South America. The following day, Goebbels and his wife poisoned their six children and then themselves. Those were the last deaths in the bunker."

Hooks nodded, waiting patiently.

"There have always been rumors, Mr. Hooks, that Hitler did not die in that bunker. That instead he was smuggled out of Germany. That is not true. Hitler died there. The Russians, although they never announced it, discovered the two skeletons and identified them both by dental records as the remains of Hitler and Eva Braun. The Russians were wrong."

Hooks interrupted. "I thought you said—"

"The Russians were wrong," Kohl said. "Hitler died, yes. But Eva Braun did not. The woman who was poisoned in the bunker, whose body was carried out facedown by Martin Bormann, who was incinerated until there was no flesh left on her bones, was not Eva Braun."

"She was Anna Mueller," Hooks said.

"Yes. A poor young woman whose only crime was that she resembled Eva Braun. It had been Bormann's plan. He had personally selected Anna Mueller for the role after seeing her on the street."

"But the dental records?"

"Dental records can be made to lie. You spoke to Frau Winkler," Kohl said. "Her husband, Anna Mueller's dentist, was seized by the S.S. and then was shot. Between the time he was seized and the time he was shot, he worked on Anna Mueller's mouth, making hers match the dental record of Eva Braun. Eva Braun did not die. Instead, she was spirited off, and soon after joined Bormann in South America."

"But why? Why all that trouble for Hitler's mistress?"

"His wife now, remember? After sixteen years of being his mistress, she was suddenly wed to him in that bunker."

"Right. His wife. But why all the subterfuge?"

"Because Eva Braun was pregnant," Kohl said. "She was carrying Hitler's baby."

Hooks sat back heavily on the seat. He looked across at Sellers. "This is all true?" he asked.

Sellers nodded. "It's true. One of the S.S. officers who helped burn the bodies . . . even though Bormann tried to hide it, this officer saw the woman's face. He saw it wasn't Eva Braun, and on his deathbed he told the story to the professor. One of Bormann's drivers was with him the day that Anna Mueller was selected off the street to be Eva's stand-in. He provided the professor with the name. The dental records, however, were the stumper. Why shouldn't the Russians have believed she was Eva Braun? The records proved she was. Then one day the professor found out about this dentist who had been killed in the last days of the war by the S.S.. He talked to the widow, and it all started to come together."

"What happened to the baby?" Hooks asked. "Was it born?"

Professor Kohl nodded. "Yes. It was born in South America where Eva Braun went to live under the protection of Bormann, a man she hated and despised. She delivered a son. But a few years later, Bormann was in danger. Nazi hunters were trying to find him. It became too dangerous for Eva and her son to stay with him. So, using the name of Anna Mueller, she came to the United States with her son . . . with Hitler's son."

The professor was suddenly racked by a coughing fit. It was almost a full minute before he was able to speak again.

"And there we lost the trail," Kohl finally said. "It was Otto who suggested the answer. I had been planning to write another book on the rise of Nazi thinking in the world—the many regimes in South America and Africa and elsewhere that have so much of Hitler's philosophies in their manner of government.

"Otto suggested that I announce that my next book would bear the title *The New Messiah*, and at the same time publicly begin seeking information concerning the fate of Anna Mueller. This would force those who knew the story, who knew the secret, to come after us. It would verify the truth, and it would lead us to this new Hitler. And that was where you came in, Mr. Hooks.

"Our trail had grown cold, and I decided that I would come to America to pursue it. We knew it was dangerous, but it was also essential. It was at that time that my brother received his medical death sentence. His cancer was too advanced to be operable. He would die in weeks. He, therefore, came to the United States in my place, after I had gone to all the American agencies in Germany asking for protection in your country while I went there to search for Anna Mueller. It was our hope that this word would get to someone in your government, if there was someone there, who knew what that name meant. My brother came in my place, you were selected to guard him and . . . well, you know what happened."

"Why didn't they kill me at the time?" Hooks said. "It would have been neat. I thought Nazis were always neat."

"I guess that while you were out with my brother for dinner, they broke into the room and reviewed his notebooks. They were careful frauds which really told nothing. I think you were kept alive so that they could find out if my brother had told you anything. So they could find out what he knew. When it became apparent that you knew nothing, they decided to use you to see if somehow you might not give them a lead to what I was supposed to know."

"They were using me," Hooks said.

"Yes. But so were we," said Kohl. "When you came to Germany, Marta became close to you. She reported that you knew nothing. That is why we kidnapped you. To make sure."

"I recognized your voice tonight. And now I finally realize why one of those kidnappers was making clicking sounds all night. It was Bockler and all that junk he wears on his vest."

"I shall have to warn him of that," Kohl said drily.

"The only information I gave you that I didn't give Marta was the name of Bob Pardin."

"Exactly," said Kohl.

"I gave you the name, Burt. Why the charade?"

"Because I wasn't sure of you," the young American replied.

"Just what's your place in this?" Hooks asked. "I thought you didn't like Germans."

"I don't like Nazis. I've been working with the professor for a couple of years. Very unofficial and I was a goner if I was found out. We couldn't take a chance of my being exposed."

"So I was kidnapped, and I mentioned Pardin, and then I came back here," Hooks said.

"And Marta followed you to find out what happened between you and Pardin," Sellers added.

"God, you don't think that Pardin is . . ."

"No. But we began to think that he knew who Hitler's kid was. Marta came here and saw you, and she told us that she was on the trail of something important. I guess she followed you to California. And now maybe you can tell us what happened there."

"All right," Hooks said. "Pardin got me a job doing security at the ranch of some congressman. Jack Kinderman from California."

"Beg pardon," said Kohl. "What was his name?"

"Jack Kinderman. I was there at the ranch when

Marta called. We had dinner that night. She promised to tell me everything that night."

"She trusted you," Kohl said. "She knew you were not one of them."

"We got back to her room and, she told me to stop and get a bottle of wine. When I got back to her room, she didn't answer. I broke the door down, and I found her dying on the floor. She'd been stabbed. That's when she told me to tell them 'he is the beast.' I didn't know what she meant."

"During the night," Kohl asked, "did you tell her anything that might have ended our search for us? Think hard. What do you remember?"

Hooks did not have to think hard. He had gone over the matter in his mind for days. He remembered everything about the evening and final dinner with Marta Kohl.

"She was interested in the congressman," he said. "There was a strange look on her face when I mentioned his daughters. She wanted to know their names."

"What were their names?" Kohl asked.

"Eva," Hooks said, and as he pronounced the name the meaning of it suddenly sank into him, and he felt his body chill.

"Eva," he repeated. "And Francesca."

Kohl let out a long sigh. "Eva. For Eva Braun. Francesca was the name of Eva's mother. Do you know what the word *kinder* means in German?"

"No."

"Kindergarten," Sellers said. "*Kinder* means child."

"Then Jack Kinderman is . . ."

"Hitler's son," replied Sellers.

"The search has ended," Kohl said.

CHAPTER THIRTY

"SO WHAT'S NEXT?" HOOKS ASKED.

"The world must know," Professor Kohl said. He rubbed his hands together in a washing motion, like a surgeon preparing for the operating room.

Hooks shook his head. "I don't understand. Maybe I'm missing something here, but why all the killing? Okay, so Kinderman didn't choose his parents very wisely. Who the hell has that choice, anyway? And so the facts come out and no, I don't think America's ready to elect Hitler's kid as president. So he doesn't get to be president. Is that worth all the killing?"

Sellers nodded and said, "You're right, Steve, there's a lot you don't understand. If Kinderman were just here and living and minding his own business, so what? But it isn't happening that way. Not in the last handful of years. We've got tunnel vision in America. Something goes wrong, and we immediately blame the Russians or the PLO or Qaddafi, but a lot of what's going on has nothing to do with them. As often as not, you check some group that's moving into power, or suddenly winds up winning enough seats in a foreign parliament to tilt the government in one direction or another, and you look hard and you'll find Nazi money behind it. It's hidden, sure. But you can track it down. The professor has. And it turns up Nazi. And you know, they don't care whether the movement they're putting in power is left wing or right wing. They're backing people who can win, who can swing the government in all these countries. They're piling up a lot of IOUs and someday they're going to call them in. I only know about Kinderman what I read in the papers. You know the guy. What's he been doing?"

The image of the newspaper clipping he had seen at the ranch flashed into Hooks's mind. Kinderman in El Salvador, his arm raised over his head, haranguing a crowd that responded by cheering "Kinderman for President." Hooks had thought it was a Roman salute, but now it took on a more sinister appearance. It was a Nazi salute, a young new Hitler with his arm raised high above his head as though he were challenging the gods to strike him down.

Hooks said, "Kinderman's been doing the international tour."

"Exactly," said Sellers. "And I don't know a damn thing, but you can bet that in every country he's going to, he's buying up allies. Maybe with his money. Maybe with promises of American money. But he's buying them."

"For what?" Hooks asked.

"For one day when he'll need them," Sellers said. His voice crackled as if electrically charged. "For one day when he calls out 'march' and they all march. For one day when the Fourth Reich, as sick and evil and demented as the Third, rises up out of the ashes. Steve, I can see that look on your face. It can't happen. They said that in Germany, too, in the thirties. And it happened. It's happening again. Right now."

"I don't see it," Hooks said. "It just sounds too much like whacko conspiracy theory to me. Old Nazi money buying the world for new Nazis. I just don't see it."

Professor Kohl cleared his throat and then interjected softly, "Mr. Hooks. No matter what the Bible says, we do not believe in visiting the sins of the fathers onto the third and fourth generation of children. But these are fresh sins, committed by the child. You may say, Why bother? Leave Kinderman alone. He's not doing anything. And I say to you that my dead brother's body, my daughter's body, they tell you that yes, something is going on. Something is going on. And it must be stopped."

Hooks was silent. For a moment, he had forgotten the professor's two relatives who had been murdered, and now he felt guilt filling his mind. He had been lecturing Kohl and Sellers on the improbability of their position, and the professor had two dead family members whose spilled blood proved his position correct.

More than a little confused, but still angry with himself, Hooks asked Sellers, "What's your role in all this, Burt?"

The CIA man's light-colored eyes were as sky-pale as Hooks remembered them from their first meeting, but there was no warmth or humor in them now. They were eyes of ice, eyes of death.

"I didn't exactly tell you the truth when you visited Berlin," Sellers said. "I got to Germany because I wanted to get to Germany. My family was German on both sides, and we lost relatives to the Nazis because they wouldn't play dead when Hitler and his goons started marching down the streets. My master's thesis at Harvard was entitled 'Nazism: Could It Rise Again?' I had read all the professor's books, and when I got to Germany I looked him up. After a while, I learned what he was doing, and the Company didn't know it, but I started to do some work for him. I think that what the professor is doing is the most important work in the world, and I'm proud to be part of it."

"The kidnapping?" Hooks said. "You didn't need to kidnap me to get any information out of me. You had everything I knew."

"Maybe. And maybe not," said Sellers. "I didn't even know who you were. Sure, I heard that somebody in the Secret Service named Pardin had sent you. But was that true? I didn't know, and I couldn't check in Washington without compromising myself. I thought the kidnapping scare might shake some more apples out of your tree. The other part . . ." He shrugged. "We were still looking for your American link. I didn't know if it was Pardin or somebody else or a lot of somebody elses. I didn't know who might be involved. We thought that having you kidnapped might flush them out."

"That's pretty damned cynical," Hooks snapped.

"Sorry, Steve, but that's the way it was, and it worked. We flushed out Pardin and Kinderman and . . . well, here we are."

"All right. How many people do you think know who Kinderman is? Really is? If I learned one thing working in government, it's that a gang can't keep a secret."

"I'd be surprised if more than a couple of people know anything, and they'd be the ones closest to Kinderman. The others don't have to know. Maybe Kinderman will tell them at the right time and maybe he won't. Maybe he won't have to. He's got money at his disposal, and money'll buy a lot of friends."

Hooks lit a cigarette and thought for a moment, then asked, "What's next? Do we go public?" The words were out of his mouth before he realized he had said "we." He had just dealt himself into the game.

Sellers recognized it immediately and grinned. "The first thing *we* have to do is get the professor back to Germany. Then get this thing moving."

"You're not going to be safe there," Hooks said. "Neither of you."

"Why not?" Sellers asked. "They don't know the professor's alive, and they don't know that I've got anything to do with anything. And the only one who could tell them is you. You going to hand us up?"

"Not now. But they're after me already. If they get me, maybe they can make me talk. I don't know," he said honestly.

"There's a solution to that."

"What's that?"

"You can come to Germany too," said Sellers. "We can hide you out there, and you'll be safe. We can arrange it. You could even work privately with the professor. God . . ." He paused. "Listen to what I just said. Did you ever think you'd hear somebody say go to Germany so you can escape the Nazis in America?"

Hooks thought of Joanna, lying unconscious in her hospital bed. He thought of Patti, and he said, "I don't know. I've got a lot of loose ends around in the United States." He puffed hard on the cigarette and a question dug into his mind like a sharp pike. Would Sellers kill him if he refused to go to Germany? It was the way the game was played in the real world. Sacrifice the one for the good of the many. Steve Hooks's life, on balance, counted for nothing. The mental picture of Sellers, the blond Philadelphia rich boy, as a killer with a smoking gun in his hand, just didn't seem to ring true. But it could be true. Hooks knew it. And where did that leave Hooks?

His flashing train of thought was interrupted by the telephone ringing. Sellers answered it with a soft "Hello," then handed the phone to Hooks. It was Patti.

"Two men just checked out that room you're in. They're on their way up," she told him.

"Bring the car in front. Wait for us," he said.

He slammed down the telephone and said, "Two guys are on their way up here."

Sellers pulled his pistol from his shoulder holster, and Hooks took his from his pocket.

"No good," Sellers said. "If they're connected, they can flush us out. Call the feds, and we'll be on somebody's hot seat."

Hooks moved quickly to the door and opened it. The hallway was empty. He walked to the middle of the hall and pressed the elevator button. He glanced back and saw Sellers watching him from the doorway.

Hooks heard the elevator whirring its way closer to him. The sound grew constantly louder, then stopped. He held his gun at his side as the elevator door opened. The car was empty. He held it open with his foot and called out, "Hurry up."

Sellers and the professor bolted from the room and ran toward the elevator. They were ten feet away from Hooks when the shots rang out. Two men had jumped into the hallway, one at each end of the hall, and started firing.

Sellers and Kohl groaned as they fell. For a split second, Hooks was frozen in place, and then a bullet hit the elevator door over his head.

A muffled voice shouted, "What's going on out there?"

Hooks fired one shot in the direction of the man at one end of the corridor and then fired blindly over his shoulder in the other direction. The shooting stopped for a moment. He darted into the elevator and looked back at Sellers and Kohl. Blood was oozing from their clothing and each had half a dozen bullet holes in him. Hooks knew there was nothing he could do there except get killed himself. He pressed the button for the lobby, the elevator doors closed and the car started down. He still held the gun in his hand. Would the men try to get him in the lobby? Or was their assignment only to get Sellers and Kohl? He could beat them to the lobby if the elevator didn't stop. If it stopped, he decided he would get off and try to work his way down through the stairways.

A cold anger gripped him. He wanted to be the first into the lobby. He wanted to wait for the two gunmen and then shoot them down in cold blood.

And then what? Get himself arrested? Get Patti killed?

The elevator expressed down the four floors to the lobby. Hooks stepped out and looked right and left. The lobby was almost empty, and he say no one coming out of the two small passageways that led to the stairs. He limped rapidly across the lobby and went through the revolving door into the street. Patti was parked in the no-parking zone in front of the hotel. He lumbered into the car and said, "Get out of here fast."

She pulled away from the curb immediately. "What happened?" she asked.

"The men I was with just got killed," he said.

"Oh, Steve." Her lower lip trembled, and she caught it between her teeth.

"And I think we're next. Let's move it."

CHAPTER THIRTY-ONE

BACK IN THE MOTEL ROOM IN VIRGINIA, HOOKS LAY AWAKE most of the night, one arm across Patti's shoulder, his hand resting reassuringly on her bare breast, while his mind relived the sudden, deadly bloodbath he had just escaped. He saw again the final spasms of Professor Kohl and Sellers as the fusillade of bullets tore their bodies into tiny fragments and scattered them about like wet confetti. And it brought back the pain he had felt when that madman's bullet had torn through his knee.

He had told Patti the whole story on the ride back to the motel, but she had said nothing, and when they got to their room she had gone about the business of getting ready for bed as if she were in a trance. Later, she had suddenly burst into sobs and had cried helplessly for half an hour as Hooks held her tight and crooned meaningless reassurances to her. Then she had fallen into a deep sleep.

Hooks suspected that she had awakened after a while, but she said nothing to him, possibly believing that he was asleep. It was nearly dawn when he finally did doze off.

Out of habit, he awoke at his usual early hour feeling as groggy with fatigue as if he had spent the entire night madly pedaling an exercise bike, burning up energy and getting nowhere.

He slipped cautiously out of the bed and went into

the bathroom to brush his teeth. His mouth felt as if he could have done the job with a hairbursh. When he came out to dress, Patti looked at him through bleary eyes, her face swollen and tear-streaked.

"I guess I'll get up," she said in a dead tone of voice.

He leaned over and kissed her. "No, stay there for a while. Try to get some more rest. I'm going to walk over to the diner and get coffee. I'll bring you some back."

"Okay," she mumbled and closed her eyes obediently.

The early-morning air was crisp, and the brief walk made Hooks feel a little more alive. He put a coin into a *Washington Post* newspaper dispenser and carried the paper in to read at the counter as he drank his coffee.

The story was at the bottom of the front page, subordinated to trouble in Ethiopia, a plane crash in Denver, the impending failure of several major banks that had made extensive, extremely rash loans to the Third World nations, a White House announcement concerning unemployment and the divorce trial of a Hollywood star.

TWO MEN SHOT TO DEATH IN AIRPORT MOTEL.

The story that followed identified the men as Burton Sellers, a Foreign Service official, and Otto Kohl, a retired West German businessman and brother of Professor Edward Kohl, noted anti-Nazi author who had been slain in Washington last month. The details of the shooting were vague, but the police said that the two men were apparently ambushed coming out of their room, and two men were being sought for questioning.

The reporter went into more detail concerning the earlier murder of Professor Edward Kohl and devoted several paragraphs to Hooks's involvement in that killing, noting that efforts to reach Hooks had been unsuccessful.

Hooks was glad that they had not run his picture with

the story, but he decided that they would probably make up for the omission in a later edition.

He ordered two coffees to go and took them back to the motel room. Patti was in the shower. When she came out, wearing an outsized old terry robe, he handed her a container, and when she sat down on the bed to drink it he gave her the newspaper and pointed out the story.

She read it through slowly, sipping at her coffee, then smiled wryly at Hooks.

"I know this is going to sound stupid," she said, "but when I was taking my shower, I couldn't stop thinking that maybe this was all a dream and it never happened. But it happened, didn't it?"

"Yeah, it happened," Hooks said bitterly. "God rest their souls. The poor bastards, they never had a chance."

"Do we?" she asked quietly.

"I don't know if we do," he said. "But you do."

She looked at him apprehensively.

"I have to believe I'm on their kill list, Patti. I know too much. That means I'm going to be living always looking over my shoulder. Maybe I'll have to change my name, maybe go into hiding. Maybe just a few months, maybe the rest of my life. But there's a chance that they don't know about you. Or if they do know, that they don't care. What you've got to do is pack up and get out of town. Go somewhere else. Start using your maiden name again. Get a job, make a new life and all of this will fade away someday, just like a bad dream."

She frowned, staring intently at the empty coffee container in her hand.

"We've never lied to each other before, have we, Steve?"

"What are you talking about?"

"I don't want you to start lying to me now," she said.

"I—" he began.

"Yes, you do," she said. "You're not going into hiding.

251

You're not just going to run away and forget all this. I know you too well, Steve. Somebody's going to have to stop them, and you just elected yourself."

"I don't want you involved," he said.

"It's too late now," she said. "I am involved." She grabbed his hand and pulled him over to the bed next to her. "We may not be married, Steve, and maybe we'll never be married. But I couldn't mean the words more. 'For better or worse.' I'm staying with you. We'll worry about the 'happily ever after' part later."

He closed his eyes in pain, then lowered his face to kiss her.

"There will be a 'happily ever after,'" he said huskily. "I promise you." And then he pressed her back onto the bed.

They spent the rest of the morning making plans, and Patti called her employer to say that she was called away by a family emergency and didn't know when, or even if, she would be able to return to work. She apologized for inconveniencing him and said she would not bother to claim the week's pay that was currently due to her.

Hooks called his lawyer and made an appointment to see him late that afternoon.

It took them almost an hour to find all their banking documents that were hidden in their luggage, then they loaded their rental car and checked out of the motel. Patti paid the bill with her credit card.

They drove into Washington and went to Patti's bank where she closed out her savings and checking accounts. Her total worldly wealth amounted to fifty-one hundred dollars, which she converted into traveler's checks under the watchful eye of a bank officer, who was clucking disapprovingly at the large cash withdrawals.

"Is there anything we really need to get at your apartment?" Hooks asked her.

"Well, my four Balenciaga gowns and my entire Halston evening wardrobe. My diamond tiara and the family jewels. Of course there's nothing we really need to get. Pots and pans and blue jeans and dirty laundry. You into dirty laundry, kid?"

"Only if I help dirty it," he said.

Hooks could tell that Patti was embarrassed by her disheveled appearance when he introduced her to Cy Schonhaut, but the lawyer fussed over her as if she were visiting royalty.

"She's usually a pretty good looker," Hooks said casually, "but I made her sleep in the street last night."

"Lucky street," Schonhaut replied. "What's on your mind, Steve?"

"Cy, we've got some complicated work to do," Hooks said, "and I can't answer a lot of questions about it."

"You're in trouble, aren't you?"

"You saw the story in the *Post* about the shooting at the Airport Motel?" Hooks asked.

"I saw it. And I saw your name. What's it mean?"

"I was there, Cy, and they almost got me too. I'm on somebody's list, so Patti and I are going on the run. Maybe for a long, long time. No more questions, now."

"What do you want, Steve?"

"I don't want to go to my bank for a lot of reasons. But I've got my checking account and savings and a couple of CDs here. I want to sign a power of attorney turning them all over to you so you can cash them in, and I want you to give me a check for forty six thousand two hundred dollars. Actually, it's forty-six two twenty-four, but I thought you could keep the twenty four dollars for your trouble."

Schonhaut picked up the phone and told his secretary. "Molly, we can go on vacation now. We've finally got a big spender for a client."

He hung up without waiting for an answer.

"Anything else, Steve?"

"Yeah. I want to sign a handful of papers in blank for you. Then, whenever you need to, you can just type in whatever kind of power of attorney you need. I've got some loose ends that I won't be able to deal with. My federal pension should come to you. You take your fees out of it and hang on to what's left for contingencies."

"No fee," Schonhaut said sharply.

"Thanks, Cy. And Joanna's got her medical insurance paying for her, but the premiums still have to be paid every six months or so, so you'll have to take care of that."

"You're really going to disappear, aren't you?"

"Cy, for the time being, start thinking of me as if I died and you had to try to clean up the mess I made," Hooks said.

Schonhaut nodded. "Okay," he agreed. "I'm going outside and dictate all this stuff to Molly. There's coffee over there in the pot. Help yourself."

After the lawyer had left the office, Hooks noticed the attorney's wallet was out on his desk. He quickly picked it up, rifled through it and removed the man's driver's license.

"Steve, what—" Patti began.

"Shhhh. I'll explain later," Hooks said as he replaced the wallet, then rose to pour coffee.

Schonhaut returned to his office five minutes later and his tall, gray-haired secretary brought in the papers for Hooks's signature ten minutes after that. Hooks signed them all and the secretary and Patti acted as witnesses to his signature. After the secretary left, Schonhaut took the checkbook from his desk drawer and wrote a check for $46,200.

"Isn't this wonderful?" Hooks told Patti. "You're in on

a first. I've just swindled a lawyer out of forty-six thousand dollars."

"Steve, I don't know what kind of trouble you're in," Schonhaut said with a grin. "But hustle me, and you'll find out what trouble really is. There is no vengeance like that of a lawyer who's lost money."

"You're safe," Hooks replied. "Cy, you may not hear from us for a long time. If ever again. But if it ever comes to that, someday you'll get a letter that tells you everything. Then you decide what to do about it."

"You can't tell me now?" asked Schonhaut.

"It could only get you into trouble," Hooks said.

When they were in the car, Patti said, "Okay. Why are you a driver's license thief?"

"Cy can always get another one when he finds out he lost this one. The worst thing that can happen to him is maybe he gets a twenty-five-dollar ticket. But you and I, I don't know what we're going to do or how. We can set up other identities, but it takes time. In the meantime, we've got a driver's license for identification."

"He would have given it to you if you'd asked," Patti said.

"Right. And he would have been involved. I don't want him involved."

They checked into a small, inexpensive hotel in suburban Maryland that night, registering under the name of Mr. and Mrs. Cy Schonhaut. They stayed up to watch the eleven o'clock news, but there was only a brief synopsis of the killings at the Airport Motel, and Hooks's name was not mentioned at all.

Feeling relieved, they went to bed and fell asleep in each other's arms almost immediately.

CHAPTER THIRTY-TWO

HOOKS WAS AFRAID HE MIGHT SPEND ANOTHER NIGHT tossing and turning sleeplessly. Instead, he slept as deeply as if he had been drugged, waking only once shortly before dawn, shaken by a dream that was fading by the time he forced his eyes open. All he could remember was running . . . running . . . and knowing something was gaining on him.

Even as he tried to recapture the "something," he felt himself falling asleep again. When he woke up, it was an hour past his usual rising time. Patti still slept deeply, and he quietly put on his clothes and left her a note that he had gone to get coffee for them.

He sat at a booth in the hotel's small coffee shop and read the *Washington Post* he had bought in the lobby. The story on the motel killings was still on page one, and when he saw the reason for it, his stomach seemed to jump, and he felt a lump of nausea in his throat. He covered his eyes for a moment with his hand, then looked at the story again. It was still there. The facts had not changed.

The new development was that Frau Kohl, Herr Bockler and several other people who had not yet been identified had died in a fire that had swept through the small Kohl home in suburban West Berlin. The fire was of suspicious origin, according to authorities, especially after the recent murders of Frau Kohl's husband and brother-in-law.

The story said that the woman and Bockler, perhaps assisted by the others found in the gutted residence, had earlier that day moved several file cabinets of records from the Institute for Contemporary Historical Studies, which her late husband had founded and directed. The contents of the file cabinets had been incinerated in the blaze.

The story transposed into exhaustive rundowns on the killings in Washington and the blunt speculation that Frau Kohl, Bockler and the others had also been murdered. Hooks's name was mentioned, as was the fact that efforts to reach him had still been unsuccessful.

He sat through three cups of coffee, staring at the newspaper story and realized with a shiver that he might now be the only person in the world besides Patti who knew the secret of Anna Mueller's death.

Except the murderers, who were still loose and still free to kill again. Would he and Patti be next? he asked himself, even though he knew the answer. Of course. Unless he did something to stop it. But what?

As he ordered two containers of coffee to take back to the room, he thought that he had postponed this moment as long as he could. Perhaps he had done it in the hope that if he left it alone, it would all go away and he and Patti could get on with their lives. But it wasn't going away. Not by itself. Not unless he acted.

Patti was up when he went back to the room. He gave her one of the containers of coffee, then looked into the local phone book.

"Good," he said. "There's a branch of Cy's bank in town. What I want you to do is hop a cab over there today and cash that check. Get cash."

"What are you doing?" she asked nervously.

"I've got a few things to clean up in the city," he said, and she came toward him with a rush.

"Steve, you're not going to—"

"No. I'm not doing anything yet. Just tying some things up."

"I don't want you to forget," she said. "We're in this together."

"I won't forget," he promised. "I won't."

When he got into town, Hooks parked the rented Ford in a garage and stopped in a corner stationery store to use the telephone.

First he dialed his office number. After just one ring, his tape-recorded message clicked on. "Hello. You've reached the Hooks Security Service. We're all out right now, but if you leave your name, number and message, we'll get back to you as soon as we can."

He hung up without leaving a message. He had found out what he had wanted to know. Someone was in his office. He could tell because his tape-recorded message had suddenly gotten louder halfway through, which happened when someone turned up the volume control to be able to hear the incoming call.

Next he dialed his apartment. He let the telephone ring half a dozen times and was about to hang up when the phone was picked up and a male voice he had never heard before said, "Hello."

There were people at both his apartment and his office. He dialed Patti's number and let the telephone ring for a full two minutes before hanging up. Thank God, he thought. They had not yet made the connection between him and Patti. She could still be out of this and out of danger, if he handled things correctly.

He went to the clerk at the counter, bought a pack of unneeded cigarettes and got a dollar's additional change, then returned to the phone booth and called Mrs. Bordino, the nurse at Joanna's hospital.

"Mrs. Bordino?" he asked.

"Yes?"

"Don't mention my name, but this is Steve Hooks," he said.

"Oh."

"Is there anybody there waiting for me? That you think I might not want to see?"

She lowered her voice and almost whispered into the phone. "There was someone here all morning, Mr.—" She stopped herself short of speaking his name. "But he just left. He said he'd be back in an hour. What's going on?"

"Mrs. Bordino, do you trust me?"

"Yes."

"Please do. I haven't done anything wrong, but people are looking for me. Bad people. If I come right over, can I see Joanna?"

"Yes. He shouldn't be back for three-quarters of an hour, anyway."

"I'll be right there," he told her.

"Go in the emergency room entrance and call me. I'll let you know," she said.

"Thank you," said Hooks.

He stepped out of the stationery store and lucked into a cab that was stopped at the corner in front. Fifteen minutes later, he was standing at his wife's bedside.

Inside the sterile room, nothing seemed changed, and Hooks found that oddly disorienting, since so many other violent changes had been taking place in his life.

He kissed Joanna's cool forehead. The woman lay in bed, immobile, connected to life only by tubes and wires.

"Hi, Jo, it's me," he said. "I just wanted to see you and let you know I'm still alive. Patti and I may have to go away for a while, but I wanted you to know we're thinking of you all the time."

Suddenly he found himself at a loss for words. There seemed to be nothing he could say to his wife. In the past, he had been able to talk to her—or, more accurately, talk aloud to himself. He could ease his own loneliness and bitterness, his anguish for Joanna, by rambling on about anything and everything. It might have meant nothing to the woman, but it had been a kind of therapy for him, and although he was saddened anew by each visit, he had always felt better afterward for having done it.

But now, when he had so much to tell her, he could find no words.

He took a deep breath and forced himself to talk.

"Patti and I are making a life together while you're here in the hospital, Joanna. We're . . . well, we're looking out for each other, helping each other . . . until you come back to us."

He paused, but there was no flicker of expression on Joanna's face, no change in the rhythm of her shallow breathing. "We want you to come back to us, Jo," he said urgently, reaching down to put his hand on her head. "We love you, Jo. Both of us. We always have and we always will. I don't know when we'll be able to come back to you. Or even if we'll be able to come back. But you're never out of our minds, and we'll never leave you."

Joanna slept on, far away from him. He sighed and kissed his wife softly on the mouth. "I love you," he said.

He picked up the room's telephone and dialed the three-digit number that rang on Mrs. Bordino's desk.

"It's Steve," he said. "Is it okay to leave?"

"Yes," she said.

He stopped at the doorway and looked back at his wife. She had not moved. He left the room silently. There was nothing more to say.

Mrs. Bordino met him in the hallway and led him to a flight of steps that would take him out through a side entrance, then walked partway down with him.

"The man who was here. Did he say who he was?"

She shook her head. "He had a badge. I think he was the local police. I know you didn't do anything, Mr. Hooks."

"Thanks, Mrs. Bordino. I didn't."

She left him at the bottom of one of the landings and pressed a business card into his hand. "I know you might not be able to come back very soon," she said. "My home telephone number's on there. Call me anytime if you want to talk about Joanna."

"Thank you," he said.

When he got back to the hotel room, Patti was lying on the bed. She was surrounded by stacks of hundred-dollar bills, and she winked at him as he entered the room.

"I'll tell you," she said. "This life as a single working girl isn't bad. All this in just one afternoon." She glanced at her watch. "I can only give you fifteen minutes, sailor. My next John's due at six o'clock."

"Call him and cancel," said Hooks. "Tell him you've got a better deal."

"Money talks but bullshit walks," Patti said with a smirk and Hooks walked over to her side of the bed, fished out his wallet and dropped a five-dollar bill on her stomach.

She looked at it, jokingly bit a corner to see if it was real, then lifted her arms up to him and said, "I didn't like the John anyway."

But her good mood didn't last through dinner.

They sat in a small restaurant two miles from the hotel, and Hooks was telling Patti how easy it was to set up a new identity.

"What you do is go into a large city, buy a newspaper and find an obituary of somebody about your age. Then telephone the funeral home and make believe you're a newspaper reporter doing an obit. You find out the parents' names of the dead woman and where they lived and so forth."

"Fascinating," she said sarcastically, as she popped a piece of lettuce into her mouth.

"The next day you go to the Bureau of Vital Statistics and tell them you need a new birth certificate. That all your papers were lost in a fire. You tell them the date of your birth and your full name and your parents' name, and you pay them five dollars, and they give you a new birth certificate."

"I'm thrilled," she said, chewing noisily.

"You can use that to get a Social Security card. You tell them you never worked before and this will be your first card. Rent an apartment for a month or so, and they'll mail you the card. From then on, it's a new driver's license and a new checking account in your new name and that's it, you're a new person."

"How do you know all this?" she asked.

"I read a book once. It was turgid but fact-filled," Hooks said.

"More important. Why are you bothering to tell me?" Patti asked. Her dark eyes were riveted on him, and he had the feeling that if he tried to look away, magnetism would draw his eyes back to hers.

"Because it's what I want you to do. You don't have to worry about remembering it all. I'll write down all the steps and—"

"And you can shove them down your throat and swallow them, for all I'm concerned," she snapped.

"I've been thinking about this a lot," he said. "I don't want you hurt."

"And I've been thinking about it a lot, too, and I've

decided that you and I are a team. That's it. No ifs, ands or buts. What you do, I do. We do it together." She reached across the table and put her hand on his. "I'm not letting you get away, Steve. Not after all these years. I know you've got to do what you've got to do, but I'm going to do it with you. I love you, and I'm staying with you."

"But—"

"And besides. You'll need somebody to drive the getaway car." She gave him a grim, tight-lipped smile and a curt nod. "Count me in," she said.

He tried to bring the subject up again several times during the meal, but each time she ignored him and launched into a vivid, organ-by-organ recitation of the plot of *Night of the Living Dead*.

"Stop it or I'll throw up," he warned.

"Don't throw up. Shut up," she said. "No more talk."

He finally gave up, and as they left the restaurant he squeezed her tightly and said, "God, I love you, Patti."

She snapped an imaginary piece of gum and said, "It's not getting you any discount, sailor. The price is still five bucks."

They went to bed and made long, elaborate love, but after Patti had finally drifted off to sleep, Hooks lay awake a long time, smoking, his heart torn between wanting Patti with him and wondering if he had the right to endanger her. He finally fell asleep, promising that he would not let her get directly involved, no matter how she complained. For a moment, it seemed like a frivolous decision made about some subject of relative unimportance, until he reminded himself he was talking about confronting a murderous pack of goons who would not rest and who would not stop killing until they had turned the evil son of the most evil man who had ever lived into the most powerful man on earth. The thought chilled him and sleep came slowly.

Patti had gotten up before him. He heard her moving about the room, but he forced himself to keep sleeping, and when he finally woke up Patti was standing, fully dressed, alongside the bed. Tears streamed down her face, and she was sobbing.

He sat upright in the bed and reached out to her.

"What's the matter, Patti?" he said.

"Oh, Steve. Joanna's dead." She handed him the newspaper, then sank to her knees, burying her face in the bed covers and sobbing. He patted her back, even as he looked at the story on page one of the *Washington Post*. The story was all rehash of old facts, except for the one that reported the death of Joanna Hooks (née Ridley), the wife of the missing former Secret Serivce agent. It told how Joanna had been injured by the assassin and reported that she had died of natural causes after being in a coma for a year.

He tossed the paper aside and leaned forward to wrap his arms around Patti and comfort her. Even as he did, he felt his own eyes grow wet.

"Don't cry, Patti," he said thickly.

She did not look up as she said, "Oh, Steve. I feel so sorry for Jo, and I feel glad for her too. Glad that it's finally over at last. But I feel guilty, too, 'cause I kind of feel glad for us and that's just horrible. It's like I wished this death on her."

"You didn't do that," said Hooks.

"Tell me I didn't," she said, lifting her tear-streaked face to look at him.

"Jo didn't just die," he told her in a cold low voice. "She was murdered."

"Steve. No."

"When I went into town yesterday, they had people

at my office and my apartment waiting for me. They had somebody at the hospital, too, but I sneaked by him to see Jo. They're getting desperate, and they figured this was how to flush me out. You didn't kill Jo. I did by blundering around. By waiting too long."

"I don't—"

"They wanted to flush me out," Hooks repeated. "Now they have."

That evening, he called Cy Schonhaut at home.

"Hello, Steve. I'm sorry about Joanna," the lawyer said.

"Cy, I want you to take care of the arrangements to bury her. I won't be able to do it."

"Are you all right?" Schonhaut asked.

"I'm fine," said Hooks. "Cy, there's something else."

"Name it," the lawyer said.

"If anything happens to me . . ." Hooks hesitated. "If I turn up dead, I want you to claim my body. I want to be cremated, immediately. Throw my ashes in the Potomac. If you need authorization, fill in one of those blank sheets of paper I signed for you."

"What are you expecting?" Schonhaut asked him.

"You've been my lawyer for years," replied Hooks. "I've learned to always expect the worst."

"Prick," Schonhaut said jovially.

"Cy. Please take care of Joanna."

"I will, Steve."

Hooks and Patti left their room later that night and found a Catholic church in the nearby town where they said prayers and lit two candles for the woman they had both loved and lost.

CHAPTER THIRTY-THREE

"LET ME TALK TO BOB PARDIN, PLEASE."

"Who may I say is calling?"

"No name. It's a personal call. Just tell him an old friend."

There was a pause and then Pardin's voice, sounding a little tentative, said, "Hello."

"This is Steve Hooks."

"Steve. Where the hell have you—"

"Cut the buddy-buddy crap, Pardin. I know and you know I know. I think we ought to talk."

"I think you're right," said Pardin. "I won't insult you by asking where you are."

"Don't," Hooks agreed.

"All right. What's your plan?"

"Do you have your car at work?" Hooks asked.

"Yes," replied Pardin.

"All right. I'll call you at seven o'clock sharp and tell you where to go and when. You just follow my instructions."

"Listen, Steve. We could just meet out in the open, you know. Nothing's going to happen to you."

"Just like nothing happened to Joanna? Sorry, Pardin, but you're a murderous liar. I'll call you at seven."

Hooks hung up, left the roadside telephone booth and drove off in the rented car.

He stopped at a drugstore, then consulted the map in

the car's glove compartment and finally drove out over the Arlington Memorial Bridge where he found a small boatyard on the Virginia side of the bay. He rented a cabin cruiser for an overnight trip, paid the attendant in cash and tipped him to make sure that there was extra gasoline stored on board. He signed a registry form with his full name and address and made sure the attendant knew he had a bad knee and wore a support brace.

Then he drove back to the hotel, where he picked up Patti and had her return with him to the city. He ransomed his Porsche from the parking garage for ninety dollars and drove out to the boat basin, where he parked the Porsche in the lot.

As he got into the rental car with Patti, she said, "Mind telling me what's going on?"

"All you need to know is what you need to know," he replied. "We'll stop now and get a sandwich, and then I'll drop you off at the theater. You know what to do?"

"Yes, dammit, but I don't know why I'm doing it."

"You don't have to," he said. "You'll understand when the time comes."

They shared a bottle of wine along with veal Parmesan sandwichs, and then drove to a motion picture theater near the boatyard, where Hooks parked at a meter and turned off the car's ignition.

"Hey, look," he said. *Night of the Living Dead*. That should keep you busy barfing for a couple of hours, anyway."

"Steve, don't joke. This is going to be dangerous for you, isn't it? I mean, you're going after them, aren't you?"

Her voice was so plaintive and her manner so vulnerable that he could only nod, and after a moment he said, "It's something I've got to do. I can't . . ."

"You can't what? You can't just let the dead be dead

267

and forget about them? I've been thinking about this today, Steve. Why us? Why our lives?"

"Patti, you can turn and run now. I told you how to hide. You've got a lot of money. I'd understand. But they've killed too many, and they'll kill us if they get the chance. It only stops when we make it stop."

"I love you, Steve. Wherever thou goest—"

"This is what I've got to do," he said.

They looked at each other, and he saw fear in her eyes, not for herself but for him. It touched his heart, and he said, "We start our new lives after this."

"If we're alive," she said bitterly.

With a confidence he did not feel, he said, "We'll be alive. Don't worry about it. I love you."

"I know it. Nothing better happen to you. I'll kick your ass if anything happens to you," she said.

"Nothing will."

"I love you too," she said. She opened the car door, then leaned back in and kissed him long and hard on the mouth. "I'll be there," she promised.

"So will I," he said grimly.

At seven P.M., he called Pardin's office. Pardin answered the telephone himself on the first ring.

"This is Hooks. I want you to go to Charlie's Place on M Street. You know where it is?"

"Yes."

"Drive there and sit at the bar. You'll get a phone call at seven-thirty sharp."

"I don't know if I can make it there on time," Pardin said.

"I've done it a lot. You can just make it if you hurry and don't waste a lot of time making phone calls. Three things, Pardin. One. There'll be somebody watching you at the bar. If you get my call and make a call yourself, I'll know. Two. If you're followed, I'll know and you won't see me at all, except maybe in the news pages. Three. If you're not there for the phone call, the deal's off."

"Good-bye. I'm leaving now."

Hooks hung up the telephone in the tiny Chinese restaurant down the block from Charlie's and went back to the bar to have another drink. When the bartender showed up, he ordered another bourbon and water, then changed his mind and switched to club soda. He didn't want alcohol to be fuzzing his brain.

At seven-thirty sharp, he called Charlie's.

"Is there someone at your bar named Pardin?" he asked.

"Yeah. Right here," said the bartender. "Hold on."

He heard Pardin's voice come onto the phone and Hooks asked, "Where's your car parked?"

"Two blocks from here. It's why I was almost late. I couldn't park."

"All right. Go out the front door, turn right and walk to the corner. Make another right there. On the next corner, there's a phone booth. Wait there for my call."

"Is all this necessary?" Pardin asked. There was an acid note to his voice.

"You tell me," said Hooks. "Just do it."

He dropped a twenty-dollar bill on the bar then walked outside and started his car. Down the block, he could see Pardin leave Charlie's and start walking toward the corner. Hooks could see no one following him. Hooks pulled out of the parking space and drove slowly down the block. He rolled down the window as he drove, his eyes darting from side to side, looking to see if anyone was watching Pardin from a parked car. He saw no one and caught up with Pardin at the corner.

He called the man's name through the open window, and when Pardin turned around Hooks made sure that he could see that the pistol in Hooks's hand was aimed at him.

"Get in," he ordered.

Pardin got into the car.

"Hello, Steve," he said and tried a smile.

Hooks answered by pressing the gun into Pardin's side.

"Open the glove compartment," he ordered.

Pardin complied and Hooks said, "Put your hands inside it. And keep them there."

The other man inched up on the seat to get his hands deep into the glove box.

"Good," said Hooks. "Keep it that way." He drove away, still pressing the gun barrel into Pardin's side.

They parked in a far dark corner of the boatyard's parking lot. Hooks turned off the motor but left the keys in the car's ignition switch.

The two men had driven to the area without conversation. Pardin had tried several times to talk, but Hooks had silenced him each time by pressing the gun harder into his side.

"All right," Hooks said. "Now be careful. I want you to take your hands out of the glove compartment and open the door. Leave it open. I'm coming out behind you. This gun'll be pressed into your spine. Don't screw up."

Pardin opened the door carefully and stepped outside. He left the door open and turned toward Hooks, who still leveled the gun at his stomach.

"Back away," Hooks ordered. "That's good." Hooks slid across the seat, stepped out onto the ground and closed the door behind him.

"All right," he said. "Now lean against the car."

"I don't have a gun," said Pardin.

"You'll forgive me if I don't trust you," Hooks replied.

He carefully frisked the Secret Service official until he was convinced that the man carried no weapon.

"All right, start walking," Hooks said.

"We are going for a boat ride?" Pardin asked.

"Yes."

Hooks stopped outside the boatyard office and opened the door just a crack. As he leaned inside, he kept the gun pressed against Pardin's back. Hooks called to the man behind the desk, "I'm Hooks, remember?"

"Yeah."

"Okay. I'm taking that boat out now."

"It's all gassed up, and the keys are in it. The poles are stashed in the front cabin."

"Good," said Hooks. "Keep an eye on my black Porsche until I get back. It's in the parking lot."

"You got it. Good fishing."

"Thanks," Hooks said.

He held the gun at his side where no one would notice it and herded Pardin down the long finger pier to a thirty-foot cabin boat.

He untied the bowline, then told Pardin, "This is it. Get aboard."

Pardin put a foot on the boat's railing and hopped lightly onto the back deck. Hooks followed slowly, having to work his way into the boat in a sitting position because of the lack of mobility in his left knee.

The boat was tied up parallel to the pier, facing out across a spit of land toward the Potomac. Hooks asked, "Do you know how to drive one of these things?"

"Grew up with them," replied Pardin.

"Take it out, then," Hooks ordered, as he reached back and unhooked the sternline while holding the gun unwaveringly on Pardin's midsection. "And no lights," he said.

Hooks ordered Pardin to cut the boat's twin motors and drop the anchor when they were about three miles from the boatyard. Night had filled the sky, but off to the right Hooks could see the landing lights of Washington National Airport and behind him a few dim lights from Hains Point, a little spit of land that jutted out into the river from East Potomac Park.

The two men sat on deck chairs on the open rear deck of the boat, eight feet away from each other. Hooks kept the gun in his hand, but Pardin casually crossed his legs, resting one ankle atop the knee of the other leg. It seemed odd to Hooks, seeing a man wearing a business suit sitting on a boat.

"So," said Pardin. "Here we are."

"Why, Pardin? I want to understand."

"Do you like the world?" Pardin asked.

"Not much. Not with you and people like you in it," Hooks replied.

"I'll let that slide by. I don't like the world either. But I'm not like you."

"Thank Christ," said Hooks.

Pardin's voice snapped in anger. "Yes, thank Christ. That's right. That goddamn lunatic put a bullet in your wife's brain and crippled you and what did you do, you went around whining about it. Not for me, Hooks. Not for a lot of us. We used to say the world was going to hell in a bucket? Well, that's not right anymore. It's already gone to hell in a bucket, and we're going to do something about it. At least, those of us who aren't afraid to do something."

"You're building a bigger bucket?" Hooks said.

"No. We're building a better world. There are people all over the world who are waiting for one. People who'll move when the time comes. People who'll get involved and do something about building a new order in this world. Not sit back, like you, and click our tongues and talk of how terrible things are, and then go back to the barbecue and fry another steak." He took a deep breath as if to gain control of himself again. "This organization's been building for years."

"Yeah," Hooks said. "Forty. Since the last maniac killed himself in Berlin when *his* new order turned to sawdust."

"He was the right man at the wrong time," said Pardin. "This time we have the right man. And we have him at the right time."

"Oh, that's right. I almost forgot Shicklgrube, Junior."

"You can forget him if you want," Pardin said. "The world will never forget him."

"How'd you get tied up with him anyway?" Hooks asked.

Pardin reached down and held his foot across his leg.

"I met Jack when I was with the Service in California."

"When'd you find out who he really was? When he started chewing on rugs?"

"We were friends for a long time before he took me into his confidence," said Pardin.

"That must have been thrilling. What a bright chapter to write in your memoirs," Hooks said.

"It *was* thrilling. He took me into his confidence because he found out that we shared the same values and the same vision about what the world could become with new leadership."

"Like Henry Mack?" Hooks asked.

"Henry is a tired old bore," Pardin snapped. "But give him his due. He raised Jack and protected him. And he still plays an important role in the movement."

"Of course. He's your chief intellectual theoretician, isn't he?"

"Very funny. Henry's the treasurer. Did you ever wonder how the owner of a small brewery becomes one of the richest men in the world? Nobody drinks that much beer, Hooks."

"Nazi money," Hooks said. "The Nazis always liked beer. Tell me, Pardin, are there many more like you stuck around in the government?"

"Not many. Maybe half a dozen who know the truth, but we're in good places. When Jack comes to power, we'll be there to run the government."

"First he has to win an election," Hooks reminded him. A boat passed far off in the darkness, and their boat rocked back and forth with the swell. "Or are you planning a revolution?"

"No. Jack will be elected. He'll give the people in this country what they want. He'll give them strong leadership. And we've got our people in country after country around the world. The network's in place. No, they don't know who Jack is. All they know is *what* he is—a leader. The world's ready for him, Steve. I'm sorry you're not."

"It'll make a great headline," Hooks said. "'Hitler's Son To Run for President.'"

"Very funny. So that can't be announced. Not at the start, anyway. But maybe someday when the country is ready for it. When the weaklings and the soft-hearts who run things now are buried so far behind us that no one can hear their wimpy whining . . . maybe then."

"And it's all worth it, isn't it?" Hooks asked sarcastically.

"Yes, it is. There's a world to save. That's worth it."

"And nothing about it bothers you? Killing off the whole Kohl family? Sellers? My wife? How many others? None of it matters?"

"People who meddle where they don't belong get what they deserve," Pardin said coldly.

"And Joanna? She was meddling in your affairs too?"

"I'm really sorry about that, Steve," Pardin replied.

"You were getting troublesome, and it was a way to smoke you out. It wasn't my idea."

"I know. I've heard that song before. You're not really a Nazi, you're just a fun-loving Bavarian, like all the rest were."

"I'm sorry, Steve. I really am. But you couldn't be allowed to run around free. Right now, you're the most dangerous man in the world."

Far out in the river, a ship's horn blew. The powerboat began to rock again.

"Dangerous? Me? Only to you and the other nuts who think like you."

"There's nobody else in the world who knows this," Pardin told him. "You're the only one left."

"Me and the editorial board of the *Washington Post*," Hooks said. "I sold them my memoirs. If Hitler's fake diaries are worth a million and a half, I'm worth a hundred million."

In the dim light from the cloud-shrouded moon, he saw Pardin's face frost over, before he realized that Hooks was only taunting him.

"I want to talk to you, Hooks," said Pardin. "I want to offer you a chance to come aboard."

"Can I be in charge of the ovens? Or is that being saved for Henry Mack?"

"Think about it before you answer," Pardin urged. "You're young and bright. There'd be room for you."

"That's so disgusting it doesn't even deserve an answer," replied Hooks.

"That's right," Pardin said. "Be a loser like you've always been. Rub your hands together when the courts free lunatics like the one who shot your wife. Turn the other cheek until you run out of cheeks. Let America get kicked around by all the degenerates and the misfits of the world. You make fun of the ovens? Some people aren't even good enough to waste ovens on."

"How'd you find out about Sellers and Kohl being in the country?" Hooks asked.

"Casey, Sellers's boss. We didn't know about Kohl. He was a bonus."

"Casey's one of you too?" Hooks asked.

Pardin shrugged. "Have to have a man in the CIA," he replied.

"You know what I don't understand?" Hooks said. "Who decides who lives? You? The other brown shirts? Who lives? The rich and the powerful? The weak, the sick, the old, they all die?"

"If they get in the way," Pardin said. "If they get in the way." He leaned back momentarily in his deck chair, then came forward again. "It's too bad, Steve. You know, you and I were kind of friends."

"I know. I just don't know where we went wrong," said Hooks.

"You went wrong by being weak. And it's too late for you. No one can stop us now. No one."

"I'm going to try," Hooks declared.

"How are you going to do it?" Pardin asked. "You kill me, so what? I'm just a small cog. Even if you somehow manage to kill Jack, it wouldn't matter right now. Another leader would come forward to take his place. That organization we're building? A lot of them don't even know yet that Kinderman will be their leader. Maybe later, maybe then, his loss would hurt us. But not now. There will always be someone who can lead." He spat on the deck. "And there'll always be people like you. Too frightened to lead, too stupid to follow."

"I want to know one thing. Who killed Joanna?"

"You want to know," Pardin growled. "I'll tell you who did. I did. I went into her room while one of my men was talking to a nurse, and I pushed a pillow down over her face and held it there until I choked the breath out of her body." He was shouting now. "I did! How does that make you feel?"

"Like you're a mad dog that needs killing," Hooks said.

Pardin smiled. His voice grew soft and cold. "It's too late for you, Hooks. Too late for you even to try. I killed Joanna. Just like I'm going to kill you."

And then his two hands, which had been resting casually upon his shoe, came up and in the right hand was a small pistol that had been built into the heel of his shoe.

Hooks saw it and started to raise his own gun.

But Pardin fired first.

CHAPTER THIRTY-FOUR

THE LATE EDITIONS OF THE NEXT DAY'S *WASHINGTON POST* carried the story on Hooks's death:

The body of a former hero Secret Service agent, sought by police for questioning in connection with a string of murders, was recovered today from the Potomac near the Naval Research Laboratory.

Police said the burned and mutilated body of Steven J. Hooks, 42, was spotted near Marbury Point by an electrical workman in the area. Hooks was killed when a pleasure boat he had rented last night somehow caught fire and exploded.

According to harbor police, the thirty-foot pleasure craft, *The Chill Wind*, had been anchored near Hains Point when somehow it caught fire. Workmen at National Airport saw the flames and called harbor police, but before they could respond the boat exploded.

Police were able to identify Hooks from the registry he signed when renting the boat, and from the metal knee brace that he wore ever since being injured in an assassination attempt upon the president. His black Porsche was also found in the boatyard's parking lot.

(Continued on Page 4, Column 1)

The next day, the ashes of Steven Hooks were scattered in the Potomac.

A day later, Joanna Ridley Hooks was buried in the green rolling hills of Our Blessed Lady Cemetery. The only mourners were Cy Schonhaut and his wife.

The following week, in California, a press conference was called to announce the formation of a new national committee whose sole purpose would be to begin a movement to draft Congressman Jack Kinderman into becoming a candidate for President of the United States.

Fred Maier, chairman of the committee, said that "America sorely cries out for new leadership. And only Congressman Kinderman can provide that leadership for a troubled nation in a dangerous world."

Kinderman, asked for comment, said that he was flattered but that the election was still two years away, and he would wait before making any decision.

EPILOGUE

A LONG CRUEL WINTER HAD FINALLY ENDED AND GIVEN way reluctantly to spring. In Washington, D.C., the cherry blossom festival was only several weeks away, and, as if in preparation for it, the city was rolling out a green carpet of lawn.

The combination of spring rains and warming suns had worked its magic on the city, filling it with color and vibrancy, and few places were more beautiful than the rolling hills of Our Blessed Lady Cemetery, a place dedicated to death but blooming with spring life.

A tall man stood in front of a small headstone, engraved simply with the name of a woman and the all-too-brief span of her life. It was midmorning of a weekday and no one else was visible in the cemetery as far as the eye could see in either direction.

The man was speaking aloud. It was a habit he had not been able to break.

"The baby's ten months old now, Joanna. We named her after you and she's going to look like you too. Another beauty.

"We knew you wouldn't mind, and in a way it's like Patti and I have you back with us again. We know you'd want us to be happy, and we are. And neither of us ever stopped loving you, Jo.

"But you know that.

"Oh, I forgot to tell you. I'm blond now. And I've got

a mustache. It's a pretty scraggly-looking thing, but I'm used to it. I don't think you would have liked it, though, and whenever I kiss the baby, she scrunches up her face like I'm scratching her. So maybe someday I'll shave it off.

"Isn't it strange, Jo? How you hated violence? How we both did. Neither of us wanted anything to do with it, and yet our lives wound up filled with it. Professor Kohl told me a long time ago that Anna Mueller was just another poor victim of the war. I guess you were too.

"I haven't been here since they brought you here, Jo, but it wasn't because I wasn't thinking of you. I just didn't want to take a chance being around Washington anymore. But now this may be the last chance I'll get.

"It looks like Kinderman will be nominated for President this summer, and I've been waiting for that. Pardin said it on the boat. He said the movement was growing, and if Kinderman didn't lead it, somebody else could. I didn't want that to happen. I wanted Kinderman to be the head. I wanted everything to revolve around him. Now he is the head, and I'm going to cut that head off, and then, maybe, the rest of that monster will die. So that's why I came to see you now, just in case I can't make it some other time.

"I told you that Pardin is dead, didn't I? He took a shot at me on the boat, but a wave slapped the boat just then, and he only creased my shoulder. I didn't miss. I know you don't like to hear about this, but I've got to tell you to let you know that we didn't just forget you, Jo. Not your life and not your death. I won't tell you the details 'cause I know you wouldn't care for them, but I put the extra knee brace I bought on him, and then I used the extra gasoline— Well, anyway, he was hard to recognize when they found him.

"The brace, the rental, my car, all of it, they decided it was me, and I guess everybody was happy to let it go at that. Funny. Knee braces aren't a better way to identify the dead than dental records are sometimes. They could ask Anna Mueller.

"There was never a word about Pardin in the paper. I can guess what the Nazis think. They figure he went out with me on the boat, killed me and died in the explosion. Another martyr to their glorious cause.

"And the Secret Service? Well, I don't know. I called his office a few times after . . . after the accident. At first they told me he was on vacation, but after a couple of months they said he was no longer with the Service. I guess they wrote him off as a guy who just got fed up and quit. I made sure that night that the boat attendant never saw him, so they never had reason to suspect that he was with me. And he had no family to ask a lot of quesions.

"Anyway, he's dead, and good riddance to bad rubbish.

"So Patti was waiting for me in the park when I swam ashore, and we left. This is the first time I've been back. We live now in one of those pretty upstate New York towns that you and I always talked about visiting and never did. Now we've got different names and different lives. Even our old lawyer—remember Cy?—even he thinks I'm dead and that's for the best.

"You know, Jo, I owe you an apology. All that time you were in the hospital, I kept promising to read you *The Brothers Karamazov*, but I never really got to it. And now I guess I never will.

"But I read it myself. There's something in there that I want you to hear."

The man fumbled in his jacket pocket and pulled out a worn paperback book which fell open to a familiar creased page.

"The old man is talking, Jo, about whether hell has a ceiling and if the ceiling's got hooks in it to hang sinners on, and he says, 'After all, what does it matter whether it has a ceiling or it hasn't. But, do you know, there's a damnable question involved in it? If there's no ceiling, there can be no hooks and if there are no hooks, it all breaks down which is unlikely again. For then, there would be none to drag me down to hell, and if they don't drag me down, what justice is there in the world?'

"Jo, there *is* justice in the world. Maybe you didn't see much of it in your short life, but I believe there is. And I believe that sometimes we have to mete out our own justice. Kinderman, that misbegotten animal, is on top of the world now, but I'm going to drag him down to hell. I am, Jo.

"You know, when I did that security work for Kinderman at his ranch, I thought I missed something, but then things got so confused I just forgot about it. It was only a long time later that I remembered what it was. It was the ranch's water supply system. Anytime I want I can get into the ranch through the protective piping. Young Hitler can have a hundred guards, but I can still get in there.

"So that's about all the news, I guess. I'm working, I don't think I told you, as a personnel manager in a small electronics plant. It's not much, but we make enough to get by on. This year we're even going on vacation.

"We're going to California, and I don't know if I'll ever be here again."

The man put his book back into his jacket pocket, looked at the gravestone again and said softly, "Goodbye, Joanna. I'll always love you. Until death reunites us."

Then he walked away, limping heavily, favoring his injured left knee. It always seemed to hurt most in the spring.

ABOUT THE AUTHOR

WARREN MURPHY IS THE AUTHOR OF ONE OF THE WORLD'S leading action series, THE DESTROYER—a tongue-in-cheek man's adventure series that has sold millions of copies around the world. He and his wife Molly Cochran, who is also a novelist, live in New Jersey. Three of his books were nominated for awards by the Mystery Writers of America and the Private Eye Writers Association. His last book for Fawcett, *The Red Moon*, won the Gold Medal Award from the West Coast Review of Books as best adventure novel of the year.